THE DOCTOR

MAGIC & STEAM: BOOK THREE

C.S. POE

Published by Emporium Press
https://www.cspoe.com
contact@cspoe.com

Cover Art by Reese Dante
Cover content is for illustrative purposes only and any person depicted on the cover is a model.

Edited by Tricia Kristufek
Copyedited by Andrea Zimmerman
Proofread by Lyrical Lines

Published 2022.
Printed in the United States of America

Trade Paperback ISBN: 978-1-952133-39-8
Digital eBook ISBN: 978-1-952133-38-1

For Declan.
Thank you for lending your voice to this world.

I

In the middle of the East River, between Manhattan and Long Island City, was a two-mile-long island called Blackwell's. This unescapable, disease-ridden plot of filth was where New York sent undesirables—its poor, its criminal, its incurable, and its disturbed. On the northernmost end, isolated from the workhouse, penitentiary, almshouse, and hospital, stood the Asylum for the Magically Insane, a three-story, two-winged structure of agony and despair and my Hell on Earth.

"Fitzgerald is loose!" a matronly nurse shouted, her voice ringing off the stone walls. "Wake Dr. Ashland at once. No, no—it's *Simon Fitzgerald*!"

I raced down a dark corridor on my slippered feet, the freezing winter air leaching what little warmth remained in my body, causing my toes to go numb and feel as if I were running across a bed of sharp rocks. Between the city's budget perpetually underfunding even the most basic necessities in which to keep innocents in their care alive, and the tender mercies shown by abusive and cruel staff, the asylum wasn't lit or even warmed by steam during the nighttime hours, save for the nurses' station. Violent patients bullied the meek for ownership of threadbare blankets lousy with fleas and lice, and nurses—many of whom were actually criminals serving sentences at the penitentiary and working at the asylum as a means of saving every single penny—mocked, beat, and starved the helpless who begged for warmth to see them through the night. It was like owing money to a gang-run gambling hall. You were most *certainly* going to die; it was simply a matter of *how* that would make the experience one of interest.

Thrusting a hand forward, I conjured a wind spell and blew the lock plate from a door, tore hinges from the wall, and sent the heavy wood crashing deeper into the unlit east wing. I ran through the opening, the shouts of staff growing in volume as they stormed the second floor after me. The wails of the insane echoed from within the dozens of locked rooms I passed. A sudden uptick in the bitterly cold draft that clawed through my ill-fitting institutional clothing informed me I'd reached the activity room. In theory, doctors and nurses were supposed to supply a number of stimulating mental exercises for patients, in either an attempt to rehabilitate or at least settle the worst of disruptive behaviors, but like the rest of this madhouse, there was no funding. Instead, the large room was empty, save for several long and uncomfortable benches where patients were left to sit all day with nothing but their delusions. A well-meaning man of the cloth had managed to set up a meager library for patients, but between the Irish who couldn't read and the Germans who begged for titles in their mother tongue, the books saw little use.

I skidded to a stop in front of the nearest window, wiped frost from the warped glass, and studied the black water that separated me from hope, from freedom, from the life I'd lost. The twinkling skyline of New York was so close—and yet word among those locked away and left to rot behind these walls was that no one had ever survived the crossing.

I'd been dismayed upon learning that security had been the one sound investment the city took to heart when the residence opened in 1841. After all, magic had been illegal then—was illegal for over another twenty years, in fact—and this hadn't been an asylum but a *prison*. Upstanding citizens, criminals, and lunatics alike had been locked up together if they were found to be magic-wielders. City officials had to be certain our kind couldn't escape, couldn't return to the streets of Manhattan, couldn't pose a threat to the society that didn't want nor care to understand us. And it didn't matter that *now* this space was used only to house the insane outcasts of the magic community—every window was still reinforced with bronze on the second floor and iron on the third, with the patients separated into groups whose magics were inherently weak against these metals.

But Dr. Ashland hadn't heeded the warnings of the Federal Bureau of Magic and Steam when officials from D.C. dumped me here—warnings that I was more dangerous than any patient he'd dealt with thus far. Because without being magically inclined himself, Dr. Ashland hadn't understood the severity of what it meant to be a caster whose abilities broke the scale that'd been used in the oversight and regulation of an entire population. He hadn't comprehended that simply because lightning was my default elemental skill, it didn't mean I wasn't gifted in every other known spell, even illegal magics like gravity.

And why *should* anyone consider me a threat? I was freshly thirty years of age and had the stature of most women, with brown hair mottled with gray that was at odds with the youth of my face. I was not an intimidating man, and my survival had depended for years on being respected, but in the end, entirely forgettable.

But I suppose that had really just been *one more lie*.

Dr. Ashland had housed me on the second floor because

the bronze reinforcements weren't conductive to my lightning spells.

Not an issue.

I took a few steps back from the window, raised my hands, and flames erupted from my palms. The fire painted the benches and walls and windowpanes of the room with a radiant red to orange to yellow glow as the spell intensified. If only I could feel the effects of my own magic… I was so goddamn cold. But it was a cold that went beyond the bitter February night. It harkened back to Fort Donelson, Tennessee—submerged in the icy waters of the Cumberland River, cries of dying men, so chilling that I had expected to see psychopomps with my own two eyes, haunting the snow-covered and blood-spattered battlefield, severing the souls of soldiers from their ruined bodies.

My nightmares hadn't begun in 1862, only amplified into something more, something *worse*, but those days and nights of frozen waters and frozen terrors at the fort had put me on the trajectory to Antietam—to becoming the monster I was today.

"Fitzgerald!"

I looked toward the ruined door on my left as the open threshold filled with women in white aprons and burly men on loan from the penitentiary. I shifted my vision to the magic plane and watched tendrils of raw power blossom and unfurl around two men. *Great.* Criminals with casting abilities. I turned back to the window, and without a moment's more delay, released a massive fireball. The flames shattered the glass, melted the bronze reinforcements, and cracked the stone wall.

One of the men cast a water spell, and the deluge barreled toward me. Still focused on my escape route, I sent a powerful gust of wind through the opening, blowing the flames outward and removing debris so I could climb out.

Without meeting the caster's gaze, I invoked lightning in my other hand and let my magic find him. My storm of electricity slammed into his magic, enveloped the water entirely, and then he was screaming and his flesh was cooking and I was completely numb to another murder being heaped onto my shoulders.

That same matronly nurse—Louise, that was her name—was screaming another warning, perhaps to the arriving Dr. Ashland, that I was casting multiple spells at once.

It was a cautioning well worth the air in her lungs, because I could count on one hand the number of casters with such skill and control. The problem with this particular ace up my sleeve was that the energy required to harness two distinct elements pushed my body's threshold to the maximum quite quickly, even when I wasn't already exhausted, starving, and half-frozen. Another minute of this and I'd overtax, pass out, and wake up with another streak of gray in my hair.

I dropped my hands and both spells ceased immediately.

A second nurse crouched beside the criminal caster on the floor, but when she touched him, electricity sparked from his steaming body and she yelped in surprise before falling onto her backside.

I stepped toward the gaping hole and leaned my head out. Winter winds whipped my short hair. Snow cut at my exposed skin like thousands of tiny razors. I gripped the scorched walls on either side, leaned back for momentum, and prepared to thrust myself into—

A sudden wind spell, like cannon fire, slammed into me from the second caster. As I was flung across the room like a ragdoll, I heard the *snap* of my fingers breaking, the blood-curdling *cries* of the dying, and embalmers—the vultures of the army—*swearing*: he's a goddamn butcher!

I crashed into one of the benches, splintering the wood, then fell to the floor with a *thud*, the air knocked from my chest.

"Sometimes I can't breathe. I—I hear sounds from memories, and they repeat over and over and it makes me sick."

I began to sob—pathetic, breathless little gasps—as the staff loomed over me. The second caster yanked my arms up and behind my head in a lock. Louise held a long-sleeved, blue-and-white garment that could be mistaken for nothing but the horror that it was. And Dr. Ashland, a clean-shaven, dignified man with neatly parted silver hair, pressed a sodden rag, sweet with the scent of chloroform, over my mouth and nose.

I wanted to die.

II

February 18, 1882

I was not mad.

I did, however, suspect I was on my way to becoming so.

Time ceased to pass in a dependable or entirely believable manner when locked in a reinforced cage in the asylum's cellar, denied even the smallest window by which to discern day from night. The basement stank of the rotting foods that were being prepared in the kitchen, which supposedly constituted as meals for patients. The malodorous aroma of green meats mingled with the scent of mold and mildew and a parade of never-ending bodies. New patients arrived not through the grand rotunda entrance of the asylum, but instead marched through the cellar, where they were bathed in the same filthy brown water as those who came before them, were dressed in clothing intended for prisoners, and then locked away forever.

I had gauged the transition of the last three days by sound and smell alone. Every morning, the new patients, confused and frightened, were stripped of the last of their dignity, and every evening, noxious cooking preceded suppertime— which promised to quell the ache in your belly, if only briefly, before you were up 'til the early hours vomiting and shitting until you were convinced cholera would be the end of you. I knew these routines to be true, because I, too, had been forced to undress in front of an audience. I, too, had bathed in the same cold, slimy water. I, too, had been fed molded breads and rancid meat scraps and deeply regretted it.

On January fourth, special agents of the Federal Bureau of Magic and Steam's headquarters in Washington, D.C., had arrested me on charges of falsifying identification and knowingly misrepresenting magical skills. It had happened once D.C. had begun investigating the death of Old Money son and fellow agent Henry Bligh, who'd turned out to be moonlighting as the city's newest gangster, Tick Tock. Director Loren Moore had reported the events of the New Year exactly as he knew them to be true, which unbeknown to him, had raised suspicions regarding his best agent.

Gillian Hamilton's control and influence on natural elements had seemed to be on par with those of Simon Fitzgerald's, a war criminal who hadn't been seen since September of 1862. Fitzgerald had been presumed dead all these years, but what if that was a lie? Because who *was* Hamilton? A man with no home, no family, no past. He had been eighteen years old, applying to the federally mandated regulation because he had hoped to be chosen for the FBMS. He needed a job. And his skills had been rare enough— impressive enough—that he'd gotten that badge and that paycheck, but he'd tempered his formidable magic so as not to present a threat to the government.

For a decade, I'd lived that lie.

And I'd lived it so well that there were nights I *almost* believed I was Gillian Hamilton.

A special agent.

A lawman.

A *good* man.

Except, I wasn't him, and I wasn't any of those things.

I was Simon Fitzgerald.

A murderer.

A monster.

A *bad* man.

And they were going to make certain I disappeared.

After residing in an asylum for over a month, my breaking point had been three days alone in the dark and damp, arms pinned by the sleeves of a pinstripe straitjacket, and forced to get on my knees to eat from a plate on the floor like a dog. I began screaming, and I *kept* screaming. I screamed until I ran out of breath, until my throat was raw, until I spat up blood. And then I screamed some more. I twisted and tore and fought against my restraints, but without the use of my hands, I couldn't cast properly. At one point I had managed not so much to create fire, but smoke, and fully intended on singeing the garment, thread by thread, until I could escape, but the cook picked up on the scent of burning cotton and had thrown a bucket of ice water on me.

Afterward, I lay on the floor and cried.

I cried for each and every lie that had, if only briefly, allowed me to glimpse a better life. I hadn't lived as Gillian Hamilton for fame or riches, but for stability. For a sense of purpose. For perhaps, even, love. I'd been asked by the FBMS as to why I felt the path of deception had been worthwhile, and my response had been that, as a child, I hadn't ever had a dream, but instead only nightmares of torment, abuse, and horror. The council of top FBMS officials hadn't understood, and it was then that I knew any further word I took in my own defense was a waste of breath.

Because if you grew up being loved, it was impossible to

imagine a childhood of the contrary.

"—very nearly escaped." That was Dr. Ashland speaking as he entered the room immediately outside my cell. "So we've placed him in isolation."

I quieted and raised my head to listen.

A stranger replied, his voice soft and gentle, "I was under the impression that Simon Fitzgerald was a casualty of the Great Rebellion."

"That no longer appears to be the case. It seems he deserted after Antietam and has been living in the city under an assumed name ever since."

"Why is he not at Sing Sing?"

Ashland answered, and there was a particular sense of cruelty in his casualness, "He's completely without his faculties—frenzied about supposed wounds in the magic atmosphere and something he calls *quintessence*."

I rolled onto my knees and climbed to my feet as the men sounded like they'd come to a stop at the cell door.

Ashland continued. "Of course, the FBMS has conferred with the best casters and architects on staff regarding his claims. Fitzgerald's raving mad."

Best they have.

I'd have laughed if I wasn't so offended. Not even Director Moore had had an inkling as to what the artificial spells in Tick Tock's magic ammunition were doing to the raw undercurrent of power, and aside from myself, I'd have considered him one of the top casters on the East Coast. No, the FBMS wouldn't understand the true danger until they were handed tangible proof by someone of *my* caliber. And considering my reputation was now worth less than the shit that covered the streets of the Five Points, and other casters on par with myself were, let's just say, extremely rare, there was no one to warn the Bureau of the imminent threat to the magic community.

I had to wonder if the Bureau would even care if they *were* presented evidence…. Well, of course, the casters and architects and scholars would very much care. Because that tear in the atmosphere, that gross refuse that was building up like a barrier, it affected us all. But the nonmagically inclined? The politicians who'd put the Caster Regulation Act into effect and founded the FBMS? The ones who held positions on the council? Those were the same bastards who had fabricated the story of my lunacy so as to have a proper place to isolate and confine me until I was needed. I knew it. Could feel it in the marrow of my bones. And until that day came, I was going to be a plaything for Ashland, a sadistic man who'd sooner slice me open to diagram my inner workings than work to cure my supposed madness. Under his continued watch, I'd be lucky to survive until the time came that the US government called for me to kill again.

"It's my personal theory," Ashland said to his visitor, "that Fitzgerald's high levels of magic have had a direct impact on his mania."

The stranger asked, polite but unconvinced, "How, then, do you explain patients with relatively low casting levels but confirmed and documented lunacy?"

"Well, it's also worth noting that he's a known sodomite," Ashland answered. "And that, of course, will be a factor. But it'll take further research."

It was that one word—*research*—the threat of something worse than the shocks, beatings, ice baths, and isolation that pulled me back from the brink of giving up. I could hear words spoken to me on New Year's, repeating over and over in that husky monotone….

"Whatever you've lived—"

I drew myself up straight, squared my shoulders, and listened as the tumblers in the lock turned and the reinforced iron door swung open. I studied the self-satisfied expression on Ashland's face as he stared at me from the threshold. He wore an afternoonified suit with the white coat of a physician over it. His companion was about a decade his junior—midforties, I suspected—and very dashing, with auburn hair parted severely on the left side, a touch longer and thicker than how most men allowed theirs to grow these days. He was cleanshaven, with a dusting of freckles along his sharp cheekbones. His eyes were undoubtably his best feature: a bright hazel that shone with an emotion my tired and abused mind couldn't quite pin down.

Inquisitiveness? Tenderness? A combination of the two that had no apt description in the English language?

"How are we feeling this evening, Mr. Fitzgerald?" Ashland asked.

Drawing my attention away from the second man, I answered frankly, "The cook threw a bucket of water on me." I shifted within the straitjacket so as to stress its cold and sodden state.

"You were misbehaving," Ashland chastised, his tone sickeningly sweet, as if speaking to a red-cheeked babe still in its infant dress and not one of the most formidable casters this country has ever seen.

The stranger said solemnly, "He's likely to catch a chill, Dr. Ashland." Then, with growing concern, added, "How long has Mr. Fitzgerald been wearing that jacket?"

I looked at him and answered, before Ashland had a chance to speak, "Three days. Of course, the asylum claims to not employ the use of such inhumane constraints." I redirected my stare to Ashland. "Don't they?"

"Mr. Fitzgerald killed a staff member, Dr. Barrie," Ashland said without any sense of perturbation. "There are times that the more severe restraints are necessary."

"I was defending myself," I said.

"While attempting to escape," Ashland replied.

I glanced at Barrie a final time and said, "Wouldn't you do the same?"

Barrie's eyes glittered as he considered me for a long moment, as if he were trying to convey words without speech. But eventually his gaze shifted, and he studied the bare stone walls before lingering on the putrid, hay-stuffed mattress at my feet. "I'm afraid I must ask that we remove Mr. Fitzgerald from the straitjacket." He said to Ashland, "Surely a pair of platinum gloves will suffice?"

Ashland's expression darkened, soured as this new, younger doctor who appeared to hold some kind of power that he, the resident physician, did not, made polite demands to better the well-being of Ashland's latest curiosity. "I suppose that can be arranged." And with that, Ashland stepped out of the cell.

Barrie remained, watching me.

I shifted my perception to the magic plane. Tendrils of glittering light ebbed and flowed and unfurled around Barrie, marking him as a caster. The raw power shifted, undulated, lapped back and forth between us—a calm and placid creek around him, a storm at sea around me. Underneath the show of energy, I could feel the atmosphere over the Lower East Side pulsating.

Like a heartbeat.

Like blood pumping to an open and festering wound.

"I'm not insane," I said into the quiet between us.

"No," Barrie agreed. "You don't have the eyes of a madman, Special Agent Hamilton."

It'd been the first time in over a month I'd been called by the name and title I *wished* were mine, and it sent a sickening rush through my body.

"You don't remember me," Barrie said with a smile that might have been disappointment. "You'd been given a good deal of laudanum for pain at the time." He raised his hands, palms out, and clarified, "Tucson."

My heart thudded hard against my rib cage. "St. Margaret Hospital?"

He lowered his hands and pressed one to his chest. "Eugene Barrie."

The doctor who'd salvaged my hands—my very ability to cast—after Milo Ferguson had nearly blown me to kingdom come last October. But how was it that a magically inclined physician, operating out of a scant, church-run hospital in Arizona territory, now found himself in New York City, at the Asylum for the Magically Insane, of all places?

A tear followed the salt tracks staining my cheeks, and I awkwardly wiped my face against my shoulder before asking, "Why're you here, Dr. Barrie?"

Barrie countered, "Why are *you*?"

"I falsified my identification to the federal government. I lied about the extent of my casting abilities. The FBMS told Dr. Ashland I was mad, because if I am without my faculties, it's much easier to oversee and control my actions."

Barrie frowned. The twinkle in his eyes sharpened like the glint on the point of a knife. "Your skills are incredibly rare," he said in defense. "Why would the FBMS want to endanger that? One of their own?"

"My skills make me a threat, Doctor. Not only to enemies, but to my own country. The order to lock me up came from the council in Washington."

"Whatever you've lived, it made you a survivor."

I'd been lying to survive my entire life.

It wasn't until I'd become Gillian Hamilton that I began walking a tightrope of absolutes, of black-and-white, of law versus lawlessness. I rejected the notion that I could live a morally gray life because I had lived that corruption firsthand my entire childhood. When my country had called abled men to crush the Rebel foes, Congress had agreed that the sacrifice of one for the betterment of the Union was a necessary evil. That they could do the wrong thing for the right reason.

But *I* had been that sacrifice. *I* had lived with those consequences.

I had never wanted to be morally gray again.

So in my time at the FBMS, I'd enforced every code and upheld every law. That had even included denying my own tendencies and allowing myself nothing more than the occasional indulgence on the Bowery—but only to be seen and never touched. Because a lawman—a good man— couldn't admit to such inclinations. My new life of security and stability was also one of penance. I would never be able to atone enough for the crimes I'd partaken in, and so I did not *deserve* affection, despite how often I had cried myself to sleep wishing for that very thing.

And then I'd met America's most-wanted outlaw. A deadeye marksman vigilante who robbed and killed and yet was still, *somehow*, the most observant, kindest, gentlest man I'd ever crossed paths with.

Gunner the Deadly, who reminded me to breathe.

Gunner, who skirted the truth for my own safety.

Constantine, who loved me and told me to never feel guilty for being alive.

Because I was a *survivor*.

"Gray looks good on you."

I would not die today.

I would not die inside these walls.

I would die free and on my own authority.

To Barrie, I demanded suddenly, "Get me out of here."

He blinked in surprise. "Mr. Fitzgerald—"

The sharp echo of heel on stone warned of Ashland's approach.

I hastily said, "I have done terrible things in my life, but if there's one thing I excel at, it's self-flagellation. I do not need Ashland's barbaric practices to hate who I am. What I reported to the FBMS was true—artificial magics were introduced to the city during the New Year festivities. I have no evidence but my own account, but I swear to Christ, it's polluting the raw magic stream and will inevitably cripple casters like us. *Yes*, Dr. Barrie, I knew you were a caster the moment you stepped foot in this room. I have to stop that barrier from spreading before it's too late. If you hold no compassion for a fellow magic-user, please at least consider empathy for an ill-treated patient."

Barrie looked like a man coming undone—his sense of duty as an upstanding citizen at war with his obligations as a doctor and whatever affinity he might have felt toward a fellow caster. He wrung his hands together while opening and closing his mouth like a landed fish.

And then Ashland reentered. He carried a massive pair of mechanical gloves, similar in construction to those worn by street gangsters, but these absurdly heavy concrete blocks were used to imprison the magically inclined and were often reinforced with the element most opposite their nature. In the case of someone like myself, where no magic was too difficult to master, they invested in platinum, which didn't melt like brass, nor conduct like silver, and took acids like *aqua regia* to dissolve. There was a lock located on the wrist that, when turned, forced the hands to ball into fists, hindering casters from blasting free from the confines.

The magic in the room bloomed as a burly staff member entered fast on Ashland's heels, and I figured him to be the same caster with the impressive wind spell that'd blown me on my backside the night I'd nearly escaped. The bastard on loan from the penitentiary shoved Barrie out of the way and rounded on me. He put one massive arm around my neck in a chokehold while he began to unfasten the jacket with his other hand. I was forced up onto my toes with the motion, trying in vain to claw at his arm but was hindered by the long sleeves of the jacket. I coughed, *gasped* for air—all the while Ashland watched, completely devoid of emotion, whereas Barrie's face was that of poetic tragedy. I'd be so lucky to survive the transition of jacket to gloves, as the closer this brute got to freeing me, the harder he strangled me.

Please, I screamed in my head. *Please, please, get me out of here!*

And just like that, almost breathless, Barrie blurted, "Dr. Ashland!"

Ashland turned his attention to his younger counterpart.

The final clasp on the jacket popped free.

And I flung my arms wide, wrenching stones and mortar from the walls with a formidable earth spell. The thick, crude edge of gray gneiss struck the man at my back with a sickening snap of bone. His chokehold released and he collapsed to the floor. Ashland shouted for help, stones volleyed back and forth, colliding and bursting and raining shards of sharp rock, quarried by the very prisoners of this island, down on him and Barrie. I lowered my arms to my sides with a jerk, a gale tearing the jacket in two down my front and ripping the long sleeves from my arms.

The wind screamed.

The earth shattered.

I crouched down beside Ashland, who was cowering on the floor, grabbed him by the thick silver hair on his head, and forced him to look at me as I said, "'Cowards die many times before their deaths.' Consider this your first."

I let him go with a shove.

And ran.

Night on Blackwell's Island was a frightening sort of darkness. Shadows were so thick that there was a density to them as they slid between my fingers, like holding hands with the dead—those who tried and failed for freedom before me. The vestiges of the poor, the criminal, the insane, leading me toward the skyline of Manhattan to continue my atonement. To keep righting the wrongs I'd contributed to in the past. To protect the magic community from this same abuse so the next little boy born into the squalor of the Lower East Side, testing at unfathomable casting levels, wasn't subjected to the same horrors that had befallen me.

If my breaths were to matter, if I were to look good in gray—let it be for the next generation.

For their dreams to be of marshmallows and peppermint candies, hopscotch and marbles, reading and arithmetic. For their nights to be warm and their days bright. For their bellies to be full and their hearts loved. For their fathers and mothers to kiss their fingertips.

Snap, snap, snap.

I stumbled over an upturned root in my slippered feet and nearly tumbled head over heels. I caught myself on the trunk of a tree within the thicket surrounding the edge of the island, leaned over on my knees, and took deep breaths of freezing air. The pale glow of the lighthouse shone from the most northern tip of the island. The asylum stood at my back, and the wails and screams of patients echoed all the way to the water's edge. There was no doubt I'd scared them after literally shaking the foundation of the building, but I couldn't linger on that thought. The staff was already searching for me, their calls and whistles steadily growing louder.

"*Fitzgerald*," hissed a voice somewhere in the nearby darkness.

I spun, raised one hand, and produced enough of a glow—like embers in a dying fire—to see who'd followed so close on my heels. "Who's there?" I demanded.

And then the outline of Eugene Barrie's face appeared from the tangle of bare tree limbs. His hair was in disarray, and dark blood seeped steadily from his nose, like he'd been swiped by one of the stones in the cellar. He held both hands up in an act of submission, saying, "Apologies for startling you." He was breathing hard, like he'd been in hot pursuit from the moment I'd escaped.

"I'm not going back," I cried.

"*No*," he hastily agreed. "No. I believe you."

The glow in my hand dimmed until Barrie was nothing more than a black smudge on a canvas already smeared with charcoal.

Barrie further clarified with "I can feel it—the barrier. Like there's a struggle to borrowing the raw energy. Isn't that right?"

Relief like I hadn't felt in so long coursed through my body, my knees nearly giving out. Barrie must have been more powerful than I'd initially suspected, in order to have picked up on the still-subtle changes to the barrier's state. "Yes. Exactly. And it's getting worse."

"What will you do?" Barrie asked.

I'd begun to shiver and chafed my arms as I said, "I need to get to California."

"Where can I find you?"

"Wh-what?" I instinctively took a few steps backward as Barrie began to loudly tromp through the dead and frozen underbrush toward me.

"You don't have proper attire," he explained, his face illuminated briefly by the distant and rotating lighthouse lamp. "Let alone the means in which to book charter on an airship." He delicately dabbed at his bloody nose with the sleeve of his suit coat. "Isn't that so?"

I'd only had two objectives that night: escape and survive. Because if I could accomplish those, pilfering clothes off a frozen wash line and pocketing a drunkard's wallet were skills that, once learned, a street rat never forgot. But there was no denying that boarding a continental airship as a wanted man would be… difficult.

Barrie said, "I'll report to Ashland that I didn't find you—but I heard splashing. You underestimated the cold. And with the current, they might not find your body washed up 'til daylight. I'll catch a ride on the morning steam shuttle back to the city, but you must tell me where I can find you."

My gaze shifted momentarily over Barrie's shoulder. The screech of metal whistles grew to ear-piercing volume. "Why?" I finally asked.

"Why what?"

"Why are you helping a criminal?"

Barrie wiped his nose again. "I don't believe it's fair to call twelve-year-old Simon Fitzgerald a criminal when, as far as I understand it, it was not your will to join the Army."

"I was ten."

Barrie motioned with one hand in a "my point exactly" gesture. "And Gillian Hamilton saved an entire town of good, God-fearing people from an engineer hellbent on blowing them up. Neither of those men sound like criminals to me."

My throat had nearly seized up. "I'm a sodomite."

Barrie glanced at his shoes, at me, and then said with a note of finality, "I don't much care about that."

Perhaps the glimmer I'd caught in his eyes had been that of humanity.

"Pilly's," I answered. "On the Bowery. Ask for O'Dea."

Thunder rumbled ominously, lightning flashed overhead, and the air whipped and cracked and tore around me. I was lifted off my feet just as Barrie was thrown backward from the onslaught, and he toppled into the snow and underbrush.

"If you try *anything*," I called over the gale, "you won't find me. Understand?"

Barrie nodded solemnly from his prone position on the ground.

With that, the wind screamed and I shot through the air across the East River, like the magically charged bullet from a Waterbury pistol.

III

February 18, 1882

The wind magic piggybacked on the gales of the thunderstorm I'd manifested. Coupled with the static charge of lightning in the air and my very nonmagical rush of adrenaline, I'd not only crossed the cold and choppy expanse of the East River, but the dark structures of modest German-family homes in the Yorkville neighborhood. Steam-powered light seeped from the outline of windows, curtains drawn taut against the cold, the diluted yellow glow like the eyes of a sleepy monster.

The Second Avenue El was awash in a kaleidoscope of streetlamps—reds and greens and purples as far as the eye could see—and the incoming rumble, screech, and whistle of a South Ferry-bound train told me it was still early—before eight o'clock, when the line closed for the night. I altered my trajectory, and in a final burst of energy before my body could falter, could protest, shot south ahead of the train, following the steel tracks and steam pneumatics all the way to the Lower East Side.

I could hear the nightlife of the Bowery before reaching it—fiddles, concertinas, and bodhráns from Irish dance houses, and raucous laughter and shouts spilling onto the streets from bars that mingled with Yiddish singing and dandies hawking club scenes to passersby. The thunderstorm was abating as sheer exhaustion set into my bones. My magic gave one last pathetic thrust and flung me over the Third Avenue El tracks. I hit a roof, skidded and stumbled, careened head-over-heels, and fell off the opposite side. I grabbed at a fire escape, but its grates were so icy, I lost my grip and dropped into the alley below.

I struck the frozen, slushy cobblestones like a sack of potatoes. Remnants of wind magic followed me to the ground, picking up debris in its spiral. I coughed smoke and sparks from my lungs.

"Jesus, Mary, and Joseph!"

I'd know that blaspheming mouth anywhere, and looked up.

Addison O'Dea, tall and lean, with fiery red hair and a face smattered with kisses from the Cliffs of Moher, hastily rubbed the ember of his cigarette against the brick façade of Pilly's before tucking it behind one ear. His hazel eyes grew in the muddy lamplight as he approached. "*Hamilton*?"

"Addison," I croaked, and more brilliant yellow sparks spewed from my mouth and bounced along the cobblestones.

He crouched at my side, mindful of the magic remnants, and grabbed both shoulders. "Oy, where the fuck you been? I ain't heard from you since the New Year."

A hiss of pain escaped my lips as Addison aided me first to my knees, then to my feet. Through the exhaustion and debilitating cold, I managed to say, "H-hide me."

"What?"

"*Now*," I all but begged.

Addison's charming features were distorted by blatant confusion, but he didn't again question me. Instead, he got one shoulder under my arm, gripped my waist, and because his height forced me onto my toes, practically dragged me through the unlocked door that led into the Fighters Only room.

The warmth was immediate, like a clumsy girl's poke while practicing her needlework, only felt *all over*. The steam-powered lamplight was low, which probably had as much to do with the owner being cheap as it did an effort to hide the dirt and grime and blood. A few men, in various states of bruised and undressed, mingled around wash basins, laughing and boasting. Addison didn't stop to speak with any of them as he hurried me into Pilly's proper.

The scent of wet wool, sweat, and beer hit me like an exotic and expensive perfume after the rot, mold, and shit of Blackwell's. The hall was doing a brisk trade of drink and cheap meals at the bar near the front door. Tables and benches were filling up with the evening crowd—men, and a few women, all of my own inclination, were there to bet and cheer over the bare-knuckle matches before passing a fighter a few coins for some of the private entertainment that went on upstairs.

Addison wove around an empty table near the Fighters Only entrance and dragged me up the first few steps of a staircase. "I've hefted barrels of flour more cooperative than you, Hamilton," he said with a grunt.

"S-sorry," I said, but it came out so softly that I couldn't be certain he'd heard. And when I tripped on another riser, Addison scooped me up in his arms without further comment.

I worried we'd pass any number of people in the dingy stairwell and have to explain my questionable state. If I'd been able to make the ascent on my own, I supposed it'd have been easy enough for Addison to claim I'd gotten into the drink early and we were turning in for some evening pleasures, but not like this—not with Addison carrying me like a babe. Never mind that I was still wearing a wet and filthy prison garment too. But the upstairs was silent and still, and I supposed the night's work was only just beginning for the fighters.

On the landing of the third floor, Addison turned left down a hall pockmarked with doors on either side. He came to a stop outside the second-to-last room on the right, gently set me on my feet, and dug a skeleton key from his trouser pocket. Addison unlocked the door, turned on the light, and gave a nod of his chin for me to enter.

I stepped inside and took in the less-than-modest setup: a dented and discolored brass bed frame with a lumpy mattress, a table big enough for a wash basin and pitcher, one of its legs broken and propped up with a brick, and a beaten-to-hell trunk, dated enough in design that it might have been in Addison's care since he left Ireland as a boy. There was one window, a curtain pulled over the glass, and the walls had remnants of a once maybe blue wallpaper that had since been stripped away by both man and time.

Addison closed the door and said, "Rumor on the Bend is you don't work for the FBMS no more."

I reached back for the shoulders of my drab shirt and yanked it over my head. I dropped the stinking, sodden material to the floor, kicked my soaked slippers off next, then began on my trousers.

"The state of ye!" Addison exclaimed at my back. His steps grew close, and then he darted to stand before me. "You're skin and bone!"

Addison set his hands on my bare shoulders, and the weight, the warmth, the texture, the concern—it undid me entirely. My still-numb fingers fumbled weakly with the tie at my waist while hot tears spilled down my cheeks. I could only imagine what I looked like through his eyes—a once-healthy man, an unbeatable special agent, as ornery as himself—now broken, bloody, filthy, starving, like the poor streetcar horses that'd been left in the gutters to die before the advent of steam technology.

"I—I can't—"

Addison brushed my hands away and worked the knot of my trousers himself.

I wiped my eyes with the back of my shaking hand and asked, "If someone lied to you, would you feel betrayed?"

"Lied how?"

"Does it matter?"

"Aye, it matters." Addison got the knot free and looked up.

"About everything," I clarified.

Addison's grip on the drawstring loosened, but he didn't let go. "What are you—a spy or something?"

"No. Just a wretch."

Addison held my hand for balance as he helped me step out of the trousers. He yanked the quilt from his bed and hastily threw it around my shoulders. "*Athair* was a drinker. *Ar deargmheisce—máthair* would say that."

"What's it mean?"

Addison shrugged and said, "Something like, mad drunk. He was always fallin' down and pissin' himself. Mad drunk."

"Lovely," I muttered.

"One night, the bastard comes home ravin' because he's short coin for the pub. He's demanding to know where it is, right? I weren't more than a wee brat then, Hamilton, and my family was starving. My baby sister had already wasted away." Addison paused, and the spirited light in his eyes became subdued. "She cried until she weren't strong enough to keep cryin'. Took a long time for her to die…. So I tell *Athair* I took the money. I'd bought a handful of shit potatoes.

They had the blight, but it was better than starving, so I cut all the black parts off and we had supper for the first time in days." Addison tilted his head to the side and motioned to a slash of lighter skin along his jaw. "See that? Cut me right here with a broken bottle. He was aiming for my mouth. *Ar deargmheisce.*" He turned and busied himself filling the basin with water from the pitcher.

"Your point?"

Addison opened a weathered satchel on the tabletop, and inside were a few toiletries. He plucked a sliver of soap free and said, "I ain't never been honest about money since. But a lie or three don't make *you* a wretch." He turned, put the soap in my hand, and started for the door. "I've got a match tonight, but I'll be back as soon—"

"You don't understand," I said over him. I watched Addison pause at the door and look toward me. "I was born at the Old Brewery."

"I don't know what that is."

"It… it was a tenement. In the Five Points," I whispered. "Demolished that same year, in '52. My family moved to Gotham Court afterward."

Addison's brows rose, but he asked in a careful, neutral voice, "On Cherry Street?"

"Now aren't you curious as to what else I've lied about?"

"Do you judge *me* for lying?"

"You were born into a world of famine. You were lucky to survive. No, I don't judge you."

Addison opened the door and said, "You know something, Hamilton? I'm a grown man, and yet you couldn't pay me to venture into the Court. As far as I'm concerned, whatever you had to do to survive that shithole, it ain't no one's business but yours."

The bare-knuckle boxing began shortly after Addison's departure, if the echoes of whooping and hollering through the thin floors and walls were anything to judge by. I set the quilt aside, and soap still in-hand, limped naked to the basin. I scrubbed my hair and face clean with cold water, then moved the soap more gingerly over the rest of my body, every ache and welt protesting as I bent this way and that, every bruise making itself known as the grime was washed away. By the time I'd finished with the dirt under my nails, I'd gone through the entire pitcher and the water was a sudsy, muddy brown. I returned the quilt to my shoulders as if it was a king's mantle, sat on the edge of the mattress, and sighed very, very quietly.

What now?

If I hadn't been a criminal before, I most certainly was after escaping confinement.

Had I meant what I said to Barrie? That I intended to reach California in order to track down the architect who'd built the spells we'd seen in the ammunition employed by the mechanical men?

Yes, I did. It really wasn't even a question.

The threat to the magic community hadn't stopped with the deaths of Milo Ferguson or Henry Bligh. They were but two cogs in a greater mechanism already activated—petty criminals in an underground that Christ only knew went how deep. I'd begun a job in January, and with or without the backing of the law, would see it to its conclusion.

I figured there were two avenues to explore. The first was this supposed doctor—Sawbones—who'd been reconstituting Whyos into grotesque mechanical men with the ability to use the magic weaponry Bligh had been purchasing from out West. Sawbones had clearly been on payroll, considering he'd also transformed Bligh—at the gangster's own behest. And I was certain Sawbones had been, at the very least, in communication with the mysterious architect and wanted caster, Luther Jones. Luther had worked for Carl Higgins, formerly of Grace Gallery, before being brought into the illegal enterprise Bligh had been building. There was too much knowledge Sawbones would have required regarding the artificial magic and how it interacted with the precious metals used to build the mechanical men to not converse with an architect in advance. That being said, the last intel I had on Sawbones was that he'd been building Bligh's mechanical army in a warehouse on Bayard and Mulberry but had hightailed it before my arrival. I'd lost over a month's time and now Sawbones might have been *anywhere*—working for *anyone*.

He was most certainly a danger, but for now, would remain a secondary concern.

Because the other path led to who was arguably the FBMS's greatest fear: the architect. He had succeeded in embedding elemental magic into a tangible item, and granted, the only current way to control the spell inside the bullet was to have it shot by a mechanical man, properly reinforced to withstand the magic, it was only a matter of time before this forbidden knowledge became fine-tuned. Before anyone and everyone could control magic and further imperil the atmosphere as raw magic was taken and never restored by casters. Before casters like myself were kept prisoners to do nothing day and night but pump our magic into household items or—God forbid—more weapons of war.

The architect was who I had to stop. At any cost.

At least I had the basics to work with: the architect went by the alias Weaver. He had been recruited in California by Luther Jones in order to construct the illegal spells. And due to prototype weapons ending up in the hands of Ferguson last October, Weaver might have known the madman engineer.

I closed my eyes and then his husky monotone was right

there, at the forefront of my memory, blotting out the shouts of the audience downstairs, the sighs of the wind outside, the groans of the old building—almost like I could reach a hand out and touch him again….

"What is your name?" Gunner had been so quiet.

My voice had shaken when I said, "Simon Fitzgerald— I'm the Butcher of Antietam. And they've finally found me."

I'd taken one last look out the bedroom window, watched the D.C. agents step out of view as they made for the entrance of the building, and began to cry as I'd said to Gunner, "Please go. *Please*. If you love me, you won't break my heart by staying."

Gunner's stunned silence had a wrecked quality to it. He'd said, after a long moment, "But you'll break mine by leaving?"

He'd said nothing else. Gunner had stepped out of the bedroom, collected his coat and hat, and walked out of my life.

I had done it to *protect* him.

I had severed what I thought was an actual courtship in development, with a man who had only existed in my wildest dreams until recently, to keep Gunner's neck out of the noose. Because surely that's where he'd have ended up when the agents came upstairs to take me into custody.

Except that hadn't made the hurt any more bearable. If anything, I felt as if I'd stabbed myself in the chest—my own words like a blade. And the look in Gunner's eyes—distress? defeat?—it had been enough to bury me six feet deep.

But I had done it to protect him….

Goddamn it. I had to find Gunner while I was out West. To apologize. To explain that my cruelty was an act of love, and my demand that he leave was a last-ditch effort to save the life of the only person who'd ever called me his. But I also needed to prepare my heart for the very real possibility that he would not renew his affections for me. Having Gunner in my thoughts had been all that kept me alive on Blackwell's—his soft mouth at odds with that rough, husky voice, his tough, callused hands juxtaposed by how gently he held me, grounded me in the present when the past tried to sweep me away—but I had hurt him. I couldn't be selfish and demand he return his heart to me if he no longer wished to.

He owed me nothing, and I owed him *everything*.

"I'm sick to death of being afraid…. If I cannot be both an agent and happy, to hell with them."

I had talked a good game until I had been caught off guard, forced to confront Simon Fitzgerald and thirty years of tragedy all in that single moment. It couldn't have gone more wrong.

I rubbed my tired eyes and considered: How was I supposed to find a vigilante who roamed from Helena, Montana, to Tucson, Arizona, and as far east as Dodge City, Kansas? A vigilante who carried no Personal Discussion Device and who called nowhere home?

My spiraling thoughts were halted when the doorknob rattled. I scrambled to my feet, drew the quilt tight around me, was ready to fight my way out—

Addison stepped inside, two mugs pressed to his chest by his forearm and a steaming bowl balanced in his free hand. He'd lost his shirt since I last saw him, and his braces hung at his sides, dragging his trousers low. He was sporting a split lip, and the knuckles of one hand were scraped and bloody. But he looked at me, smiled that crooked smile of his, and said, "Now that's much better." He kicked the door shut with his heel.

"I used all of your soap."

"A worthy cause." He moved around the bed as I sat once

again, and said, "It ain't roasted lamb with mint sauce, but it'll fill you." Addison offered the meal.

The sharp and gamey aroma of boiled sheep reawakened the month-long pain in my belly, and I grabbed the bowl in both hands. I stirred the contents—a fat-heavy broth thickened with a bit of oatmeal, wedges of carrot and turnip, and the available scraps of meat and parts from the creature's head that respectable upper-class citizens recoiled at. I shoved a spoonful into my mouth, then another, and another. I couldn't even taste it I was swallowing so quickly.

"Hey," Addison chastised. "Slow down. Make yourself sick eatin' like that." He passed me one of the mugs.

I accepted the beer and drank down half of it before coming up for air.

Addison was watching me in between sips of his own drink.

"I never thanked you," I stated.

"No? For what?"

"For everything I should have thanked you for over the years but never did."

"You ain't trying to get a free tussle in bed, are you, Hamilton?"

"God no."

Addison chuckled and set his mug beside the pitcher and basin. "You've always been good to me." He reached for my chin, tilted my head back, and studied my face. "You need a shave."

I laughed weakly. "That's really the least of my troubles."

"Aye, maybe. But wherever you've left, they're searching for a shoeless, fever-eyed bastard who smelled like he crawled out of a sewer." Addison let go and made for the door. "They won't be expectin' a handsome and wonderfully uptight special agent."

"I'm not an agent anymore," I admitted, mostly to the bowl of poor man's winter stew.

Addison opened the door at my back and called, "Once a lawman, always a lawman."

He was only gone a moment, but I finished the rest of the warm beer and ate every grisly cut of meat and mushy carrot chunk before he returned with a second set of toiletries. The habit was a bad one—eating like an animal, uncertain of where its next meal would come from, and it heralded back to my childhood—but after Blackwell's, I couldn't help myself. I tipped the bowl, drank the last drop of broth, and wiped my mouth on the back of my hand. My stomach did ache some, but I felt full and warm for the first time in over a month, and had Addison not insisted on further grooming (it was more a colorful threat, if I was being honest), I'd have curled up for a long, long sleep in his bed.

Addison stood before the bed holding a palm-sized mirror in one hand and a shaving mug in the other. He asked, "So you're done with the FBMS?"

"It wasn't my choice," I said as I finished lathering my face with a shaving brush. I replaced the brush in the mug and opened the straight razor.

"You break the law?"

I wiped soap from the blade onto a ratty hand towel. I took another pass or two on my face before asking, "How much do you know about the Caster Regulation Act?"

Addison shrugged and shook his head.

I didn't follow up until I'd finished shaving my neck. I said, while wiping the blade again, "Magic users are tested on a scale of one to five—five being the highest."

"You a five, then? I bet you are. I've seen you lay 'em out."

There was a sense of freedom in speaking of this now.

I was no longer undermining my skills and padding reports with lies so those in positions of power above me didn't suspect something was… *off*. I sighed, and even to me, it sounded so tired. So fed up. "My abilities break the scale."

The mirror in his hold lowered a touch. "What's that mean, then?"

"I lied about my level and the FBMS found out last month."

Addison lowered the mirror the rest of the way, and I met his puzzled expression. "They punished you for—being *too* skilled?" Then realization sparked in his eyes, like a flame brought back to life among dying coals. "FBMS is afraid of you."

I reached for his hand with the mirror and raised it up.

"You were arrested?"

"Among other things."

Addison muttered some Irish cusses he'd picked up in the surrounding establishments over the years before asking, "Why'd Moore sit on his fuckin' thumb while they hauled you off to the Tombs?"

I allowed Addison to believe I'd only been inside the walls of Manhattan's jail and not deep in the trenches of Hell in the middle of the East River. "Moore had been relieved of his position while D.C. investigated the death of Henry Bligh."

"The rich fellow who flaunted around the Bend as Tick Tock."

"That's right. Moore never knew about my skill level. He had no idea D.C. was coming to arrest me—only thought they were going to interview me regarding my involvement on the case." I finished shaving and used the towel to wipe away bits of leftover suds. "I haven't spoken to Moore since last month."

Addison crammed the supplies onto the already-too-crowded side table. "He's still with the Bureau."

"Is he?"

"Aye."

"But as State Director?"

Addison agreed a second time before he took the razor from my hand and said, "None of the other lads had scissors—"

"What're you going to do?"

"Cut your hair."

"No."

"You look ragged."

"I look fine."

"Don't be so hard-mouthed." Addison kept one hand atop my head as he sheared the sides in the manner I typically wore my hair, as it hid a great deal of the premature gray. He was trimming the top the best he could with only a blade when he asked, "What will you do, Hamilton?"

"Finish the job I started."

"As an outlaw?"

"If I must."

"Will you send word to Moore tomorrow?"

"It'll only endanger him."

Addison made a sound of disapproval under his breath before saying, "Then what about Gunner the Deadly?"

I glanced up as cuttings brushed my nose and cheeks. "What about him?"

"I don't think it's smart—whatever you're planning—to go at it alone. And Gunner was aidin' your office in January, weren't he?" Addison stopped trimming and met my eyes with a wry smile. "Unless that was blarney too."

I felt warmth pool in my cheeks.

Addison laughed low and said, as he made a few final passes, "I thought so. He's a real belvedere."

"Can we not talk about this?"

"Why not?" Addison finished with a ruffle of my hair before he set the straight razor aside.

"I would just prefer not to discuss Gunner."

"You do something daft?"

"But you'll break mine by leaving?"

I pinched the bridge of my nose and took a breath. "I'm going to fix it." But in a less sure voice, I added, "I'm going to *try* to fix it."

IV

February 19, 1882

The ruckus and uproar of bare-knuckle boxing continued into the night, whereafter the commotion transitioned upstairs as fighters sold their beds and company to whichever man offered enough coin—but I slept through it all.

Well, nearly all of it.

Addison had returned to the main clubroom for another round of boxing—he had a living to make, after all—and I'd turned in. I'd only acknowledged the grunts and groans of fucking mingled with drunken laughter emanating through the too-thin walls when the mattress had dipped at my back sometime during the night. I'd jerked to attention as the quilt was raised and a rush of cold air snaked around my naked body, but then Addison murmured it was only him as he settled in behind me.

I'd met Addison here at Pilly's, when I first dared a visit because I was so desperate to be seen, to be acknowledged, by a man of my own inclinations. He'd been a newly hired fighter—a mouthy rascal who demanded the spotlight, whether he won or lost a match—and Addison had caught me staring. Being the flirtatious bastard he was, Addison had joined me at the bar, drew up real close, asked if I'd buy him a beer, and I'd panicked. I still remember how hard my heart had pounded, how my underarms sweated, how I couldn't formulate a single word in the English language. I had been saved when I caught the manner in which Addison had side-eyed a known Whyo gangster—not with joy, but disgust—and that was when I'd taken him on as a street informant.

For years, Addison relentlessly tugged at that loose thread, determined to pull my stitching free and prove I'd lied to him that night—that on the inside, I was just like him, and only used my badge as an excuse to deny my tendencies. And now, here we were, crowded into a too-small-for-two bed that he'd had sex in with more men than I could probably imagine. A mere month ago I would have panicked at being this close to Addison, despite him doing nothing more than trying to catch forty winks. I squeezed my eyes shut, and in my mind, I was in the hallway of the FBMS field office again, pulling Gunner close, his body melting into the contours of mine, and I was kissing him in front of a dozen scholar special agents.

There was something to be said about the relief in finally admitting aloud who I was.

Accepting that this was who I was.

I only had to keep working at loving who I was….

The next time I awoke, wintry sunshine was pouring in through the paltry curtain at the window, illuminating the bedroom in a clean, bright glow. The brisk air had a touch of body odor and a general closed-up mustiness to it, but compared to the malaise of Blackwell's, it might as well have been pristine, untouched oxygen. I rubbed the sleep from my eyes and realized Addison was leaning over me, a hand on my shoulder.

"You awake?" he asked.

"I am now."

"We might have a problem."

I pushed up onto my elbows.

"There's a man downstairs—says you told him to inquire after me," Addison explained as he straightened his own posture.

"Did he give you his name?"

"Nah. He ain't of the neighborhood, though, that's for sure. He's one wrong block away from being robbed. And that's if he's lucky."

I sat up the rest of the way. "Older than myself? Auburn hair and freckles?"

"That's right." Addison was staring inquisitively.

"He's alone?"

"Aye."

"Bring him up."

"Who is he?" Addison asked.

"It's not important."

Addison put his hands on his hips. He was dressed in simple black trousers with braces and a white shirt, sans collar, with sleeve garters, indicative of its mass-produced size and that someone such as Addison was unable to afford custom tailoring. "Tell me who he is, or he ain't getting past Oliver."

"The dandy who hawks the exploits of your bloody knuckles for five cents a head?"

"He's stronger than he looks."

"Eugene Barrie. A doctor—"

"*Doctor*?" Addison echoed with renewed interest.

"Yes, from—from Blackwell's."

Addison's hands slowly slid from his hips and a sickening sort of realization crossed his features. "You were—"

"Just bring him up," I said over him. "Please."

"Okay," he agreed, his tone notedly subdued as he stepped out of the room.

The light of a new day brought with it the realization that I was in no proper state to be called upon. I wouldn't be coerced to put that filthy prison garment back on my person, but even as I looked about for it, like the way one must keep an eye on a mad dog, lest it attack you unawares, I realized it was gone. Good. I hoped Addison had burned it. But that meant I was utterly naked, without even a touch of Macassar oil for my hair. I pulled my hand free from the cocoon of the quilt, snapped, and orange-and-yellow flames licked my scarred fingertips.

At least that was something.

The creak of floorboards under two distinct treads in the hallway drew my attention. I moved across the mattress to the edge nearest the door, planted my feet on the floor, and attempted to look as dignified as one could after just waking nude. The doorknob turned and Eugene Barrie was ushered inside by Addison, who was right—the doctor was dressed too nicely and lacking any sense of street smarts in his bright eyes to realize he was a walking target in a poor neighborhood.

"Mr. Fitzgerald," he said in greeting, a smile on his face. "Goodness. You're looking much better."

"I think it's best we use Hamilton," I corrected as Addison shut the door and shot me an inquisitive stare. "And I'm afraid I'm not sure if I should say good morning or afternoon," I continued.

"Afternoon," Barrie politely answered.

"Good afternoon."

Barrie was still smiling, and the silence that followed

wasn't uncomfortable, but awkward. It reminded me of conversations I'd attempted in the past with women I'd worked with, never knowing what to say that wouldn't give something about myself away. But before I could attempt to rescue him with some trivial nicety, Barrie seemed to acknowledge the carpet bag he held by the handles and quickly thrust it in my direction. "You'll need this."

I reached for it, but the quilt slipped to reveal my bare chest and shoulder. I hastily righted it, saying, "Apologies for my current state."

"Not necessary." Barrie instead drew close enough to set the bag beside me on the mattress. If it wasn't for the cold weather and drafty old clubhouse that brought color to everyone's cheeks, I'd have said he was blushing. "May I take a look at those contusions?"

"No." I stared at him until Barrie reluctantly nodded and took a step back. I directed my gaze at the bag—rich red and maroon roses stitched in an almost geometric style, with leather handles and a skeleton key still tied around them. I picked up the cold metal, stuck it in the lock, and peered at the contents. "This is mine," I said, almost like I didn't believe my own eyes.

"Yes, sir."

I looked at Barrie. "How?"

"It was confiscated upon your arrival at—" He hesitated, glanced at Addison, and said instead, "The island. I took it from storage on my way to catch the steam shuttle. I know it's only a few changes of clothes…."

I found Gunner's brass and purple-tinted goggles sitting atop the neatly folded articles. I took them out, worried that dent over one of the lenses, and smiled as I said, "It's nice to have something familiar. Thank you."

Barrie's hesitancy, a sort of stiffness he held in his

shoulders, loosened. He reached into the inner pocket of his suit coat and removed an airship ticket. "I've booked passage on the Ora Continental for San Francisco. It leaves this evening on a rapid route—only one stop in Dodge City. We can make the trip in two days instead of three."

I'd begun to reach for the ticket, but froze and repeated, "*We*?"

Barrie glanced up from the printed details before saying, "I think it would be best if I was to accompany you. After all, they'd be looking for a man on his own, right?" He thrust the ticket into my hand and said, "See, I've booked you under Malcom Ackerman."

"Who's Malcom Ackerman?"

"He's an eager student I've met while visiting Bellevue," Barrie explained, seemingly quite proud of his skullduggery. "And I've agreed to taking him under my tutelage as I continue my lecture tour on the uses of aether in medicine."

"Hang on, hang on," Addison said, putting his hands up as he butted into the conversation. "All this shit—it's happenin' because Hamilton's a magic user, ain't it? And the best backstory you got *underscores* his ability?"

I reassured Addison by saying, "It's best not to deny magic abilities. You never know who you might cross paths with that can call out the lie. An agreed-upon explanation of those skills is the best option here."

Barrie removed his pocket watch and consulted the face. "I still need to collect my belongings at my hotel."

"I'll dress and join you," I answered. "We can go to Grand Central Depot together."

"A sound plan," Barrie concluded. He opened the door, stepped into the hall, and waited.

Addison lingered, but I gave him a firm nod and he reluctantly left the room as well.

I blew out a quiet breath before climbing to my feet. A wash, hot meal, and sound sleep had done wonders for a body that'd been barely clinging to life, but I still had to move with caution. A month of unprovoked assaults from the mad, as well as gleeful beatings of the staff, had left me with bruises on bruises, and I felt stiff and sore everywhere. I folded the quilt, set it on the bed, and began pulling clean, if slightly stale-smelling, clothes and a toiletry satchel from the carpet bag.

I dabbed Crown perfume onto a few pulse points, and the rich scent of lavender and sandalwood and cedarwood went a long way toward making me feel like a gentleman again. I added a touch of Macassar oil to my hair, then drew on undergarments and dark-gray trousers, tucked in my shirt, and buttoned cuffs and collar. After seeing to a blue tie and light-gray waistcoat, I dug to the bottom of the bag, but was unable to find my pocket watch. The criminals on Blackwell's must have stolen it, but at least they'd had the courtesy to leave my Richmond Bros. shoes. I pulled on a suit coat, Gunner's traveling goggles, and my scally cap, then locked the bag. I had no winter coat, but considering the state I'd been in only yesterday, it was an inconvenience in comparison.

I was mindful of my footfalls as I exited the room and made for the stairwell. Most of the fighters and staff kept a nocturnal schedule, and while it sounded as if only a few were awake behind closed doors, I didn't need to draw any attention that could further compromise Addison's position. As I turned the corner to make down the final flight of stairs, I saw said redhead at the landing, leaning against the wall with his arms crossed. Barrie stood a few feet away, looking very out of place and trying to mask that discomfort.

Addison glanced up and smirked as he pushed forward. "Handsome bastard," he stated.

My cheeks grew warm and I said, "A touch in the right

direction."

"I should say so." Addison nodded for us to follow, and we went through the Fighters Only door and exited Pilly's through the alley. Addison knocked a bottle into the doorjamb before turning to me. He reached into his trouser pocket and removed a cloth bundle. "Bought this for you. Pretty lass over on Grand sells 'em."

I held my hands out and accepted the piping-hot parcel. "Chestnuts?" I guessed.

"Aye."

"Thank you."

"I won't say a word about this," Addison continued, with a wave of his hand between us, "but you need to tell the FBMS I ain't workin' for no one but you."

"I appreciate the sentiment."

Addison said nonchalantly, "It ain't no sentiment. I like the way you bully me."

I rolled my eyes.

"The Whyos have been in a tizzy since Tick Tock and those mechanical men made a scene last month." He leaned in close to whisper, "They're afraid it might happen again. I ain't trustin' anyone at the FBMS with my gossip but you."

"You think the Whyos are fortifying their defenses."

Addison nodded. "*Do* you think it'll happen again?"

I looked over my shoulder at Barrie before saying, "That's what I intend to put a stop to."

"Be careful, Hamilton. Send word when you're back in the city, yeah?"

"I will. And in my absence, I want you to trust Director Moore."

Addison made a face.

"Should you require anything."

"I'll think about it."

The February air whipped up, and both of us shivered and hunched our shoulders in response. I reached a hand out. "Thank you."

Addison shook with a firm grip. "Us wretches stick together."

In my haste to get underway and provide my restless mind with more immediate challenges to untangle, so as to avoid any further opportunity to dwell on the very dark thoughts that, only a few days ago, had led me to the serious consideration of suicide, I hadn't asked Barrie what address he was a guest of until we'd arrived at the Third Avenue El station on Houston Street.

"Fifth Avenue Hotel," he'd answered.

And thank God I'd finished eating all of the hot chestnuts on the walk; otherwise I might have choked. The Fifth Avenue Hotel was five stories of opulence, counting the ground floor. Much like Grand Central Depot, it hosted a number of conveniences for travelers, including a telegraph room, reading room, barber shop, even a reception area exclusive to women. I had never been inside myself, as it was the sort of establishment that had hosted the likes of Prince Edward, General Ulysses S. Grant, and even that Tammany Hall monster, Boss Tweed, but I'd read plenty of articles in the *Daily Cog* about its imported marble, austere carpets, rosewood-and-walnut furniture, and its nearly half a dozen dining rooms, tea rooms, and bars.

But perhaps what was more alarming than Doctor Eugene Barrie being able to afford a stay in such a place was that the Fifth Avenue Hotel was on Twenty-Third Street and Fifth Avenue—the same intersection as the New York field office of the Federal Bureau of Magic and Steam. In fact, before I'd been arrested, my private office boasted a north-facing window, with a view of Madison Square Park on the right and the grand hotel on the left.

"You know the neighborhood is rife with special agents, don't you?" I'd asked.

Barrie had looked comically perplexed, then downright aghast after I explained the hotel's proximity to the FBMS. He'd apologized profusely, as if the presented danger was a fault of his own, and suggested I go ahead to Grand Central without him and he would catch up. I immediately shot the idea down, because now that the federal government was aware I'd never been a casualty during the war so many years ago, they'd certainly be dispatching agents and coppers alike to the Depot and piers to look for a stowaway, while the staff on Blackwell's continued to search the island and surrounding waters. No, splitting up was a surefire way for me to stand out to the wrong people.

Besides, I thrived where I wasn't welcomed.

So, lost in a sea of passengers, we'd ridden the uptown El to Twenty-Third Street and walked west, cutting through the park so as to avoid boldly strutting along the sidewalk directly outside my former place of employment. Madison was bustling with men and women dressed in the latest winter fashions, enjoying the golden sunshine of late afternoon, even if it wasn't warm enough to melt the thick snow weighing down the bare branches of English elms towering alongside the walkways. And even I, without a proper coat, didn't mind the cold, because the air was sweet and crisp, the light sanitizing, and walking about my old neighborhood allowed me a sense of freedom I hadn't felt since the New Year, even if I were, in all reality, skulking.

"How'd you do it?" Barrie eventually asked, his smooth and tender voice breaking the long silence between us.

"Do what?"

"Pilly's is so far downtown," Barrie explained. "And the strongest wind spell on record levitated a grown man for precisely twenty-seven seconds."

"Yes. I believe a level-five caster in Chicago holds that particular record," I answered in a tone suggesting I wasn't actually all too interested.

We reached one of the westside exits of the park, and Barrie stopped walking to study me. "You've always had that record broken, haven't you?"

"There are some things which are better left unspoken, Dr. Barrie."

He said nothing more on the subject.

We crossed the street crowded with steam-powered motorwagons and touring automobiles, their chrome exhaust pipes spitting hot steam into the air and their pressure gauges whistling in time with the copper directing traffic on the busy thoroughfare. I followed Barrie through the front door of Fifth Avenue Hotel and, I must say, the splendor of the establishment hits differently when experiencing it with one's own eyes.

The white marble was buffed and polished within an inch of its life, and the mellow yellow light from the steam lamps strategically placed among the columns bounced off its surface, supplying the lobby with a sort of ethereal quality. Porters rushed this way and that, schlepping the considerable number of travel trunks that the ultra-rich never left home without. The corridor was full of mingling guests as well, most still dressed for the day, but I could already pick out a few men in top hats, ready for an evening of oysters, roasted grouse, and grapes before whiling away the hours with cigars and cognac, rubbing elbows with the elite of the city.

Barrie approached the reception desk to request his bags

be brought down from his room, and I made myself entirely forgettable to passersby—leaning against the far wall, carpet bag at my feet and a complimentary copy of the *Daily Cog* opened wide. It appeared that the city of Brooklyn wished to open another water well, at the cost of one million dollars to its citizens. An unknown man committed suicide on Mercer Street and had been sent to the city morgue in hopes of identification. Miner's Theatre on the Bowery experienced some smoke excitement the night before, but thankfully it was only coming from a stove in the adjoining poolroom. And it looked as if the Widow Vanderbilt and General Grant were to both attend the Martha Washington Reception tomorrow at the Academy of Music.

All in all, I hadn't seemed to have missed much in my absence.

"Mr. Ackerman."

I lowered the paper enough to look over the top. Barrie was walking toward me with a porter carrying a carpet bag similar to my own. "Is that all you have?" I asked, closing the paper and folding it into something more accommodating for travel.

"I've asked they ship my trunk home. I only need the essentials for our trip."

The porter, a young lad in uniform, approached and held his free hand out. "May I take your bag, sir?"

"I thought we could take an auto directly to Grand Central," Barrie explained.

We wanted to avoid any undue presence in the public eye, and even the short walk back to Third Avenue to once again catch the El was a risk, given the FBMS being just a stone's throw away, but requesting a ride in one of the private commuter autos had never crossed my mind. It hadn't even been a luxury I'd indulged in when gainfully employed, because not only were they costly, but I had a certain aversion to automobiles. I found them as hazardous as they were ostentatious. And while they were certainly better for the city than the horse-drawn carriages of my youth, I was much more a proponent of public transportation. I supposed if I knew how to properly drive one, I might not be so hesitant, but the opportunity had never arisen.

"No matter what you handle, you look good doing it."

"Now I know you're flirting with me."

"Sir?" the porter tried a second time.

I shook myself of the memory of Gunner behind the wheel of the automobile he'd procured during our chase of Gatling Man through the Lower East Side. How handsome and utterly rakish I had found him to be as he handled the massive piece of steam-powered machinery with elegance and ease. To the boy, I said, "Yes, thank you."

The porter accepted my bag, directed us out the front doors, and hailed one of the many autos that lurked alongside the avenue where money was no object.

V

February 19, 1882

The number of uniformed coppers patrolling the immense hall of the Depot had led me to the assumption that our ruse was up before it'd even began. But as Barrie and I moved through the people coming and going in all directions, with the telescopic roof overhead rolled back to accept the constant traffic of airships, the wintry air causing our breath to turn gold under the glow of steam chandeliers, I realized we were invisible to the metropolitan police—just two well-dressed gentlemen with reasonable luggage, making for the lifting apparatuses without any undue caution or alarm. Addison had been right: they were looking for an escaped convict, someone manic and destitute—or at the very least, the thick-headed brutes had seemed to only focus their attention on men commuting alone.

When we reached the fifth level, where the Ora Continental ship bound for San Francisco was docked and boarding passengers, I shifted my sight to study the surrounding magic. The glittering tendrils continued to light up Barrie at my side. They wove around a crewmember overhead, who hung from a steam-pneumatic grappling hook as he performed his routine double check of the steam-filled canvas. More magic glowed around a mother and her daughter presenting their first-class tickets ahead of us. I peered around them in line, toward a man farther down the dock with his back to me who appeared to be studying those boarding through the third-class ramp. I nearly second-guessed myself, but when his partner turned to face our general direction....

"FBMS," I murmured, tugging the brim of my flat cap lower.

Barrie stiffened at my side but asked calmly, "Where?"

"Third class. Special Agent Watson is the caster. Special Agent Plunket is his bruiser—the woman with short hair looking this way."

"I see her," Barrie said. "The caster hasn't sensed you, though."

"No, he wouldn't. Watson's a strong level three."

"Does the FBMS not hire agents who can sense magic signatures like you can?" Barrie murmured as he fetched his ticket from his coat pocket.

Sense? If he only knew.

"It's not a typical skill, Doctor."

"Are they the only agents here?"

"It appears so," I murmured. "I suspect more teams have been directed to the piers. More likely a fugitive would be among cargo airships than pleasure cruisers."

"A valid point."

"Tickets, gentlemen," said the crewman at the ramp. He accepted both our papers, studied the information briefly, then smiled and said, "Welcome aboard, Dr. Barrie, Mr. Ackerman. Your sleeper is number three, and the first-class dining car can be found toward the bow."

Barrie thanked the crewman and stepped onto the

gangway with the confidence of a man who'd been about luxury a time or two. I took a breath and followed a few steps behind, the enclosed glass and brass and silver of the airship's gondola catching the final rays of the setting sun. As I reached the entrance, I glanced over my shoulder.

Rachel Plunket, who in my absence had obviously been found innocent of any involvement in Henry Bligh's underground doings and assigned a new partner, was striding along the deck in her men's trousers and shoes, quickly approaching the first-class gangway.

I ducked inside and pressed myself to the bulkhead just to the right. If there was one agent at the New York field office who had legitimate reason to despise me, it was Plunket. I had had her arrested and seen to her partner's… removal. If Moore or D.C. felt she'd had even an *iota* of knowledge regarding Bligh's gangster activity… well…. I was certain her every action was still being heavily scrutinized regardless. I leaned to the window on my right and peeked out. Plunket was standing several feet away from the crewman who'd been checking tickets but was now moving up the gangway in preparation of taking off. Her winter coat was unbuttoned, so when Plunket put her hands on her hips, I could see the handle of the axe she kept buckled to her waist.

She was staring at the gondola windows.

And even at a distance, our eyes locked.

Agent Watson was moving to join her as the last of third class had boarded. He called something, and she looked at him, back to me, and then she shook her head. Plunket motioned for Watson to follow, and they walked along the dock toward the bank of lifting apparatuses.

"The hell…," I whispered, then startled as the crewman who'd just entered began to crank a set of very loud gears that retracted the gangway. I didn't move from the window until the door had been locked and my safety all but confirmed.

Plunket saw me. Recognized me. Christ Almighty, why had she lied to Watson when he'd clearly been asking if she'd seen something? She had nothing to gain by letting me escape the city. As I walked through the passageways toward the private rooms, I considered what I knew of Plunket that could shine light on the decision she'd made, but I couldn't come up with anything beyond, perhaps in her mind, it was as simple as *good riddance* and now I was California's problem. I opened the door to sleeper number three, and I must have had a look about myself, because Barrie's voice immediately filtered in.

"Is everything okay?"

I raised my head and smiled politely, automatically. "Yes, of course."

I took in the details of the room, noting the private luxuries offered to the first class were a far cry from the shared sleepers and water closets of second class that I used to travel by when dispatched on jobs outside of the city. There were large chairs on both the left and right, cushioned and upholstered in a bright, emerald-green velvet, and sleeping compartments directly above, the beds already made up of several layers of quality sheets and quilts in more green, gold, and royal purple. The sleeper had stained-glass windows, steam-powered lamps in a warm tungsten, and just beyond the beds was the open door to a water closet—indoor plumbing and steam radiators included.

"This is very nice," I said, setting my carpet bag on the floor beside the chair on the right side of the room.

"I'm an unenthusiastic traveler," Barrie explained. "If comfort is an option, I'll opt for it." He made a vague motion with one hand and asked, "Would you like to join me in the dining car for supper?"

The locks keeping the airship docked released with half a dozen simultaneous hisses of steam, and the Ora Continental began to float upward to exit out of the telescopic roof.

We were officially underway.

I removed my cap and hung it from a hook. "I'd like to lie down." Reluctantly, I added, "I'm still not feeling quite myself."

"Of course. Sleep first, and a hearty meal tomorrow." Barrie smiled, offered an uncharacteristic wink, and said, "Doctor's orders."

I had fallen asleep the moment my head hit the pillow, and with the many comforts extended to passengers with heavy purses, I slept soundly and uninterrupted throughout the entire night and late into the next day. Presumably, Barrie had returned to the sleeper after his dinner, but I hadn't heard him. Nor did I wake in the morning when he would have been seeing to washing and grooming and dressing for the day. What woke me from nearly twenty hours of the most sublime sleep I'd had in possibly my entire life was the hiss of steam and the release of dock locks. Again. And then I acknowledged the audible growls of hunger emanating from my stomach and the painful distress my bladder was in, and concluded we were departing from the one scheduled stopover—Dodge City, Kansas.

I climbed down from the bunk and took my time in the water closet, cleaning and shaving with hot water and complimentary soap, before I dressed in fresh clothes from my bag, collected my cap, and left the sleeper. I walked along the mahogany and gilded passageway of other sleeper rooms before reaching the parlor. A dozen cushioned armchairs lined the grand windows, allowing passengers unfettered views of the sunrises, sunsets, and distant landscapes below. Several of the seats were occupied, but Barrie wasn't among them, so I continued on until I stepped into the beautiful dining room. Tables were set with fine linens, china, and crystal, and a multitude of wonderful aromas wafted from the kitchen beyond. I approached Barrie, who sat alone midway in the room, staring out the window beside his table.

He glanced up at my approach and offered a warm smile. "I'm sorry I didn't wake you. I thought to have a meal brought to the sleeper for you."

"That's very kind. But I can do with a bit of polite company if this seat isn't taken," I replied, touching the back of the chair across from the doctor.

"Please," Barrie said gayly, motioning for me to sit. He slid a menu across the tabletop. "I've only just ordered."

I set my cap in my lap, studied the options for a moment, and when a waiter appeared to pour us water, I included my choice of roasted pheasant with currant jelly, mashed potatoes, and mince pie.

Barrie added two glasses of claret wine to the order, and when we were left alone, asked, "How do you feel?"

"A great deal better. Thank you." I ran my fingertips back and forth across the tabletop, but my scarred skin didn't pick up the sensation of high-quality cloth. Quietly, almost shamefully, I heard myself say, "Blackwell's feels like a nightmare I've woken from but still haven't been able to interpret."

"I'm very sorry you were confined," Barrie said.

"It wasn't your doing."

"No, but you deserve an apology. You've served the FBMS loyally, from what I can tell, and yet… they opted to believe an untrue narrative that you were mad."

It was difficult for me to hold eye contact with Barrie, and it was due to any number of reasons. Shame, certainly. He had first known me as a good lawman, and the next time our paths crossed, I was covered in filth, restrained, and he was made to believe I was insane, even if Barrie hadn't known the FBMS were the ones who concocted that lie. Embarrassment, of course. Even at my best, physically, I was hardly much to look at. Undressing in front of Gunner that first time in Arizona had been nearly unbearable, and I hadn't been half-starved and black-and-blue—and that's what Barrie had seen of me at Pilly's. And of course, there was the matter of him knowing my tendencies. I hadn't shied away from the truth, had in fact been rather brutal in my honesty. But being able to admit a dark secret wasn't the same as loving said secret. I was still scared of my inclinations—scared of the danger it presented, scared of the happiness so many men like me failed to find in their lifetime, scared of being judged, of being thought of cruelly… of so many things.

But I think what I found most difficult about meeting Barrie's gaze was the absolute intensity of his eyes. A hazel with such a spark, such a light—like stars in a desert night sky. They had a concentration to them that left me with no doubt that Barrie was well versed in the study of human emotion. In a sense, they reminded me very much of Gunner's eyes—beautiful but shrewd. Barrie's expressions might have suggested a sense of naïveté, but his eyes said otherwise.

"You never told me why you were in New York City," I stated into the lull.

"I'm on a lecture tour."

I glanced up.

"I suspect you're quite adept at calling out bunkum when you hear it."

"I am."

Barrie laughed under his breath. "It's your stare—a man who's heard it all and has time for none of it." He paused when the waiter dropped off our wine, took a sip from his glass, then said again, "I'm on a lecture tour."

"A lecture at Blackwell's?"

Barrie set the glass aside. "Yes and no. I'm researching the extent of aether's healing properties in medicine."

I tried some of the wine and asked warily, "At whose expense?"

"That's the thing," Barrie said with a smile. "Currently it's up to the physician to cast aether if they wish to incorporate it into their method of healing."

"And aether is too demanding in its energy level to be of much use beyond healing superficial wounds. You shouldn't even be considering research or experimentation into something further, Doctor."

"There's been no harm in it."

"Yet."

Barrie's smile steadily grew. "Some of us are a touch more skilled than superficial wounds." He inclined his head in the direction of my left hand resting on the tabletop. "May I see how your hands have healed?"

I leaned back in my chair and put them both in my lap.

"Okay. I get it. You're a very private man and my prodding is unwelcome." Barrie took another sip of wine. "I'm researching methods in which to use aether that won't overtax a physician, when medicine alone won't save the patient. I've had some promising results with syrups and tablets thus far—"

"That's illegal," I pointed out, and my mind went to the warehouse on the corner of Bayard and Mulberry—Warner's Quality Medicinal Remedies—where Carl Higgins mixed illegally imported aether into a simple syrup to sell under the table to the upper-class women of the city.

"Yes, but—"

"It's illegal for good reason," I interrupted again. "When casters and architects learned how to manipulate aether in '71, it opened a door that should have remained closed. It's allowed the nonmagically inclined of society to take advantage of a spell they don't understand."

Warily, Barrie said, "Aether is being added to *medicine*."

"But not exclusively. It's also utilized for weapons," I corrected. "Its use in tangible items was key to unlocking how to manipulate other elemental spells and… and there are also the ethical concerns," I reprimanded, and clearly, I wasn't finished with warning Barrie of what a profoundly dangerous path he was on, even if he thought it was for the greater good. "Medications spiked with aether and being sold aren't regulated by the FBMS or overseen by doctors. They can kill people if the spell is cast incorrectly. Never mind what is arguably the biggest danger: aether medicine might not put a strain on the physician, but what about the caster who infused it? *Someone* has to perform the spell, and if this medication is sold at drug counters, becomes a daily demand by society, who does it fall on to fulfill the need? The magic community. It's a swift and dangerous path to abusing casters and forcing them to perform against their will."

"This is obviously a sensitive topic for you."

I snorted. *"Obviously…."* I looked away and studied a shower of falling stars out the window.

Our meals arrived, and an uncomfortable and incomplete silence fell over the table. I ate a few bites of the pheasant and currant, and the rich game bird mixed with the sweet-tart jelly was absolutely delectable. I was hyperaware of my table manners this time, and in order to pace myself, reluctantly said to Barrie, "You still haven't explained why you were visiting Blackwell's."

Barrie stopped cutting his veal and stared at me with those bright eyes. "A doctor at Bellevue had asked me a question I hadn't considered: Could my theories be applied to not only the physical aches, but the mental as well? And would it make a difference whether the mental patient was magically inclined themselves? So I requested a visit to Blackwell's, which Dr. Ashland approved. The moment I'd stepped foot on the island, he wanted to show you off."

"Like a trophy."

"Yes." Barrie glanced around the dining room before leaning forward and saying in a low voice, "Everyone in our community knows the name Simon Fitzgerald. I hardly believed Ashland—everyone thought you died in the Great Rebellion."

I nodded mutely.

"He was quite convinced of your supposed lunacy and wished to be part of any and all research on you."

I picked up my napkin and pressed the linen to my mouth as the sudden urge to vomit nearly overwhelmed me.

"Ashland thought your magic is what ultimately caused your mania, so he was quite interested in whether my magic medicine could also *reverse* it."

I swallowed a few times before I was confident in setting the napkin back down. I finished off my glass of water, picked up my fork and knife, and said absently, "I'm sorry I asked."

The second pass of silence was less uneasy—just the clink and scrape of silverware on china and murmured conversations at a few occupied tables to my back.

Unprompted, Barrie said, "I was in the war."

I raised my head.

"Seven Pines."

"Virginia?" I asked, uncertain.

Barrie nodded. "I stayed in the state as a surgeon throughout '62 and '63."

I sat at an elegant table aboard a luxury airship, swaying in sync with the gentle back and forth of the skies. But I also stood under the canvas roof of a hospital tent, gunpowder burning my eyes as I watched men carried in from the battlefield die right before me—so mangled and so bloody, no doctor could save them, no mother could identify them.

And it had been my fault.

I dropped my silverware, and it clattered to the plate as I hastily stood. "Excuse me." I left the table, yanking my goggles from around my neck and over my eyes as I stepped through a door to the right and onto the empty promenade deck. I moved to the chest-level railing, gripped the brass tightly in both hands, and dropped my head as I took in breaths of cold night air.

The mention—the mere *mention*—of those days and I couldn't breathe. A clammy sweat had broken out across my chest and underarms, and my fingers tingled almost painfully along my damaged nerves, like the blood had completely stopped pumping to my extremities. Every time I closed my eyes, I saw a different image, like those photographic negatives that'd found their way from the battlefield and into the hands of journalists. But unlike the woodblocks used by newspapers to reprint tragedy for the masses, my memories of those deaths were in full-color stereograph.

I took a slow, shaky breath. Another. And another. A dozen deep breaths later, my heart no longer felt as if it were trying to pound my rib cage to dust. I raised my head, opened my eyes, and studied the star-studded sky through my purple lenses. I straightened my posture and reveled in the cold air whipping through my hair and suit, cooling down the sickening fever that had heated my whole body.

A few minutes later, the door to my back opened, closed, and Barrie's steps sounded against the wooden deck. He stopped beside me at the railing and offered my flat cap.

I took it, thumbed the tweed, then shoved it in my suit pocket.

"Mr. Hamilton—"

"Dr. Barrie, if it's all the same to you, I'd rather we not discuss the war."

Barrie remained where he stood and said, with a sort of gentle authority, "I wonder if you suffer from Soldier's Heart."

"Are you familiar with Soldier's Heart? They say it's an invisible illness."

I laughed, but it tasted as bitter as it sounded. I looked toward the sky again, so heavy with stars that it was like a sack of flour spilled across the night. A knot tightened in my throat, and I thought of my mother, who had lived in such fear of the Flour Riots of '37 occurring a second time, that when I'd misfired a water spell as a boy—I'd had no understanding of how to control my magic!—and I'd ruined a newly purchased sack….

Smack, smack, smack.

I flinched, tugged the goggles down, and hastily wiped my face with the heel of my hand.

"Do you know this?" Barrie continued.

"It's been suggested to me," I said woodenly, and I caught Barrie nodding to himself from the corner of my eye.

"Why California?"

"I'm sorry?"

"I've done my best to answer your questions and ask little of my own," Barrie explained. "But I feel you ought to extend to me this one thing—why are we going to California?"

I ran fingers through my tousled hair before holding it down firmly with the palm of my hand. "While I was still employed as a special agent, a number of suspects I questioned indicated there were suspicious happenings out in California that relate to the atmospheric troubles. I left the case opened and unsolved."

"Ah. Would that be the investigation you were working at the New Year? The one regarding Henry Bligh?"

"Yes—*wait*." I finally looked at Barrie. "How did you know—?"

My attention was immediately drawn in two different directions, existing in both the physical and magical planes: Barrie opening a small wooden box in his hands, and the whir of aether ammunition being activated at my back.

A blast of blinding white light.

A shot cracking against the night.

And then Barrie jerked backward like a ragdoll. He stumbled and crashed to the deck. A red stain blossomed through the layers of clothing at his shoulder, and the box he'd dropped was open to reveal a hypodermic needle with a syringe.

I raised my hands, cast lightning, and spun on one heel—only to find myself staring down the triple barrel of a Waterbury pistol.

"Gunner?"

VI

February 20, 1882

Gunner the Deadly—the country's number-one wanted outlaw. The gentleman thief. The vigilante. Six feet of all-black-wearing, deadeye marksmanship skills, with a penchant for Crown perfume and Black Jack chewing gum. A learned man of literature, with a husky voice from years of smoking Virginia Brights, and eyes so blue that sapphires paled in comparison.

Constantine Gunner—the one man on God's green Earth who'd considered me *his*. Who'd adored me without fear, without hesitation, without concern for the secrets that burdened my soul. The love and light of my life, who I'd pushed away to save and broken his heart in the process.

He was here.

Right now.

Of all places, sailing through the skies, somewhere over the Eastern Plains of Colorado.

Gunner lowered his Waterbury, yanked the bandana from his face, and reached out. He grabbed my arm the moment I allowed the lightning spell to dissolve, sparks of electricity dancing across the deck under my feet as he drew me up against himself and asked, "Are you okay?" I must have been staring at him as if I'd seen a spirit, because Gunner's hold tightened on my bicep, and he said sternly, "*Gillian*?"

"Y-yes. I'm—what're you… how are you here?"

Gunner didn't answer, and instead pulled me to stand behind him as he raised the Waterbury and pointed it at Barrie a second time.

"Gunner, what the hell are you doing?"

"Putting a bullet in the good doctor's head."

I grabbed Gunner's extended arm with both hands. "No, don't! Dr. Barrie saved—"

Gunner twisted around to stare at me. "*That man* is Sawbones."

"*What*?" I peered around Gunner as Barrie reached into his coat pocket and removed a glass bottle. He tore the cork off with his teeth and drank the contents of what I could only presume to be aether syrup, while blood seeped down his arm and dripped from his fingertips. I turned toward the windows of the dining room that overlooked the promenade—several passengers watched, their faces aghast. A waiter dropped his tray and ran through the maze of tables in the direction of the bridge, presumably to inform the captain of the situation. I said to Gunner, "That's not possible."

Gunner didn't bother to argue further and turned toward Barrie.

I yanked Gunner to face me again, one hand clutching a fistful of his black winter coat, the other keeping a firm hold on his tie. "Barrie is helping me get to California to track down Weaver."

Gunner said with frightening composure, "Eugene Barrie was a bloodthirsty surgeon during the war. He performed thousands of amputations—derived pleasure from it. Soldiers called him Sawbones. They were so afraid of being put under his knife, men chose to die in the fields rather than risk the agony of his hospital tent."

My eyes stung and my vision blurred something horrible. "Why are you saying this?"

"My dear. He's been in New York—"

"On a lecture tour."

"No. Since December, when he was hired to build the mechanical men. He's not helping you. He's *kidnapping* you."

I opened my mouth—to say what, I hadn't a clue. Protest that I couldn't possibly be so dense, so naïve, so oblivious? But more likely it was to sob, because Gunner the Deadly never lied, and I had been so, so stupid. My distress caused a delay in noticing movement over Gunner's shoulder, and then Barrie was standing there, his wound no longer bleeding and his face contorted in blind fury. He looked like a completely different person from the soft-spoken and too-curious man I'd been sharing a bottle of wine with just moments earlier.

Barrie raised the needle he'd collected from the deck, stabbed it into Gunner's left arm, and hit the plunger.

The magic atmosphere was suddenly alive with that awful sensation of wriggling, like maggots making home in the cavities of man. It was the activation of a spell I hadn't felt since January, but one I couldn't ever forget: quintessence.

And it was mixed in with the contents of the syringe.

I screamed, a kind of wordless, soulless rage, and heavy black clouds manifested in the sky. Thunder boomed and crashed overhead while lightning sparked from my body, coalesced into a spell, and slammed into Barrie with a force so concentrated that it could have illuminated all of New York City. Barrie had let go of the syringe, left it sticking in Gunner's arm, and had taken a step back with just enough time to raise his hands and cast a shield of aether. Our magics exploded upon contact, and while I remained standing, the force of his spell propelled me backward several feet. When the blinding detonation let up enough that I could risk a glance, I could make out Barrie on his knees, shaking electricity from his hands and hastily patting down the smoke billowing from the sleeves of his coat. His carefully parted hair was in disarray, and he was bleeding from his nose or mouth or maybe, hopefully, both. The fact that he was still conscious was surprising, and I feared I'd most definitely underestimated his own level due to the way raw magic interacted so gently with his person.

The door to the promenade burst open, and the ship's captain stood in the threshold, a pistol in hand. "Stop right where you are!" he exclaimed. "Hands in the air!"

I shot my palm out and a squall of wind blew him off his feet, back into the dining room, and the door slammed shut in his wake. I spun toward Gunner as he holstered his Waterbury and ripped the syringe from his arm. He stared at the glass tube, shook it, but it was empty, then dropped it to the deck and stomped on it with the heel of his boot. That squirming, unnatural magic sent another shiver up my spine.

Gunner turned around as one knee buckled. He reached for the railing to steady himself.

I grabbed his chest and righted him when he staggered a second time. "Oh God. Gunner?"

"Morphine," he answered with a grunt.

"I'm researching methods in which to use aether that won't overtax a physician...."

Not just aether, I thought with sudden horror. Barrie was researching how to use quintessence outside of the mechanical army he'd been constructing for Tick Tock. Quintessence, a new and illegal spell, its casting method and usage unknown to me, other than it was sort of an antithesis to aether.

Gunner was right.

And now… was he going to die?

My heart was pounding so hard, I was light-headed. I couldn't catch my breath. There was no time to consider the limitless catalogue of possible reactions Gunner would have to the quintessence, no time to dwell in despair over something that hadn't yet occurred. I needed to get him somewhere safe, somewhere I could think for half a second without bullets flying or two-timing sadistic surgeons trying to—

"Climb onto the handrail," I ordered Gunner.

A second aether spell crashed into me, knocking me off my feet and flinging me across the deck. All of my hurts screamed in protest as I slammed into the polished wood, but I didn't allow the adrenaline rush to wane, and scrambled to my feet. Barrie stood several yards away, with Gunner between us, still leaning against the rail. The doctor's expensive suit was scorched, and he wiped blood off his face with the back of his hand, the other maintaining an aether spell the size of my head, glowing white-hot.

"You pack a hell of a wallop for such a *small man*, Fitzgerald," Barrie called.

Thunder continued to crash overhead, and I smelled ozone as lightning snapped and crackled around me. "I allowed the country to call me a butcher, but all the while, *you* were the real monster of that war." The lightning unleashed, shot forward like a rabid animal, and slammed into Barrie's aether. I tore more power from the atmosphere to feed the spell, watched as the lightning swallowed the aether, and the magics shattered like a mirror constructed from light. I shielded my eyes with my forearm, and when I was able to look again, Barrie was flat on his stomach and coughing a storm of his own.

I rushed back to Gunner and kept a hand on him as he

unsteadily hoisted himself onto the railing and turned, back to the sky. I climbed up beside him, keeping hold of the nearest baluster while swinging myself behind Gunner. I gripped around his middle and asked, "Ready?"

"Whatever you're considering, please do it before I pass out," Gunner answered.

I glanced at his grip on the same baluster I held. "Let go."

Gunner did, without question or hesitation.

And we fell backward into the stars.

Viciously strong winds whipped our bodies back and forth. I held Gunner against myself for all I was worth, while I watched the landscape below and used my free hand to cast a wind spell that would counteract the sky's attempt to tear us apart.

A streak of blinding aether light shot past us, and I craned my neck for a view of the airship—at Barrie, leaning over the rail, casting aether, his manic voice carrying on the current: "*Fitzgerald!*"

Gunner's arm wavered in the wind, but then he unholstered the Waterbury, aimed, and fired. Again and again, round after round, as a means of keeping Barrie at bay, until he was too far away to pose a threat.

The flat, frozen plains were reaching up to meet us, and I swore while pulling more energy from the atmosphere to maintain the wind spell. The magic hit the ground ahead of us, tearing prairie grass and kicking up chunks of frozen snow and dirt before ricocheting back at me to slow our plunge. Still not feeling up to full strength, coupled with having just exerted myself against Barrie, and with the added weight of Gunner in my arms, my landing didn't stick. I stumbled, tried to pick back up into the air and retry, but Gunner suddenly went limp, offsetting my balance, and we crashed.

I was pinned underneath Gunner, and it took a moment to

catch my breath and wriggle free from his height and muscle. I got to my knees, put my hands on his shoulders, and gave him a firm shake. "Gunner? *Gunner*! Christ Almighty." I leaned close, my ear to his mouth, and felt warm breath more than I heard it. He was alive, but out cold. And who was to say if it was a morphine overdose or the quintessence magic introduced to his body?

I raised my hand, snapped, and used a flame to study the dark, desolate wasteland where so many homesteaders lived these days. I had heard that these poor folk were susceptible to something called Prairie Madness, and as I stumbled to my feet and turned in a complete circle, only to realize we were utterly alone in this flat, unforgiving land, I understood how madness could be lying in wait. Afterall, I had come close to insanity after only three days in isolation at the asylum.

My breath stuttered in little plumes of white smoke as I crouched beside Gunner a second time. He was dressed appropriately, whereas I was not, but lying on the frozen ground for even a short period of time would leach the heat from his body entirely. What took precedence was examining the spot in which Barrie had injected him, but I couldn't expose Gunner's bare skin to these elements.

I could drag him, I thought. But drag him *where*? With the exception of wind—so cold, it was like my bones were being hacked open to expose the marrow—the plains were still and silent. I couldn't even pinpoint a single rock outcropping or cluster of trees that might have served as an impromptu shelter until daybreak because of how utterly black the night was.

I had been, quite literally, leaping from one chaotic mess to another for the last three days and I was... absolutely overwhelmed. I didn't know what to do anymore. That familiar, crushing weight of the world on my shoulders was back, deforming my spine, forcing me to my knees, and sooner rather than later, I'd be dead from the burden. The sense of feeling unmoored in that moment was, at least in part, due to the revelation regarding Eugene Barrie. I hadn't been given an opportunity to question him, let alone digest the truth, and now I had an entirely new problem to deal with because of it.

I squeezed my eyes shut and took a very deep breath. When I opened them, I was still in the same situation, but a sense of clarity, of truth, of devotion, had docked at the empty harbor in my soul.

Gunner had had no sense of obligation toward me.

Not anymore, at least.

And yet, he'd tracked me down. He'd rushed to my aid when I wasn't aware of the danger. He'd called me Gillian—the man I wished I was. He'd called me his dear—the man I once had been.

Gunner meant everything to me.

Perhaps… I still meant something to him.

Holding the flame in one hand, I set my other on Gunner's chest and leaned over to study his placid face. "Constantine?" I didn't know how to encompass all of my thoughts, my emotions, my past actions in a way that made sense—that was explainable—but love wasn't sensible. That's why we misspoke when we were scared, and that's why we made a scene when we didn't want to live with any regrets. I kissed his forehead and whispered, "You're loved too."

A rifle shot cracked the air, and I extinguished the flame before throwing myself on top of Gunner to shield his prone body.

A woman's voice called from the darkness, "Consider this your warning: I only miss once!"

"Don't shoot! Jesus Christ, lady!"

"Don't you be takin' the Lord's name in vain, sir," the

woman retorted, and she cocked the weapon. "You're on my property."

"*Wait*," I called, and I raised my head enough to look over my shoulder toward where I thought the shot originated from, although the vast monotone landscape made a sense of direction impossible without the sun to act as a guide, and I had always been too much of a city boy to navigate by stars alone. But then I saw a flicker of light, like a kerosene lantern being set on the ground, and a shift of black shadow against the even darker night. "I'm not trying to pull the wool over your eyes," I promised. "My friend is in need of medical attention."

The light of the lantern was then lifted from the ground, and the crunch of frozen earth and grass sounded under the woman's boots as she approached. She stopped a few feet short and raised the lantern eye-level, illuminating her face by the lick of yellow flame. She had a dark complexion and black hair pulled into what looked like a hasty bun, as if she'd already let it down for the evening. She wore a pair of men's trousers and a shirt with braces that rested against her bosom.

Shifting her hold to accommodate both the lantern and rifle, she aimed the weapon at me while asking, "How'd you get here? The road's that way." She jerked her head toward the right.

My hands were raised up, palms out, as I said, "Would you please stop pointing that gun at me?"

"I will once you disarm yourself, sir."

"I don't carry a weapon."

"I see a holster on your friend."

Keeping my sight trained on the stranger, I awkwardly leaned back and fumbled blindly for Gunner's Waterbury. "It's empty," I explained, showing her the cylinder once I'd wrenched the pistol free from Gunner's hip.

She studied me another long, hard minute, then lowered the rifle. "You got no damn sense."

"Sorry?"

"Stumbling around out here, in the dark, in winter, without even a proper coat."

"It's a long story," I answered, dropping my hands and keeping my voice low so that she didn't catch the chatter of my teeth.

"How'd you get here?"

"That's an even longer story." I shifted on my knees in order to put a hand on Gunner's chest. "I need to get my friend inside. He's been poisoned, I think, and needs to be tended to right away." I dug into the inner pockets of Gunner's coat before finding the coin purse I knew he kept on his person. "I can pay," I finished, shaking it so the heavy coins clinked together.

The woman slung her rifle over one shoulder and said, with a hint of exasperation, "And I'm sure you expect me to help carry his sorry backside too. C'mon. Lift him up—that's right—I'll take this arm."

We were able to haul Gunner's dead weight into a sitting position before each getting a shoulder under either arm and standing. Unfortunately, Gunner was a great deal taller than both me and my irritable rescuer, so his feet dragged uselessly behind him as the woman steered us in the direction of what looked like more endless night.

"I didn't catch your name, ma'am," I said, a bit breathless from both the cold and exertion.

"That's because I didn't offer it, sir."

I'd have happily traded places with Gunner at that moment, if only because he was certain to enjoy this woman's chutzpah more than me. "May I have your name?"

"Winona Brown."

Despite the probability of a nonmagical homesteader knowing the history of either Simon Fitzgerald or Gillian Hamilton being astoundingly low, I didn't dare drop those names. Instead, I introduced myself as Malcom Ackerman.

Winona made a sound in the back of her throat. "And your friend, here?"

"John Gaylord."

She made that sound again.

"Is there a problem?"

Winona looked around Gunner at me. The lantern bouncing in her right hand cast strange shadows along her handsome face. "Those really the names you want to go with?"

My heart beat a little faster, but calmly, I said, "Those are our names."

"If you say so."

Just ahead of us, another lantern flickered to life, its subtle glow outlining a structure I hadn't even realized was there. It was a squat, one-story home that didn't appear to have any windows, at least on the side facing us, and perhaps had what might have been a stove pipe sticking out of the roof. One of those sod homes, I imagined.

And then a second figure stepped out of a doorway, holding the lantern high like a beacon as she called, "Who is it, Winona?"

"Some simpleminded menfolk. One of them's in a spot. We got any brandy?"

We finally drew close enough to the sod home that I could make out the details of the second occupant and, suffice it to say, they were not sisters. Oh sure, they were both close to me in age, but this other woman was much more slight, wearing a green checkered-pattern dress and shawl draped over her shoulders, with a pale face and very blond hair. Society had a distinct lack of vocabulary for women like this and, I'd noticed, a tendency to outright ignore, even pretend it wasn't happening and that the sodomite affliction affected only men. But I had to wonder at the likelihood of these women sharing a similar tendency… given the current circumstances. After all, I could understand the appeal of moving far away from prying eyes and living life by your own set of rules, even more so for women, given the strict limitations so many were forced to endure within "polite society."

"We got some," the second woman confirmed, disappearing back inside.

Winona led the way into the home, her other half shutting the door behind me and locking out the cold. We dragged Gunner the last few feet to a bed in the corner of the one room, where Winona deposited him before moving to the small table near the stove to set her lantern down. She turned it off, likely to save fuel, and the humble home was near-dark, illuminated only by the second lantern, which outlined the other woman moving some bottles on a shelf and reading the labels.

I shucked off my suit coat so as to work without hinderance, and hastily rolled back my sleeves, asking, "How'd you know we were out there? We were less than a hundred feet away, and I couldn't see your home, it's so dark out here."

Winona said, while hanging her rifle on a hook near the door, "Went outside to make certain the chickens were locked in for the night—"

"Foxes on these plains are smart as hell," her friend piped in.

Winona was nodding. "—and I saw fire."

"Huh." I began the arduous task of maneuvering Gunner free from his winter and suit coats.

After a beat, Winona said, "But you've got no lantern, Mr. Ackerman."

"No, I don't."

The second woman moved around the table and joined me at the bedside as I'd begun working on the buttons of Gunner's waistcoat. I glanced up. She was clutching a half-empty bottle of brandy in one hand, the other extended toward me.

"Lucy Vogel," she said brightly.

"Malcom Ackerman." I reached to quickly shake her hand, unable to be rude to the strangers who'd opened their home to us, but still near panicked regarding Gunner's state, when a pop of electricity bounced and crackled between our hands.

"*Oh!*" She pulled back and shook her hand like it hurt a little, but was laughing and smiling. "I knew it." She spun to Winona. "Explains the fire."

"Sure does," Winona answered, crossing her arms over her chest.

"You're a caster?" I asked Lucy, because I hadn't picked up on any tendrils of magic lingering about her, but then again, I wasn't exactly looking for it.

"Just a touch of the gift, sir," she explained. "Hardly a level one."

"I see." I hesitated a moment, but when neither of them suggested concern over my magic-inclined presence, I returned to undressing Gunner.

Wrangling him out of so many layers was a borderline ridiculous task, but seeing as how I had no money of my own and would be entirely dependent on whatever he had in his coin purse, I didn't want to rip Gunner's clothing to shreds and force him to buy new wares because I was panicking. Lucy had been politely gathering each article as I tossed it aside, and I think she was folding them into a neat pile, when she gasped loudly.

"Oh my word. What happened to his arm?" she asked.

I put a knee on the mattress—straw-filled, it felt—and leaned over Gunner's bare chest to examine his bicep where Barrie had stabbed him with the syringe. "Hand me that lantern, would you?" I reached for the one Winona had placed on the tabletop, and after Lucy passed it over, careful this time that our hands didn't make contact, I cast a small lightning spell and slipped the bouncing energy into the chimney of the lamp. It would save using the women's limited fuel, was much brighter, and didn't release noxious fumes. I set it on the small stand beside the bed before climbing over Gunner entirely in order to study the wound up close.

His upper arm was discolored, sort of like a bruise. It didn't *seem* to be spreading, which was good, but a morphine overdose wouldn't cause a visual disturbance like this. So it had to be because of the quintessence. I steeled myself for the squirming sensation the magic gave off, and gently wrapped both hands around Gunner's arm.

And there it was—that twisting, burrowing, *not quite right* reaction I'd experienced with Tick Tock's artificial magic ammunition, as well as the various mechanical monstrosities Barrie had built. Quintessence didn't feel like aether. It wasn't attempting to heal or destroy, both of which aether could do, depending on how it was cast and wielded. Quintessence was more like… a void. A middle ground that aether couldn't exist upon. A miasma of strangeness and sorrow that weighed down—my stream of consciousness came to an abrupt stop right then.

Weighed down.

On New Year's Eve, after throwing the intruder from my bedroom window, remnants of this magic dissipated from his body following death. Eugene Barrie—call him who he was, *Sawbones*—utilized precious metals in his construction that were meant to withstand not only the usage of certain magics in the ammunition, but reinforce the mechanical man's own defense against real casters like me. Because prior to Tick Tock's investments, the danger in homemade firearms and bullets was that aether was the only magic to be safely manipulated into tangible, everyday items. Fire, water, lightning—those spells all had disastrous and devastating results. That had been, in part, what led to Milo Ferguson's deadly fate in Arizona. The artificial spells in his ammunition weren't… weren't weighed down. So by the time Barrie had been brought into the venture, he, Luther Jones, and the mysterious Weaver had devised a work-around: overlay the bullets, the guns, and the gangsters in brass and bronze and platinum infused with quintessence.

It was a heavy, black hole of a magic that didn't seem to have any sort of offensive or defensive reaction. It was like a backbone, holding everything together, reinforcing other spells and keeping them from flying apart. Or in this case, the quintessence was reinforcing the bodily response to a medication.

That shot of morphine had originally been intended for me.

It certainly would've made me amiable and pliable, but it wouldn't have lasted until we reached California tomorrow afternoon. Barrie would have had to keep dosing me, potentially even risk killing me. So the quintessence mixed into the drug was meant to weigh down the initial reaction, to prolong it without the danger of multiple doses. Barrie could have walked me right off the ship tomorrow and into a situation I'd not have been able to save myself from. But Gunner had mucked up Barrie's plans and gotten the injection instead—whether by accident or on purpose, I couldn't be certain, as the seconds that'd unfolded on the promenade were a blur in my mind.

Barrie hadn't claimed he'd perfected his research, though. What if the syringe had had a touch too much morphine and the quintessence was weighing down the reaction of losing consciousness, instead of that lackadaisical high he'd been aiming for? In the past, the only way the quintessence had dissolved was when Frank Fishback and Mechanical Man had both died. It'd slithered away, like some creature vanishing into the night. Was that the only way the spell would be lifted from Gunner as well?

If he died?

"I thought you said he was poisoned."

Winona's voice had broken the avalanche of thoughts, and when I looked up, she was leaning over the bed, peering at Gunner's arm.

"He was."

"Ain't like no poison I've seen."

I declined to comment further and instead pulled my goggles on and cast aether. I pulled at the magic, elongating it like bread dough, until one end was a shimmering white needle point. I held Gunner's shoulder firmly, punctured skin and muscle as I stuck the edge into his wound, and then began to reverse engineer the spell, like I'd done in Arizona. Because I didn't want to simply try and heal Gunner. I didn't know how the quintessence would react, if at all. So instead I was going to treat it like a festering, embedded thorn in need of extraction, and the only idea I could come up with was to pump Gunner full of aether, like I'd done to his Waterbury ammunition, until his body overflowed with the magic and physically forced the quintessence spell *out*.

Even with the eye protection, my hands glowed such a brilliant, blinding white that I winced behind the lenses. After I'd cast aether on myself enough times that I was itching with overstimulated energy, the magic began to drip, then pour from the palms of my hands, along my fingers, and through the spike of aether I'd stuck into Gunner's arm. His body soaked it up like a sponge left to rot in the sun, and within a minute, the wound was as bright as my hands. So it was no surprise that I didn't notice the black spot growing in size around the embedded spike acting as a funnel.

That is, until it moved.

I sat on my knees, so I couldn't exactly recoil off the bed, so much as startle in a mixture of disbelief and fear. My flow of reverse aether faltered, but I managed to keep going, even as the… *thing*, now protruding from Gunner's wound, squirmed like a fat, oily leech. My body began its telltale protest of overexertion from this illegal usage of the spell, but I didn't dare stop. Not yet. Not until—

The leech popped free and fell to the mattress. Nearly four inches of the most vile, disgusting magic I'd ever had the misfortune to cast my eyes upon. And to make matters worse… it was still *moving*. Here was all the proof I needed for *someone* at the FBMS to take my side and defend me against the council—a spell that maintained its energy and cohesion without its caster there to physically feed it with raw power, and the side effect was the devastating tears and wounds in the magic atmosphere. Quintessence was versatile, powerful, and deadly in the hands of someone as unhinged as Sawbones.

I snapped, terminating the aether spell, then scrambled backward as the leech contorted and slithered toward me across the blankets. I swore and toppled off the side of the bed. Lucy—I was pretty sure it was Lucy, anyway—screamed at the sight of the magic refuse wriggling its way down the bedpost after me. A head rush from the aether hit me hard as I sat up and ripped the goggles down around my neck. The leech plopped to the rough floor planks, and instinctively, I grabbed for it. It dodged to the side, and I slammed my hand down on it. The slippery, greasy substance made an audible *squish* under my palm, and the black film squirted between my fingers.

After a few seconds of strained silence, Lucy squeaked from the opposite side of the bed, "Mr. Ackerman?"

I rose to my feet and held my hand up to show the remnants oozing down my scarred palm. "I got it," I confirmed, and then my knees gave out. I fell forward, half on top of Gunner, half hanging off the mattress, and as I went under, I heard Winona shout:

"*What the Dickens?*"

VII

February 21, 1882

For a great deal of my life, I have been deeply disappointed in the miracle of waking up. Disappointed that the touch of a blanket, the smell of breakfast, the kiss of sunshine against my eyelids had a way of rousing my consciousness, when being brought about to live another day that no nightmare could compare to was the very last thing I'd prayed for the night before. Disappointed that I didn't pass in my sleep, where there'd be no fear or pain in the process and I'd finally be free of not only the physical hurts, but those in my heart and mind as well. Sleep would be the only way I could obtain death, though, because I was a coward who couldn't pull the trigger, and any attempt to allow someone else to do the same only prompted a deep, primal necessity to fight.

To survive.

So I kept waking up.

And I *hated* it.

My eyes snapped open and I sat up in a rush, the straw mattress crinkling and shifting underneath. Someone had draped a crocheted blanket over me after I'd passed out from exhaustion. The sod home was full of watery morning light coming from a far window I'd not noticed the night before. The sunshine highlighted dust motes in the air and steam rising from a coffeepot on the stovetop. Gunner sat at the table in the middle of the room, dressed to his waistcoat, sleeves rolled back to display the cords of muscles in his forearms, with both hands wrapped around a mug. He raised his head and met my gaze.

I hated waking up… until now.

In that low and husky voice that never failed to bring gooseflesh to my skin, Gunner said, "Good morning."

I shoved the blanket off and swung my legs over the side of the bed, noting that someone had also taken care to remove my shoes during the night. I got to my feet, took a few steps to reach the table, grabbed Gunner by the upper arms, and stated the obvious, as only to confirm this idyllic consciousness to be real. "You're awake."

He nodded.

I took a breath, but it sounded more like a gasp. "How do you feel? Your arm—is there any pain? Maybe I should look—"

Gunner reached a hand up between my arms and cupped the side of my face with such care, it was as if he thought I was made from dandelion fluff.

"I'm sorry," I said, and then I began crying.

Distantly, I was aware of having lost my composure so suddenly and profoundly, but seeing Gunner's face made me feel human again, and I was greedy and self-centered and wanted to wake to his blue eyes and crow's feet and the way his mouth hooked to one side when he was amused for the rest of my life.

That… sounded like happiness.

I dropped to the floor before Gunner and gripped his

thighs with both hands. "I had no time to explain to you," I said between sobs. "I wanted to keep you safe. I know that I don't deserve your forgiveness, and I don't expect you to be willing to pick up where we left off, but I've lied so much… nothing would be different if I didn't admit that I hope to God you'll reconsider me nonetheless." I was still crying as I said, "My reputation is in tatters. I'm a wanted criminal. I have nothing to offer you—no home, no money, no name—"

At that, Gunner's callused hand moved to my chin and tilted it up. All he said was "A man is not chained to one name. Be who offers you self-respect."

I'd never trusted someone the way I did Gunner. It was funny, in a sense, that the most honest, understanding, and tender man I'd ever known was, on paper, the worst class of criminal there was. Because make no mistake, Gunner the Deadly was responsible for dozens of killings. He stole thousands of dollars that weren't his. He openly defied law enforcement with that Waterbury slung around his hips. And yet, I had confided in him my tendencies, my virginity, my magic, and my real name. I had shared with Gunner some of the blackest, ugliest, scariest parts of myself, because I saw in him a man who lived to the fullest by the same code of ethics he preached: to be certain that the choices made today allow you to breathe tomorrow.

Gunner had provided me the tools to save me from myself. He had shown me how to use them and hadn't given up when my footing faltered—and God knows there were some days I could barely stand. Even now, with my world broken into too many pieces to reassemble, he didn't hesitate. Gunner was right here, reminding me to breathe, telling me it was never too late to begin anew.

I raised my gaze to meet his. "In '62, the Union incorporated magic into their war strategies, and they weren't particular with how they came about fulfilling their need for casters. My parents sold me to the Army for ten dollars and a pound of sugar." My eyes burned and my throat began seizing up. "I turned ten at Fort Donelson, Tennessee. After the battle, I jumped into the Cumberland River to drown myself. Only, it didn't work because I knew how to swim."

Gunner's mask of passivity slipped and I caught the entire range of negative human emotions reflecting back at me from the deep blue of his eyes. Rage… horror… *heartbreak*. He grabbed my face in both hands and drew me up onto my knees.

"I was in Maryland by September. At Antietam—when… it was *so loud*. The shells overhead… and the horses were *screaming*. Canister shot hit everyone. Bones broke like glass in a hailstorm. A man's head exploded and…." I struggled to catch my breath as I turned my hands palms up to rest on his thighs. They were the scarred hands of a man, not a boy. I knew this, I could see it, and yet it was as if I were looking at little broken fingers caked in dirt and…. "There was so much blood and I wanted to wash my hands—"

"My dear," Gunner interjected with an edge of desperation.

"—A soldier dragged me back to the field." I looked up at Gunner. "And th-they told me… t-to cast…."

"Please stop," Gunner begged.

"I killed so many people!" I cried, and the sunlight at the window waned as dark clouds rolled across the plains. "I was so scared, and it just happened—I couldn't control it! The men from the Sixty-Ninth called me a monster. The embalmers called me a butcher. I ran. I ran until I had to drag myself, and I kept going. Because I couldn't—I couldn't go back. Oh God… I'm a murderer!"

Gunner got to his feet in one smooth motion, yanking me to stand as he did so. He gripped my shoulders with such force that the discomfort brought me back to my senses. "Listen to me," he said with quiet intensity, his eyes burning like an ocean on fire. "You were a *child*—" He stopped abruptly and seemed to struggle before getting out, "War is man's doing, and yet the burden will always fall onto the most innocent." Gunner held my face in his hands again. "You were brutalized and dehumanized, but you're no monster, no butcher, and no murderer. Do you know how I know? Because twenty years later, I see how easily you hurt from an unkind word. I see you long for respect but refuse to abuse your incredible powers in order to obtain it. And I see the way your face glows when I tell you that I love you. I'm not saying you don't have wounds that run deep. I'm saying that in spite of it all, you survived. I've met my fair share of monsters and butchers and murderers." Gunner wiped my cheeks with his thumbs. "Not one of them would have stood in the face of federal arrest warrants in order to allow me time to slip out."

I wiped my nose on the sleeve of my shirt. "You still love me?"

"My dear, I never stopped." Gunner leaned down and pressed his mouth to mine.

This was the first moment since New Year's Day, when I'd kissed Gunner in the FBMS field office, in front of both agents and God alike, that I'd felt the vise loosen around my chest and allow me to take a full breath. I wrapped my arms around Gunner's neck and returned the kiss with such vigor and commitment that we were both left winded when our lips parted. And after, I still wanted more. All of it. Everything.

"I love you, Constantine," I said.

His eyes softened, and a small smile lingered.

"And I'm so sorry that I couldn't explain the gravity of the situation we were in when the D.C. agents showed up—and that I hurt you because of it."

He nodded and stroked the short hairs on the side of my head.

"I'm not sure I can even begin to explain the last month and a half to you without…." I wiped my nose a final time and shook my head. "I suppose it's rather tame in the grand scheme of what I've—what *Simon* went through." I considered that thought for a moment before looking up at Gunner. "I don't want to be Simon Fitzgerald anymore. I feel like Simon died in 1862, and I'd been nobody until '68, when I found Gillian Hamilton stabbed to death on the Bowery. He had immigration paperwork and an address written in pencil on a scrap of paper…. I pretended to be him for a roof over my head, and then… I kept perpetuating the lie." I moved my thumb up and down the line of buttons on Gunner's waistcoat. "And yet, Simon's guilt and fear still lingers. I'm just so tired of it."

Gunner asked, "Did you mourn Simon?"

"What?"

Gunner shrugged. "It seems, no matter how hard you try to be Gillian Hamilton, Simon follows. Perhaps it's because you haven't allowed yourself time to properly say goodbye."

"You speak like Simon and Gillian are two different people entirely."

"In a sense, they are." Gunner took a step back. He took my hand, raised it, and kissed the pale underside of my wrist. "Gillian."

I shivered from the contact but asked, "It's okay? Even though it's not my name?"

"It's yours if you want it to be."

I turned, pulled out the second chair at the table, and sat with Gunner on my left. "I want it to be," I whispered, all at once feeling utterly exhausted.

Gunner stroked the side of my head again, like he couldn't help himself. "There's nothing more you need to say on the matter, Special Agent Hamilton."

I laughed bitterly and faced the window when I felt more tears begin to well in my eyes. I hastily dabbed them away as Gunner walked to the stove behind me and poured coffee into a second mug. "I'm no longer employed with the Federal Bureau of Magic and Steam."

Gunner put the mug in front of me, returned to his seat, and said, "We'll see about that."

I stared at him, my eyebrows raised.

"Drink your coffee. Ms. Vogel might want to be your mother, but I'm certain Ms. Brown won't hesitate to use her rifle if you waste her supply of Folgers."

I grunted and took a sip of the black, too-strong coffee. "Where are our hosts, anyway?"

"Seeing to morning chores," Gunner answered. He pulled his pocket watch free, checked the face, then tucked it back into his waistcoat.

"Gunner."

He looked at me.

"How the hell did you find me?"

Gunner didn't respond right away, and I got the impression that the answer wasn't going to be straightforward. He was already deciding which details would be disclosed and which he'd keep to himself. Because Gunner never lied. He just had a way of being honest without divulging… much of anything. The entire time he considered my question, Gunner never broke eye contact. I'd nearly forgotten how his stare could strip me down to nothing.

"How far back does my file in the rogues' gallery go?"

"Pardon?"

Gunner only looked expectant.

"Uhm… '72, I believe, for a handful of minor offenses that were linked to you after the fact. The allegations really began in '73, when you took to robbing Wells Fargo airships." I leaned across the table. "Were you intending for an ego stroke?"

Gunner's mouth quirked, but he asked seriously, "The FBMS has no record of my movements prior to that?"

I shook my head. "No police department does."

Gunner leaned an elbow on the tabletop and raised two fingers, as if he were holding a cigarette. It seemed like a sort of self-soothing gesture, perhaps a way to combat an old craving. I'd have gotten up to fetch the chewing gum I knew I'd find in his suit coat pocket, but something told me if I did, whatever Gunner was going to say would be lost like a single grain of sand in an hourglass.

Eventually, he said, "I worked as a scout for a time. Those skills don't atrophy."

"But… did you know where I was?"

Gunner's expression darkened. "Blackwell's," he gritted out.

"Did you know the entire time?" I asked, quieter.

"No." He abruptly stood and moved to the bed.

I turned in my seat to watch Gunner pick up his belt and holster from the foot of the bed. He buckled it around his slender hips, adjusted how the Waterbury rested, then looked at me. "I got as far as Dodge City before turning around. The situation didn't feel right, and I felt sick having left you scared and alone. I didn't want to be another person in your history who'd abandoned you."

I felt blood rush into my cheeks. Gunner hadn't been aware of my childhood traumas in January, and even now, God save me, he hardly knew enough to fill a help-wanted advert in the *Daily Cog*. And yet, *somehow*, he'd understood that my solitude went far beyond that of a man with certain attractions, living one step removed from society for the sake of safety. Mine was a loneliness that was all-encompassing, that touched upon every sort of human relationship.

Gunner had understood that because he'd apparently been a scout—a professional observer—in his past life.

"I spoke to your doorman when I'd returned to the city," Gunner continued. "Dawson said you'd moved and he'd been given no forwarding address."

"You knew it wasn't true?"

"When I reconsidered your attitude the day the D.C. agents showed up, yes. I decided they hadn't come for an interview. Ergo, you hadn't moved—you were being made to disappear."

"Did you know why?" My voice sounded brittle, almost detached, as I spoke.

Gunner didn't reply, but an uncomfortable expression I couldn't quite put a name to flitted across his features. And then in an odd, distended second of silence, I knew that he knew, and Gunner realized I'd read his silence correctly.

"Where were you?" I asked, getting to my feet.

"I went to California," Gunner said, walking past the table and across the room to look out the lone window.

"That's not what I mean. You *know* what I mean."

"I had no practical evidence as to your whereabouts in January," he continued without missing a beat. "But there was the name, Luther Jones, the caster working with Weaver, according to the Grace Gallery manager. And I had a thought that if I could draw enough attention to the underground associated with Henry Bligh, the FBMS would be forced to reevaluate the circumstances of New Year's Day and you'd be brought out of wherever—"

"Constantine Gunner, where were you during the war?" I demanded, speaking over him.

Gunner turned sharply and said, "Is it not clear to you I

don't wish to speak on the subject?"

"After everything I just told you—"

"Where I was twenty years ago isn't relevant, Gillian." He walked back toward me, the heels of his boots nearly shaking the planks underfoot when he was typically as quiet as a cat on the prowl. "My dear," he said, gruffer than was normal, a sort of forced patience about his person. He set his hands on my shoulders.

I pushed him off and took a step back. "Tell me you knew."

"This is not the time."

"Tell me right now that you knew who I was, or we stop here."

Gunner's expression distorted, like ripples across a water's smooth surface. He said, his voice like gravel, "I knew." I'd never seen that raw emotion in his face, heard it in his voice, but as quick as it was there, it was gone as Gunner reined himself in—squaring his shoulders, smoothing the front of his waistcoat—the mask of polite indifference slipped back into place, all as if he had said nothing.

Except he had.

He knew.

Gunner had *known*.

"Since the beginning?" I asked.

"No," Gunner said in his usual, husky monotone. "I don't lie, Gillian."

"But you sure omit a hell of a lot," I concluded.

He moved toward me again, like we were the opposite ends of two magnets who always found their way back to each other. Gunner set his hands on my shoulders a second time, more gently, I noted. "What does it matter if I knew?"

"Did you tell anyone?"

"*No*," he repeated, this time with resounding absolution. Gunner drew his touch down, and I swear the hairs on my arms stood straight up where he touched through the material of my shirt.

I watched as he slid his strong, blunt fingers in between mine, interlocking us like cogs in a mechanical automaton. I didn't look up as I said, "I can't believe you've… all along…."

"It was not my place to out your secret."

I shook my head. "Gunner, I need to understand—"

With our hands still joined, Gunner raised them and gave my chin a nudge. "You have my word. But not now. Not here. We don't have the time."

"At least tell me this—" I took a breath, steeled myself, and asked, "You didn't pursue me because of who I am, did you?"

Gunner tugged one hand free from mine, wrapped it around my waist, and pulled me up against him, igniting an immediate fire between us. "I was taken by you from the moment you pulled your badge on me in the middle of a shootout. I engaged because I find you exceptionally handsome. But I pursued you, Gillian Hamilton, because I am hopelessly in love with you and will do *anything* you ask of me." His grip on my hand tightened, and his other moved to the small of my back, then lower. "It's you I'm after, not your magic."

"And Gunner the Deadly doesn't lie."

"Only if you ask me to."

A surge of relief welled up from deep inside, whipping through me like the night air, strong enough to tear me apart, so I held on to Gunner tighter, and when we kissed again, it was like I was incandescent—the brightest star in the sky.

I felt clean.

I felt whole.

I felt like I was standing on my own two feet again.

I raised myself onto my toes, tugged Gunner forward by his hips, and between hot, hard kisses to his mouth, I prompted, "Luther Jones."

"Found him," Gunner murmured. "Says he corresponded with a doctor out of Tucson while working with Weaver." He leaned down and clamped his mouth around my throat.

My vision doubled and my gasp sounded too loud for the tiny sod home. "And Weaver?"

Gunner let up and kissed my mouth again. "No luck."

"Where's Luther now?"

"He was not a good man," Gunner concluded, letting the suggestion of Luther's fate hang between us before backing me against the table and lifting me to sit atop.

I grabbed for the half-empty mug of forgotten coffee before it had a chance to spill. Gunner took it from me and set it on the stovetop, and when he returned to the table, I reached for his tie and pulled Gunner to stand between my legs. His pupils were blown wide and he had a faint flush across his cheeks. I drew him close enough to kiss but didn't, and instead whispered, "What did you do next?"

Gunner looked at my mouth and then met my gaze. "Returned to Arizona—the address on one of the letters Luther so kindly parted with."

"St. Margaret?" I asked.

Gunner nodded.

I kissed him that time and shivered as his hands returned to my body—ribs, thighs—and then he pressed a possessive touch between my legs. "Jesus… *fuck*…."

"Nurses informed me Dr. Barrie had been on a lecture tour since December. They supplied me his schedule." Gunner kept rubbing me through my trousers while he returned to kissing and biting my neck. "I sent telegrams to the hosting hospitals."

I grabbed a fistful of Gunner's black hair as I thrust my hips forward to meet his touch. "A-and?"

Gunner let up on my neck, and cool air ghosted across my spit-slick skin. "None except Bellevue confirmed his visit. If I had known he was the resident physician when I brought you to St. Margaret…. And then to learn he's been lurking around magic patients in the city, even after Bligh's death… watch the door."

I'd followed Gunner's story until that last comment, which caused me to let up on my grip of his hair. "What's that?"

"Watch the door," he repeated before unbuttoning the front of my trousers.

"Gunner!" I yelped, grabbing at his hands. "We can't—"

"We most certainly can, if you watch the door, my dear," Gunner explained calmly, despite looking like a man about to come undone himself. The corner of his mouth tugged upward in a subtle smile before he added, "Hands back in my hair, please."

I swallowed audibly and grabbed the back of Gunner's head as he freed my prick from the fly of my trousers, leaned down, and wrapped his mouth around me. After the last month and a half of being in such a state that I hadn't the energy nor desire to use even my own hand for a bit of comfort, sex felt like a novel experience all over again. But even with the immediate flush across my skin, the sweat at my hairline, the prickling sensation at the base of my spine suggesting I'd spend in mere seconds, my body remembered Gunner's. Remembered his callused hands, the grit of stubble on his chin, the warm, wet heat of his mouth. I wasn't just reacting to having a man touch me—it was Gunner.

"Hurry," I whispered, sparing the front door a glance over my shoulder. I hadn't actually expected Gunner to change his method at my request, so as to not be caught with my trousers around my ankles, metaphorically speaking, but he immediately took more of me, sucked harder, kneaded what he could reach of my backside. I swore and tightened my hold on his head until Gunner grunted. When my balls drew up, I gave Gunner's shoulder a firm push until he came off with an indecent slurp and gave me an inquisitive stare. "I'm about—to—"

"That's the idea," he answered before returning his mouth to my prick and giving the length a long, sensual suck that pushed me over the brink I'd been teetering on.

I managed to check the door a final time before choking out, "Oh my God!" as I came down Gunner's throat. I slumped forward, shaking and shivering from the release of so much pent-up emotion and the unrelenting desire I had for the man in front of me. I watched as Gunner eased off, straightened his posture, and wiped his mouth on the back of his hand. "You, ah, swallowed…." In response to my stammering, Gunner kissed me hard, and I could taste the sharp salt of myself on his tongue.

Gunner pulled away, glanced to the window at my back, then said in a voice a touch huskier than usual, "Right yourself, my dear."

I got off the table and said, while tucking myself into my trousers and buttoning them, "That was entirely inappropriate."

"You didn't protest."

"I did!"

"Not once I had you down my throat."

I was blushing fiercely as I reached to correct Gunner's askew tie. "You're a gentleman. Watch your mouth." I finished and moved my touch to Gunner's bicep. "Luther and Weaver taught Barrie the casting for quintessence when he'd been hired to build the mechanical men."

Gunner considered this, then nodded in understanding.

"He's figured out how to infuse it into other items, similar to aether. The morphine was laced with quintessence."

"He meant for that to be used on you."

"I'd have been completely at his mercy," I agreed.

"But to what end?"

The front door opened suddenly, and Lucy bounded inside as I jerked my head in her direction. She clutched the handle of a basket close to her chest, as if to ward off the cold. Inside there looked to be a few loose eggs and a small earthen crock container. She took one look at us as I dropped my hand from Gunner's arm, and she called over her shoulder, "Told you."

Winona followed Lucy inside, and she said, while shutting the door, "It was hardly a secret, Lucy."

"Pardon me?" I interjected.

Winona shrugged out of her heavy coat. "Mr. Gaylord here's been up half the night, watching you sleep."

Lucy put her basket on the table. "I told Winona you'd overexerted yourself last night. Aether does that to most casters," she explained, but I didn't think she fully understood I hadn't merely cast aether, but reverse engineered it to save Gunner's life. "When Mr. Gaylord woke, I told him as much too, but he said he preferred to keep an eye on you."

Winona tossed her jacket over the back of the chair nearest her before pointing over my shoulder. "Never known a man to care enough to see to his friend's shoes."

I looked in the direction she pointed, to the small table beside the bed. The kerosene lamp still sat there, along with my folded suit coat, flat cap atop it, and shirt collar and goggles perfectly aligned beside them in that idiosyncratic way that marked Gunner's presence. My shoes had been safely tucked underneath.

"Besides," Winona added when I turned to her again, "you've got a love bite."

I slapped a hand against my neck, covering the spot Gunner had been working earlier. I swore under my breath as I collected my collar and hastily buttoned it in place.

"I think it's awfully sweet," Lucy told me, both hands planted on the tabletop as she leaned forward. "I haven't met men like us before."

"Lucy," Winona grumbled.

"*What?*" she protested innocently before saying again, "I haven't!" She smiled, and it lit up her entire face. She rocked her hips side-to-side, and the heavy winter skirts swished about her ankles. "Mr. Gaylord said he hadn't seen you for some time and missed you something terrible."

I pulled my suit coat on, looking at Gunner. "Is that so?"

"I do believe my exact words were 'I have missed the pleasure of his company.'"

"Good lord, that's even more obvious," I replied.

Gunner merely smiled that there-and-gone smile of his.

"You gentlemen like fried cornmeal?" Lucy piped up. "Even got some molasses to sweeten them a bit. Oh!" She picked up the eggs and displayed them. "I'll boil these too. Mr. Gaylord might need more than just cornmeal."

"Lucy," Winona muttered a second time.

"Well, he's as tall as a giant, Winona," she hissed.

I patted the front of my coat before reaching inside as Gunner was thanking Lucy. I retrieved the Bartholomew Industries receipt I'd religiously transferred from suit to suit since October, and that had, by God's good graces, survived in my carpet bag while I was kept on Blackwell's. The corners were weathered, and the crease across the middle had become brittle from the hundreds of times I'd unfolded it to read, in Gunner's own hand: *Yours, Constantine G.* I held the paper for an extra heartbeat, and as I tucked it into my pocket, a sudden thought crossed my mind.

I looked up and wasn't surprised to see that Gunner had been watching me the entire time, his beautiful blue eyes shining like a polished gemstone. "You said Luther had been exchanging letters with Dr. Barrie?"

Gunner's gaze cut to the women, but Winona was pretending not to listen and Lucy was already busying herself at the stovetop and humming some tune under her breath. He took a few steps toward me, rested his hands on his low-slung belt, and said quietly, "That's correct."

"Weaver wasn't involved in the correspondence?"

"According to Luther Jones, he was tasked with finding an architect, at the behest of Tick Tock. This affiliation, of course, was due to Henry Bligh's future mother-in-law being a repeat customer of Carl Higgins's aether elixir, which was concocted by Luther and shipped from California to Higgins's warehouse in Manhattan for labeling and distribution."

"I concur."

"But as far as Luther was willing to admit—"

"Which I'm sure was a great deal," I said over Gunner as I reached out to pat his holstered weapon.

The crow's feet around Gunner's eyes were the only hint that my comment amused him. "Weaver built the artificial ammunition spells and Luther was the first to utilize them, but it led to those backfiring prototypes Ferguson mysteriously got his hands on in October. It appears Luther contacted Dr. Barrie afterward."

"Which must have been around the time Weaver devised

and constructed quintessence. He taught it to Luther, who taught it to Barrie in order for him to construct the mechanical men that *used* the artificial ammunition," I concluded.

"I suspect that's the timeline, yes. Once an architect has built a spell, do all casters learn it from each other?"

I nodded and added, "Or scholars, if one were to follow the traditional and *legal* method." I glanced to my right—Lucy was boiling water and mixing a bowl of cornmeal while Winona set the table, watching us with one eye and listening with one ear. Feeling rather defiant in that minute, I took Gunner's hand from his belt and held it in mine.

His eyebrows rose but he said nothing, merely drew his thumb back and forth across my knuckles.

"If Barrie was never in contact with Weaver—and I suppose he had no reason to be—and was in New York by December under the guise of a lecture tour but was, in fact, working for Tick Tock… the question now is, not only what were his plans with me, but *where*?"

"It wasn't his intention to bring you to California?"

"No. It was my idea. I thought to search out Weaver."

Gunner shook his head once. "I've already done that search. Weaver's a dead end."

"You know, Mr. Ackerman," Winona interrupted, "you speak like a lawman."

"Do I? Fancy that," I answered without looking away from Gunner. Quieter, I said to him, "If you say Waver's a dead end, then perhaps we should focus on Barrie for the moment. We have a better handle on his location, and he *is* actively causing damage with quintessence. He told me he's been researching how to properly infuse medication with aether, of course at the detriment of a caster besides himself. He's clearly incorporating quintessence into these experiments."

A thought seemed to cross Gunner's face at this comment, but all he said, in a tone like it was a textbook fact, was, "He's unhinged."

"The real danger is how charismatic and trustworthy he is."

Gunner frowned, just a little, as he appeared to steel himself for more unpleasant news.

"The quintessence reinforced the reaction you had to morphine. In this case, the dosage of the drug was too high and you nearly overdosed. But if the measure had been accurate, the high would have been indefinite—I think until the quintessence is either removed from the body, or death befalls the host. I don't know what Barrie plans to do with this knowledge, but I can't begin to fathom how many people he could hurt with it."

Gunner squared his shoulders and said in agreement, "We have to find Barrie."

VIII

February 21, 1882

I was not, by any means, a hopeless man when plopped into the distant, rural countryside, but I will admit, my investigative skills were more limited than how I conducted myself in a major metropolitan area. Manhattan might have boasted a population of nearly one million, but the neighborhoods had strict hierarchies among its accepted members of society. Whether Millionaire's Row or the Bowery, there were manners and speech patterns and eccentricities unique to those people, and I understood how to conduct myself accordingly. And with my formative years having been spent in the most dangerous and overcrowded portion of the island, there wasn't a street, a pier, a warehouse, or tenement I didn't know. And if I did hit a dead end, I had contacts to lean on.

But out here, among homesteaders, mining communities, or stopover towns whose sole purpose was to provide supplies and means in which to keep traveling farther west… how was I supposed to use my usual tactics and methods? There were no alleyways to memorize, no clubs to slip in and out of, and there was hardly a presence of law in some of these locations—certainly no FBMS field offices—and the closest they had to organized gangs were motley bands of cowboys.

Gunner, on the other hand, absolutely thrived among these desolate and often unruly fringes of humanity. It was like he had a mental map of this swath of untamed wilderness and could track anything and anyone, down to a single canyon or fellow outlaw. And he managed it with ease—with comfort, even. Because while I'd been learning the sewer tunnels underneath Cherry Street as a boy, Gunner had been employed, by someone unknown, as a scout.

So when Gunner had proclaimed a need to find Barrie, as much as I agreed, my stomach sank, because I didn't have a single iota of where or how to begin. This morning he'd have safely docked in San Francisco, and with Luther Jones now home to writhing, blood-red worms, Barrie had no known business affiliations in California to reach out to. Would he stay there? Disappear into a city of a few hundred thousand, that while I was confident I could navigate, would still need a bit of time to learn the ins and outs of the new urban landscape? Would he return to St. Margaret Hospital in Tucson, Arizona? Or would he hop an airship destined for anywhere in the world?

I was overwhelmed with the endless possibilities, all of which I would be forced to traverse without the conveniences my badge once produced simply by flashing where it was pinned to my person, when Gunner said ironically, "First things first," and then asked Winona how far we were from the town of First Chance, Colorado.

It turned out, we were "exactly thirteen miles, sir" from First Chance, and it was a travel route Winona knew well, as that's where she and Lucy did all of their necessary buying and selling for the homestead. And it turned out, for twenty dollars—"I wager five for the impromptu use of our bed, three for the fresh eggs, and ten for my time"—Winona would drag her steam motorwagon out from the shed behind the sod home and drive us into town.

"That's eighteen," I'd pointed out.

"I find the last two are for the couple of lies you told, sir."

"Lies?"

"I might not know who you are," she'd said to me, then cast a look at Gunner, "but I know he ain't no John Gaylord. Ain't that right, Gunner the Deadly?"

Gunner hadn't protested to the contrary. In fact, I knew those minute changes in his expression well enough now that I could discern visible satisfaction in having been recognized. He'd simply removed his coin purse, slid a few greenbacks across the table, then dropped a handful of silver dollars on top.

And that was how Gunner and I found ourselves standing outside the front entrance of First Chance Inn and Express Apparels along the north end of Main Street later that afternoon.

Similar to Shallow Grave, Arizona, in both its population density and grid system of packed-earth roads, First Chance differed notably in color. Where Shallow Grave was nestled among vivid orange sandstone and spectacular desert plateaus and canyons that caught the afternoon sun and gleamed like fire, this town suffered a rather bland color palette of underwhelming tans and half-dead greens. A not-quite desert among a not-quite grassland, with the sun hanging limp overhead.

I tugged my goggles down around my neck, removed my cap, and smacked it against my thigh a few times to scatter the debris it'd collected on our drive into town. Winona's motorwagon was an ancient thing, barely a step above a horse-drawn carriage, that Lucy needed to boil water for to help jump-start its steam engine. It had no roof or doors like the more luxurious models inundating the roads in New York, so after an hour of being exposed to the elements, I was dusty, cold as hell, and my face felt flush with wind burn. I took a step toward the inn, but Gunner put a hand out to stop me.

He removed his own goggles but kept the black bandana tied around his face. He still looked dangerous, but the effect of his character was slightly muted with the loss of his Stetson the night before, when we'd been falling through the sky. "Follow me," he said, cutting between the inn and neighboring dry-goods shop, heading around the backside to a nonpublic door.

"Do you know the concept of déjà vu?" I asked.

Gunner knocked, confident but not demanding, then looked down. "Keep that thought in the forefront of your mind, my dear."

Heat pooled in my cheeks upon realizing Gunner was remembering the same instance from last October.

The door opened to reveal a matronly woman—big hips, big bosom, a touch taller than myself—in the midst of shouldering a shawl, and she took one look at Gunner and her expression grew almost comically animated. "I'll be damned if it's not Gunner the Deadly!"

Gunner tugged his bandana down around his throat. "Hello, ma'am."

She stamped a foot and put her hands on her wide hips. "We haven't seen your handsome mug in six months, and that's all you have to say?"

His mouth twitched before adding, "My sincerest apologies, ma'am."

"*Ma'am*," she echoed, and it sounded both annoyed and amused. She looked at me and asked, "Who's this?"

"Malcom Ackerman," I answered.

"This is Margaret Adams," Gunner introduced.

"Peggy," she corrected.

I removed my cap briefly and inclined my head.

"You got yourself a partner?" Peggy asked Gunner, and while I knew she was referring to Gunner's professional career, I nonetheless got an anxious flutter in my stomach at her choice of words. "It's awfully dangerous—what you do on your own." To me, she said, "When I lived in Dodge City, this was back in '77, Billy Starr—you know him?—the weasel robbed me of my life savings and set fire to my shop. I was in the tobacco business at the time, and I'd nearly met my Maker that night! So Gunner here, a regular customer— Virginia Brights, weren't they, honey?—he goes after Billy, recovers every damn penny, then leaves him hogtied outside the jail for those Earp brothers to collect in the morning." Peggy slapped her thigh through the layers of skirts, laughing as she added, "And then Gunner robbed *him* afterward! Wyatt Earp, that is. Not Morgan."

"If Wyatt was half the lawman he thinks he is, he'd have handled Billy himself," Gunner concluded politely.

"So you robbed a city marshal to make a point?" I asked, looking up.

Gunner glanced sideways. "He wasn't hurting for money." Then he said to Peggy, "We need two rooms."

"Yes, yes. Come on in." Peggy ushered us inside.

The immediate room was nearly overflowing with what appeared to be excess stock stacked on floor-to-ceiling shelves: bolts of linen, cotton, and wool, hatboxes in several sizes and styles, case upon case of shirt collars and cuffs, and what looked like shipments of quality, premade suits, dresses, even corsets—I supposed to have on standby for those visitors passing through who held considerably more money than the locals, who, I guessed, often sewed their own garments.

Peggy didn't stop moving as she swiped a carpet bag from among the clutter and passed it behind herself to Gunner. I considered that action, then realized it was likely a reserve of supplies or belongings for when he was in the area. Which made sense. It'd allow Gunner to travel light and not worry about necessities, as he essentially had safehouses throughout half the country. And the way folks out West fell over themselves to defend his wrongdoings… he could have a dozen or more bags like this one squirreled away with proprietors like Peggy.

The tight passage opened into an overly warm kitchen. There were fresh loaves of bread on the table in the middle of the room, and a big vat of stew was bubbling away over the fireplace. A woman about my age, perhaps Peggy's daughter, glanced up from slicing squash into manageable chunks. A little boy sat in a chair beside her, doing his best to spin a wooden top across the table without it smacking into the piled squash.

She smiled suddenly and said, "Hello, Gunner."

Gunner gestured to her as if he still wore his Stetson. "Ma'am."

She tittered and shook her head in amusement, like this was a long-running back-and-forth between them and she'd since given up on convincing Gunner to call her anything else. When she noticed me, she didn't speak, but offered a cool, if somewhat guarded, smile.

I tipped my cap before following Gunner and Peggy through a door that led to the inn's front room. Its eastern-facing windows were already in shadow, and since I was quite certain a little outpost like First Chance wouldn't see steam technology on the regular for a number of years to come, Peggy would need to light her gas lamps soon. Besides the dwindling light, the room was clean and tidy and well-stocked with all of the fabrics and garments we'd passed in storage. With the quality and expansive offerings, impressive for a shop this far out from any urban landscape, I suspected Peggy did quite well for herself and had customers all across the Eastern Plains.

Toward the back was a counter, a steep staircase on the left that led to the rented rooms portion of the business, and a few small tables and simple wooden chairs shoved along the far wall, probably for anyone staying the night and hoping to buy and eat some dinner. I paused in the middle of the shop floor as Peggy maneuvered herself behind the counter and retrieved two skeleton keys. Gunner approached, took the keys, then said something too quiet to discern, but Peggy produced a scrap of paper and pencil at his words. He jotted a note, slid it back toward Peggy, and then added what appeared to me to be a fair amount of money from his purse.

Peggy said something low, laughed, patted Gunner's hand fondly, then called toward me, "Just put your clothing in the basket and leave it in the hall, Mr. Ackerman."

"Sorry?"

"Laundry," Gunner explained as he headed toward the stairs.

"Oh." To Peggy, I added, "Thank you." And then I followed Gunner to the second floor.

Gunner handed me one of the keys, pointed to the last door, then unlocked the middle door.

"Gunner, wait," I began. "We haven't discussed our next—"

Gunner winked, stepped into his room, and shut the door loudly.

"—plan."

The devil?

I let out an exasperated sigh and entered my own room.

It was quite similar to the room I'd rented while in Shallow Grave—very small, very plain, without more than a wash basin and pitcher, a narrow and slightly sagging mattress on an unadorned frame, and a side table big enough for what men might carry in their pockets. The window of this room also faced east onto Main Street, so I moved to the glass and pulled the curtain shut. I didn't need an audience while undressing, thank you.

After setting cap, goggles, and receipt on the table beside a very old and tired-looking gas lamp, I dropped my clothes into the large wicker basket that Peggy had been referring to and opened the door just enough to slide it into the hall between our two doors, in case Gunner planned to have his clothes cleaned as well. I shut the door, and suddenly feeling rather deflated, moved to the far side of the bed and sat down.

I understood now why Gunner had asked after our proximity to First Chance—it was clearly a friendly-to-him town. And it explained how Winona Brown recognized Gunner but wasn't perturbed by his presence—because these small-town folk either had firsthand experience with Gunner protecting them in a certain capacity, or had romanticized his Robin Hood-esque manners. But that aside, he hadn't told me a lick about First Chance, and it wasn't like we'd gotten much of a look. Winona had dropped us off right in front of Peggy's establishment before turning around, her motorwagon choking and coughing on its way out of town and back to the homestead. So what was here for us? Was there an airship dock to take advantage of? Public telegraphs? Who would we even send communication to? We hadn't decided one way or another what Barrie's next movement could possibly be, and until we did—

The knob rattled softly before the door at my back opened without a word of warning. I startled and clutched at the blanket, already pulling it across my lap as I whipped my head around, for some reason expecting Peggy and feeling ridiculous when it was Gunner slipping inside. He was only partially dressed, having already lost his boots, suit coat, waistcoat, and tie. His braces had been pushed from his shoulders, and his collar, cuffs, and bandana were probably with his other odds and ends in his room—all perfectly aligned on the bedside table, no doubt.

I quickly stood. "What're you—?"

Gunner raised a finger to his lips. He carefully closed my door so it didn't make a sound and then approached the bed. He tossed me a tin container, added his own skeleton key to my table, then hastily unbuttoned his shirt. "Peggy is delightful, but she's relentlessly pushed her daughter on me for half a decade."

"The daughter… who was downstairs with a little boy?"

Gunner yanked his arms free from the shirt and started on his trousers. "That hasn't stopped her before. Besides, she's a horrible eavesdropper to boot."

I glanced at the tin.

Vaseline.

And just like that, my skin was too tight for my body. The air in my lungs evaporated like dew in Central Park under the morning sun. The fire in my chest, my belly, my soul, burned bright and without remorse for this man who'd chased every lead uncovered to find me—*save me*—for the last month and a half. Constantine Gunner might still be an enigma, but wasn't I the same for him? It made no difference, anyway. I loved Gunner with a ferocity that both scared and thrilled me, and God Almighty did I *want* him.

He returned to the door, careful as he opened it enough to toss his remaining clothing into the basket before closing and locking it. He turned around, all height and lean muscle and dark hair. Gunner strode around the bed toward me, prick erect between his legs. He took my face into both hands, leaned down, and kissed me. It was rough, hot, almost obscene, and unmistakably masculine.

I put a hand to Gunner's chest, gripping hard, digging my blunt fingernails into feverish skin and defined muscle, and I rubbed my inner wrist against wiry black hair. He groaned, I gasped, and that wildfire inside me felt so raw, so powerful, I was again convinced of some ancient spell being cast between us—because how else could I make sense of feeling so *alive*? I pushed Gunner back a step, and as he sat on the edge of the mattress, I followed by putting my knees on either side of him. I dropped the tin somewhere beside us, and recalling the way Gunner's pupils grew when I showed him a bit of dominance, something he'd suggested he preferred but didn't often get with past conquests, I wrapped one hand around his neck and squeezed.

Not enough to hurt, but to… make a suggestion.

"Yes," Gunner breathed in reply. He pulled back from my touch so he could lie on the mattress, then pointed at the tin near his feet. I offered it to him, but Gunner shook his head and said, while drawing a leg to his chest, "You do it."

"*Me?*"

That rare smile of his made an appearance. "Considering what you plan to put there, Gillian, a finger is hardly worth getting worked up over."

I snorted and clasped a hand over my mouth when I thought of Peggy lingering in the hall, trying to overhear what the infamous Gunner the Deadly did in his downtime. "You're wicked," I whispered.

His smile only grew in response.

I popped the lid and removed a dollop of the jellylike substance, trying to ignore the finger tracks from the tin's last use.

And whether it showed on my face or it was Gunner's remarkable observation skills at work, he said, "It was before I met you."

I smiled automatically and set the tin aside before knee-walking closer. "I know." I put one hand on Gunner's raised leg, giving his thigh a squeeze before pressing a slick finger inside. He sighed and lazily stroked himself, so I avoided asking the obviously inane question of was I hurting him? Instead, what came out was "But am I the only one now?"

Gunner's lust-glazed eyes refocused on me. "You *have* been. That's what you've wanted, isn't it?"

My ministrations had faltered under the direction of our conversation, and hastily, I added a second finger. Gunner's hips twitched and he swore under his breath. "I want a courtship," I blurted out. "I don't know how possible that is, given a myriad of circumstances, the most problematic being we're both men, but—"

"Gillian."

"Yes?"

Gunner hooked a finger and motioned me close. When I'd leaned over, he wrapped a hand around my neck and drew me into a kiss. "That's what I want as well."

"I really expected this to be a lot more difficult."

"I'm not a difficult man."

"I know. You require very little in life." I smiled before adding, "Black Jack, Folgers, and a loaded Waterbury, wasn't it?"

"And you."

I kissed Gunner a second time before leaning back for the tin and adding a bit more Vaseline to my hand. I stroked myself with the grease while saying, "You really have a way of being terribly romantic in situations I least expect it."

"I'll save the rest of my sweet nothings for after you

make me see God."

I swallowed a laugh before drawing close enough that I could press the head of my prick into Gunner's hole. I'd done this once before, but our positions had been reversed and Gunner had done most, if not all, of the work as a way of easing my first-time anxieties. So to say I still felt a certain level of apprehension and insecurity in doing this—in trying to bring him pleasure—was a very accurate assessment.

"Okay?" I asked.

Gunner's brow furrowed a little and his grip on his knees visibly tightened. "Keep going." But once I'd pushed deeper, reached beyond that tight muscle, he sighed with what could only be mind-numbing bliss. "Jesus Christ, Gillian."

I leaned over and kissed Gunner again, thrusting as I did. "Your mouth during sex."

"You bring out the rogue in me." He nudged my hands free from the near-death grip I had on his hips and brought them to his chest. Gunner shuddered as I sank my fingers into skin and muscle and hair, and it was this unabashed way he had of taking what aroused him, in asking for rough lovemaking because it was the pleasure he'd found that best answered his needs and so there was nothing to be ashamed of… it helped me let go of the inhibitions I had over enjoying *seeing* him in such a state.

I thrust forward in short, hard bursts that gave me a pleasant ache in my own muscles, and Gunner gasped and grabbed my wrists, gripping just enough for it to be uncomfortable. I did it again and again, and Gunner wrapped his strong legs around my hips and dug his heels into my backside.

"Don't stop, don't stop."

"Shh…." The bedframe was already making too much noise, and as much as hearing Gunner beg must have been what it was like to hear the Swedish Nightingale sing in person, we couldn't afford to enjoy vocalizing to our hearts' content. Not now, not here, not where curious ears vied for gossip.

I yanked my hands free, held Gunner's throat as I kissed him, and reached between us to stroke him with the other. He dug his fingers into the longer hair atop my head, but when his nails grazed my scalp on either side, it was like he'd reached inside me and was twisting and controlling the lightning spells with just this touch. He panted against my mouth and I swallowed his moan when he came in my hand. I sat up on my knees, leaving Gunner struggling to catch his breath. My thighs and backside burned with the exertion now, but I managed a few more rough, although entirely out of sync, thrusts before climaxing.

I collapsed on the mattress beside Gunner, our shoulders touching and one leg tangled with his. I wiped my forehead, staring at the ceiling. "Goddamn."

A low rumble that was probably intended to be a laugh went through Gunner. In his husky voice, he said, "You were wild."

I turned my head.

Gunner was staring at me, looking utterly fucked and quite happy about it. "I liked it," he clarified.

"It still scares me."

Gunner reached out and combed my hair with his fingers.

"But I've been scared for thirty years. It's like being an animal caught in a trap, again and again, and I'm running out of body parts to gnaw off. I'm… so tired of it." I propped myself up on an elbow. "You told me that some men like us find happiness."

"I said *you* would."

I nodded, looked down, took Gunner's hand into mine,

and stroked it. "I can be happy with you. I know it. It's a certainty I feel in my bones, my soul, my magic… but I have to get out of my own way about it. I have to get out of my way in order to properly love you."

Gunner pulled my hand to his mouth and kissed my big knuckles one at a time. He gently extended my fingers and began kissing the tips of each, and even though I couldn't feel his soft lips, the slight pressure of them was pleasant. He reached my index finger—visibly crooked and offset from the others—and asked, "What happened?"

"Broke it."

Gunner stared at me but didn't let go of my hand.

My heart began to race under his inquisitive gaze— quick and light, like the animal caught in metal jaws, razor-sharp teeth breaking skin and bone. I took a slow breath so Gunner wouldn't hear the hitch growing in my voice, and said, "There was an old wives' tale that was prominent in the '50s—if you broke the fingers of a child caster, the magic would leave them, like clearing a possessed spirit or some such nonsense." I had to look away from the intensity of Gunner's eyes and instead focused on the half crescents I'd left dimpling his chest. I cleared my throat and said with a humorless laugh, "It doesn't work, for the record."

Snap, snap, snap.

I swallowed hard against the sudden rise of bile while the echo of breaking bones grew louder and louder in memory.

Gunner slid his fingers between mine. "These were broken more than once."

I nodded.

He drew me down, and I stretched out alongside his body, pressing my face against his hairy and sweat-damp chest. Gunner expelled a long sigh as he wrapped his arms around me, and we lay in that silence for some time. When he finally spoke again, his deep voice was a fracture to the quiet. "I was in Virginia for a good portion of '62."

"So was Barrie. Seven Pines, he said." I tilted my head back to look at Gunner's profile.

His jaw was clenched, the tendons visible, and I briefly wondered if he was hankering for some chewing gum before Gunner said, "I was a scout for the Union Army. I did a fair amount of reconnaissance in Virginia."

I jerked out of his arms and sat up. "You—? But you couldn't have been that old."

"I was seventeen. Yes, Gillian, I see you doing arithmetic. I'll be thirty-seven in April."

"Why are you telling me this?"

"I trust you," he said simply. "I want you to know." Gunner still hadn't moved from his comfortable, sated sprawl across my bed, but his eyes were as sharp as broken glass. "At New Year's, I didn't put two and two together when we first heard his name—Sawbones. But after I went looking for you, after speaking with Luther Jones and getting my hands on their correspondence—*Eugene Barrie*. It clicked. The Sawbones of Seven Pines."

"So what you said on the ship last night?"

"It's all true."

"But you witnessed it?"

"I witnessed a great many things during the war."

My shoulders slumped and I looked toward the drawn curtain at the window. It fluttered, just a little. The sash didn't meet the sill perfectly and was letting a cold breeze leak through. "I wonder how it was that Luther knew to contact Barrie for Tick Tock's enterprise. Specifically, that is."

"It's not unreasonable to assume they crossed paths during the Great Rebellion."

"I suppose not," I murmured.

"Barrie's exploits had a certain notoriety," Gunner continued, "a magically inclined doctor with a stomach for particularly brutal amputations…. He was exactly what was needed for Tick Tock's gangster army."

"But with Bligh gone, so's his grand scheme to rule New York's underground. And most importantly, his payroll has ceased. That's probably why Weaver has all but vanished. Barrie, however…." I ruffled my hair as I thought aloud. "He seems to have abandoned the mechanical men, which makes sense, since his employer is dead, and now he's taken the knowledge Bligh paid for and is applying it to a new plot." I finally looked at Gunner again. "What could possibly be his end goal?"

"He's sadistic and enjoys causing pain, my dear. I don't think he wants anything but the ensuing chaos."

"I don't buy it."

Gunner raised an eyebrow.

I shifted to sit on my knees. "Every time quintessence is cast, it leaves a residue in the magic atmosphere that, as far as I can tell, doesn't go away. It's… it's a bit like a membrane. And the more this illegal magic is woven into reality, the more the membrane gets a bit more solid."

"It affects your ability to cast?"

I nodded. "Bit by bit, it becomes more difficult to pull on the energy. I'm a level—*Christ*—seven? Eight? Who even knows, really. But if I can feel it, imagine how troubling it must be for weaker casters—those around a one or two might not be able to perform spells if it gets worse. And my point is, it'll hurt Barrie too. He *knows* it. So he has a plan, then. An end goal. He *must*."

"And it involved you," Gunner said as he sat up.

"Yes, maybe. When Barrie was explaining his research

with aether medication, I admit I went off on him about the dangers. Specifically, abusing casters for the supply of magic. He already knew a bit about Simon Fitzgerald and was presumably aware that I had been present in the war against my wishes. How can someone from my own community be informed on the history of our exploitation and still pursue whatever it is he's attempting?" I added after a moment, my voice quieting, "The federal government has used me once already—why not a second time? The council that oversees the FBMS is made up entirely of nonmagic users."

"How ironic," Gunner said dryly.

"In theory, they'd have far less sympathy than a council made up of casters." I added, "And you said Barrie wasn't really on a lecture tour. I think he'd first been at Bellevue looking for magic patients before being given approval to visit Blackwell's. What if that approval came from the council?"

"The council who knew you were on Blackwell's because *they* put you there," Gunner concluded.

I nodded. "And Barrie has influence or an affiliation, perhaps."

Gunner set a hand on my thigh and rubbed gently at a yellowed bruise for a moment or two. It was a sort of pleasant pain, a reminder that I always came back, no matter how badly the world tried to wound me. "Gillian, I'm sorry."

"For what?"

Gunner was frowning as he drew his hand up my hip, my chest, cautiously tapping each healing bruise as he went. "That I didn't find you sooner. That I didn't storm through those doors on Blackwell's and put a bullet in the head of every man who's touched you. But I will. You can rest assured of that."

I took Gunner's face and kissed him lightly. "I don't need you to go vigilante on my behalf."

"This is not a point I'm willing to compromise on."

I kissed him again, a bit longer, a bit deeper, and Gunner growled against my mouth as he flipped me onto my back. I hit the mattress and the bedframe creaked loudly. I was trying to stifle a laugh while shushing Gunner at the same time.

"Don't think another tussle in bed will be enough to distract me," Gunner said, leaning over.

"I'd never assume I'm a sufficient distraction."

Gunner narrowed his eyes a little. "You put me in the difficult position of needing to both defy your request and show you just how much you… *distract* me."

"If it helps your conundrum at all, I don't think I can manage a third time today."

Gunner's mouth twitched at the start of a smile, then vanished. His expression was placid, so the severity in his tone was off-putting when he spoke. "Barrie wasn't involved yet with Tick Tock, and you by proxy, when you were a patient at St. Margaret."

"That's right."

Gunner slowly sat back. "Barrie never salvaged what he could saw off, and we know, based on the mechanical men, his bloodlust hasn't tempered in the last twenty years. So why did he go out of his way to heal you?"

"I couldn't say." I explained my final moments on Blackwell's to Gunner in detail—the hell my jail cell had been, how Ashland spoke about me like I was a *thing*, how utterly charming and believable Barrie had been, and how I'd killed the assistant after he'd unclasped the straitjacket. "Ashland thought my high level of magic is what led to my supposed insanity," I finished. "That and my tendencies."

"The world would be run by madmen if such a statement were true." Gunner got off the bed and walked to the pitcher and basin. He poured the water but didn't move for a hand towel.

"Constantine?"

"I can't help but think Barrie, after learning the true extent of your powers, intended to use you against consent. To cast this quintessence, perhaps, in whatever scheme he's now involved in." He finally turned from studying the water's surface and said, "You're arguably the most powerful caster in this country, Gillian. You'd withstand the abuse like no other."

The realization… made my blood run cold.

IX

February 21, 1882

We didn't talk anymore of the war, nor share further conjecture as to Barrie's current objectives. Instead, we lay in bed, tangled in each other's arms, sharing endearments and silly, loving things that only exist in the whispers of two people in love. It was incredible—the moment like an island haven surrounded by an ocean of calamity—seeing, feeling, *knowing* that I was finally loved. And not despite once being Simon, but because I *was* Gillian.

It was okay to let that scared little boy go and be the man I'd always hoped to become.

I reminded myself that I'd lived my life as Gillian Hamilton for stability, for purpose, and for love. And I'd made a promise that if I couldn't live as both an agent and happy, the former was not worth the cost of the latter. I hadn't a clue what I'd do without a badge, as that career had been the only light in my darkness for a long time… but it'd be okay. I'd manage. I'd figure it out. I wasn't alone anymore.

It was Constantine Gunner and Gillian Hamilton against the world.

C + G.

The winter sun had long since set, and I'd cast lightning and dropped the small, dancing ball of energy into the lamp on the bedside table, which Gunner eyed with one-part amusement and three-parts wonder.

"How do you do it?" he'd asked.

"It's the same as if I were going to cast in an offensive manner."

Gunner had pointed at me and said, "But you're here, and the magic is over there."

"I'm still feeding it energy." I'd smiled a little and made a tiny motion with my hand to indicate as much. "You don't always need grandiose gestures to cast magic. Sometimes a snap or flick of the finger is enough."

Our privacy had been interrupted shortly thereafter, its delicacy popped like a suds bubble. Peggy had knocked loudly, announcing that my laundry and purchases were outside the door and that Gunner must have been sound asleep because he wasn't answering, but his freshly washed suit was also ready and waiting, should I manage to rouse him. I'd thanked her and only opened the door to retrieve our belongings once the sound of her footfalls reached the downstairs. Indeed, our fresh and dust-free suits were folded and waiting, but so was a large item wrapped in brown paper, which, when I showed Gunner, he'd simply said was mine.

I tore open the packaging to reveal a brand-new carpet bag, the stitches bright with color and the wooden handles glossy. I used the key to unlock it and found inside a wool coat, some changes of clothes, a toiletry satchel, including a compact mirror and means in which to shave, Macassar oil, and a bottle of perfume—Acqua Classica. I opened the top and picked up on a strong citrus scent, both lemon and orange, with hints of neroli and something pleasantly woodsy underneath.

"Crown is a bit too selective for an outpost town like this to carry," Gunner said as he buttoned his trousers and tucked his shirt into the waist. "I asked Peggy to pick up what was available, so you'd have something until we can find Fougère again." When I looked at him but said nothing, Gunner arched one eyebrow and asked with a hint of curiosity, "Is something wrong?"

"You paid for all this?"

"I certainly couldn't continue having you run all over hell and back without a coat, Gillian. It's February."

"But the clothes?"

"Peggy had your laundry to compare sizes."

I held up the Acqua Classica. "Perfume?"

"Are you not allowed to indulge in a hint of vanity? It's not like it was an effort—the dry-goods shop is next door."

I set the bottle aside, moved into Gunner's space, and wrapped my arms around him. "Thank you," I murmured against his chest.

He stroked the back of my head, saying, "If it makes any difference, the money wasn't mine to begin with."

I laughed quietly and stepped back. "Criminal."

"The best you've ever seen."

I finished dressing and was buttoning my waistcoat while watching Gunner collect the Vaseline from the mattress and walk to the door, when I asked, "Are we both in agreement that Barrie is planning something of notable proportion?"

Gunner looked over his shoulder, his hand resting on the knob. "I don't believe he's a man organized like Henry Bligh. He's always struck me as someone a touch more chaotic—more of the same vein as Milo Ferguson."

"So perhaps he's working for someone else?"

"That is much more plausible. But whoever that is,

whatever *their* plan, my gut says your escape is not a loss they'll be willing to swallow. I've been living by my gut for a long time."

"Even if I wasn't in potential danger, I'd want to see Barrie arrested," I answered.

"On what grounds? Proving those amputations were—"

"No, no. His war crimes twenty years after the fact would be an impossible argument to make. I meant, if I were still a special agent, he could be arrested under jurisdiction code S. 350: retainment, false imprisonment, or kidnapping of a federal agent. I'm not, of course, so that's out, but he had magic-infused medication on his person, being transported across state lines, which is illegal under code S. 212. He could be held on that offense alone and provide law enforcement the necessary time to investigate his doings."

"The trouble is finding him," Gunner replied.

"Yes. Well… our conversation gave me an idea. He needs a caster he can easily control, right?"

"Possibly."

"What better place than the insane locked up on Blackwell's? They're not my level, but it'd be like a starving man at a buffet," I concluded, pulling on my suit coat and adjusting my collar and tie.

"It's a reasonable theory," Gunner said. "But are we going to travel halfway across the country on nothing more than a hunch?"

I shook out the new wool coat from the carpet bag as I asked, "Is there a Western Union in this town? Or somebody with access to a PDD?" Gunner didn't reply, so I returned my attention to him and said, "We can obtain access to recent passenger manifests with the three major airship lines and determine if Barrie is, in fact, on the move again. It'll require help, though. I'll need to call Director Moore."

First Chance's nightly establishments were in full swing when Gunner and I slipped out the backdoor of Peggy's shop. Saloons one street east of Main were rowdy as all hell with two of America's favorite pastimes: drink and dance. We headed in the opposite direction of a horribly out-of-tune piano, cutting across dark streets of quiet storefronts, some signs of which I could make out by starlight alone: Jameson & Kennedy Pharmacy Counter; Miss Annie's Hardware; and one particularly grim reminder of life in the Wild West: Coffins by McCabe.

Gunner had considered me for a long moment when I'd told him of my shot-in-the-dark idea for procuring information. Eventually, all he said was "Give me twenty minutes and then come downstairs." So I had. And when I'd reached the shop's showroom, Gunner had been standing at the counter with Peggy, wearing a new bowler and calmly slotting Waterbury ammunition into his gun belt. I hadn't asked if the bullets were full of aether, because I knew Gunner would only smile to himself and say nothing, so as not to divulge his suppliers. Instead, I'd asked why a bowler when I knew he preferred a Stetson, and Gunner had once again told me it stood out too much if we found ourselves in an urban setting.

Gunner cut between two businesses and onto the next street. Halfway across the dirt-packed road, he turned left and made for a little shop standing alone on the corner, the low glow of a gas lamp in the window marking its occupancy in the pseudodesert night. We'd very nearly reached the porch steps when a shadow detached itself from the building.

"Evening, Gunner," a young man's voice called.

Gunner didn't draw his weapon or respond. Instead, he pulled a few coins from his trouser pocket and paused long enough to drop them into the man's extended hand.

"Ready and waiting on my desk," the man said, pocketing the money.

Gunner strode up the steps and opened the door.

I rolled my eyes and was about to make a passing comment regarding Gunner's tendency to conduct business without a word of explanation and how it drove me mad, when I caught the lettering of the sign overhead from the flickering light of the gas lamp: Western Union Telegraph Co. So apparently Gunner had been doing more than shopping in the twenty minutes he'd requested—like rousing the town's telegraph operator with the promise of some after-hours coin to be had.

I let the door fall shut behind me and looked around the storefront. It was quite simple: a counter with a register, stack of telegraph blanks, and courtesy pen and inkwell for writing out messages. On the private side of the counter was a worn and battered desk and chair, telegraph equipment neatly laid out on its surface, as well as a Personal Discussion Device headset and its handheld transducer. PDDs were few and far between outside of major cities, but Convey & Dispatch had years ago gone into business with Western Union, essentially piggybacking off their hundreds of locations throughout the country in order to keep PDD users—most often specialized law enforcement—in communication.

I pulled out the chair, took a seat, and set my cap on the desktop. "Moore will be able to ping this device and triangulate my location," I warned, looking up at Gunner.

"He won't do that."

I gave him an incredulous stare.

"If he still cares for you, still considers you a friend, he won't even ask where you are."

"But do you think Moore knew where D.C. sent me?" I

asked, my voice quieting.

Gunner took a breath before saying, "No, I don't believe so. He'd have raised hell. *I'd* have picked up word of your whereabouts sooner."

After a final consideration, I nodded and picked up the headset. I put it on, tapped a code on the transducer I knew by heart—33678—and waited.

The beeping was slightly staticky, but after the third sound, there was a loud *click* and a powerful, smooth tenor voice said, "Moore."

I let out a breath I hadn't realized I was holding. Moore had been my director for a decade and my one true friend since January, when he'd learned of my relationship with Gunner and, despite *hating* my decision, respected it. I missed him, a great deal. I missed working with him and talking with him and sharing drinks with him after a long day. And I hoped to God that Gunner was right, that Moore had been left in the dark about my fate and that he hadn't approved of the decision to lock me up on Blackwell's.

"Loren?"

For a heartbeat, the silence was nearly deafening. And then an astonished, "*Gillian*...? Or, I suppose it's Simon—"

"I prefer Gillian, if it's all the same to you, sir."

"I'll call you Lord Horace Periwinkle if it pleases you."

"That seems excessive," I said but couldn't help smiling to myself.

Moore didn't sound like he was trying to be all that humorous, however. "I haven't heard from you since...." His voice trailed off, and I picked up the distinct sound of his office door closing.

I closed my eyes and could see the gleam of the yellow lights atop the mahogany furniture and their refraction off the crystal decanters, felt the air warmed by steam, and smelled the cherry smoke of Moore's smoldering pipe. "Sir—"

"D.C. reinstated me on January sixth," Moore said over me. "And when you weren't at the office, I asked after you. I was informed that you… were not who you said you were, and that you'd quit the Bureau."

I snorted as I leaned an elbow on the desktop and pinched the bridge of my nose.

"I have your badge," Moore added somberly.

"That's *not* what happened." A mix of a bitter laugh and gasping sob escaped me. "The council lied to you. I was sent to Blackwell's Asylum for the Magically Insane."

Gunner, still standing, set his hand between my shoulder blades.

Moore's silence was stricken.

"I never wanted to lie to you," I said, more calmly. "It was only because I knew *exactly* what would happen. For all the legality afforded to our community since the Regulation Act—these careers with the FBMS that you and I could have never dreamed of as children—the council is still run by nonusers whose first and only priority is controlling us. Until magic users sit on that panel, society is still keeping a boot on our necks."

"They've just made magic more palatable for the masses," Moore answered with a sort of quiet defeat in his voice, like this was a truth he'd long understood and carried with him while trying to support and defend his agents in the field. "If I had known…. I'd have never—"

"You had no reason to suspect."

"But I did. You're one of the top agents in the entire nation. You would never hand over this badge—certainly not in such a cowardly manner."

"Loren."

"I wish you had been able to trust me with the truth of

your skill level, but knowing what I do of Simon Fitzgerald at Antietam—and what magic user who's lived through the war doesn't know at least a scrap of that story—I understand why you hid your identity. I do. If my report had been less thorough, D.C. might not have noticed."

"You're an honest man, sir. It's why I respect you. I've been downplaying my involvement in cases for a decade. The encounter with Bligh was just the first one I didn't have the opportunity to fix, so to speak, before higher authorities starting looking into the accounts."

Moore was quiet for another moment, the silence between our long distance crackling in the undertone. Finally he said, in a voice that still retained an almost heartbroken quality, "I'm so sorry, Gillian. As your director, I failed to protect you, and the FBMS… they betrayed your loyalty and sacrifice."

"I don't want you to despair over what is beyond your control. I called because you're the only one I can trust, the only one I can turn to who'll believe me."

"Are you still at Blackwell's?" Moore asked, voice rising suddenly. "Jesus Christ, I'm on my—"

"No, no! Sir, I'm not there. I… found my way out."

A beat, then Moore said, "I hope you gave them hell."

"Their foundation is in need of considerable repair."

It was the first moment in our conversation that I could hear a smile in Moore's words. "This is why I adore you. Even now, you're still pulling your punches. What do you need from me?"

I glanced up at Gunner, asking, "Won't you inquire as to my whereabouts?"

"I haven't spoken to Simon Fitzgerald since the New Year. I have no knowledge as to his current location," Moore replied in a professional, aloof manner, like he was addressing a question from a superior. And the suggestion in his statement, that not only was my name *not* Simon Fitzgerald, so of course he hadn't spoken with said man, but the promise that, like Gunner, he was a man of honesty and integrity and willing to put his own principles on the line as a means of protecting me… it was incredible and humbling and I didn't deserve either of them.

"Thank you," I whispered.

"Tell me what you need," Moore said again.

"Airship passenger manifests," I answered. "If he's as mad as we think, he'll travel under his own name—Dr. Eugene Barrie. I suspect he'll have a first-class ticket, departing San Francisco."

"You need his destination?" Moore guessed.

"That's correct."

"And who is this man?"

"Sawbones."

"Saw—hang on. The same Sawbones reported to be the builder of New Year's mechanical men?"

"The very same," I said.

"You've confirmed this information?"

I looked at Gunner a second time before answering, "It's confirmed. We suspect Barrie has an employer, but the details have not yet presented themselves. What is for certain is that Barrie is probably a level-five caster, quite proficient with aether, and has the ability to cast quintessence—which you'll recall in my New Year's report. If my word is worth a damn, believe me when I say he is causing irreversible damage to the magic atmosphere."

The first thing Moore said was "You said, 'we.' Is *he* with you?"

"I'm with Gunner, yes, sir."

I half expected commentary, but Moore concluded with saying, "Let me make some calls. How can I get in touch without pinging this PDD code and obtaining knowledge of your location?"

"I'll call you back," I suggested.

"Twenty minutes," he confirmed, then disconnected.

I tugged the headset off, set it on the desktop, and said, "I need to ping him in twenty."

Gunner consulted his silver pocket watch, nodded, then returned it to his waistcoat.

"He still doesn't much like you."

Gunner smiled, mostly to himself, as he removed his package of Black Jack and stuck a piece in his mouth. "I don't like Moore either. But we respect each other. That's what matters."

I stood, moved around the chair, put my hands on its top rail, and leaned back against it. "Did you respect me? When we first met?"

"Of course. You set a building on fire."

"That wasn't intentional."

Gunner slipped his hands into his trouser pockets and raised his head in a somewhat defiant manner, still smiling that coy smile. "I respected you because you presented me with a challenge. Moore does the same—in more ways than one."

"I'm not sure if 'respect' is the word I'd have used when we met."

"I'm quite aware, my dear."

I looked down at my shoes as I stifled a laugh. "You were absolutely infuriating, brash, and frustratingly unperturbed by my presence."

"If law enforcement scared me, I'd have gone into a more

practical field of work. Accounting, perhaps."

"This is exactly what I mean."

Gunner's smile softened into something private, something just for me. "But?"

"But what? You're still all those things."

He laughed, that rare and beautiful sound like a gift from Heaven. It was confirmation that I wasn't completely hopeless in being what Gunner needed in a romantic partner, in meeting him halfway in this: our official courtship.

I left the desk and went to the front counter. I plucked one of the telegraph blanks from the pile, stamped with *First Chance Western Union* across the header. I dipped a pen into the nearest inkwell and jotted a single word before signing my name in self-taught script. I returned to the desk and handed it to Gunner.

"It's a reminder," I explained as he accepted the note. "If we're ever apart."

Gunner read it, folded it, and tucked it into his breast pocket, like where I carried the receipt with his own memo. Glancing toward the front window, where the operator's shape was made visible by the interior lamplight, his back to us, Gunner leaned down and kissed my mouth.

When exactly twenty minutes had passed, Gunner motioned to the PDD. I returned to the chair, put the headset on, and tapped Moore's code into the transducer.

"Moore."

"It's me."

He wasted no time. "Bartholomew Industries confirmed that their local office in San Francisco sold a first-class ticket to one Dr. Eugene Barrie this morning."

"Bound for?"

"New York City."

I shot Gunner a triumphant look while lowering the transducer. "Barrie's going back to Manhattan."

Gunner rolled his finger in a suggestion I continue the conversation, before he strode across the office, opened the front door, and began speaking with the operator outside.

"Hamilton?"

"I'm here," I quickly said to Moore. "What's Barrie's day of arrival?"

"He left today, with a scheduled landing of five o'clock Monday evening, February the twenty-third, at Grand Central Depot. Bartholomew asked if they should make an unscheduled landing and have him arrested, but I said to keep en route so as not to raise suspicions. I'll have a dozen agents waiting to meet Barrie when he disembarks."

"That's perfect," I answered.

"He's not even traveling under a false name," Moore remarked. "The man is either fearless or he's a cake only half-baked."

"I don't believe he had any reason to suspect I'd be in contact with the FBMS. He knew I was on the lam. He has no reason to be afraid."

Moore grunted. "And what about you? What will you do?"

Even with a firm plan in place for the apprehension of Barrie, our problems didn't end with the doctor in a pair of handcuffs. Because for all the faults the FBMS had, they were still an honest organization that couldn't be bought off, nor would they make a case against Barrie without proof of his crimes, like the metropolitan police were known for doing. I needed to provide tangible evidence that Barrie had built the mechanical men in January and that his quintessence was responsible for the rip in the atmosphere. And perhaps most importantly, I needed Barrie to tell me anything and everything he knew about Weaver, because what was stopping that criminal architect from finding a hundred more casters and teaching them *all* quintessence? This didn't end with Barrie. Frankly, it only began with him.

To Moore I answered, "I'm coming home."

X

February 23, 1882

Gunner had made quick at finding us passage: a cargo airship cruising over the Front Range mountains had been scheduled for a morning refueling of water for their steam engines in First Chance before leaving the state, according to the telegraph operator. And when the ship docked in the early hours, the sky still dark and air brutally cold, we'd left the inn to meet the crew. The captain, a tall and distinguished older gentleman hauling fine fabrics from Japan, was scheduled to arrive at Pier 17 in New York City, where no doubt his payload was destined for the army of seamstresses employed at the Iron Palace. Gunner had spoken with the captain as his crew filled the water tanks, and we were onboard and being shown a spare cabin before the first mate had called for the release of the dock locks.

The trip was night and day when compared to the luxury of a first-class passenger liner. Our quarters were intended for crew, so there was hardly enough room for two grown men to squeeze around each other. The narrow bunks were also more accommodated to those not much taller than myself, and so Gunner's feet hung off the end. Add to that the noise of steam rattling the pipes, the *clank*s and *bang*s of hardware, and the general filth that came from the mouths of sailors at all hours, and it proved to be a long two days.

I would be lying, however, if I didn't admit that there were small bouts of enjoyment to be had, when the captain permitted us to walk the deck. It had become apparent that a few sailors recognized Gunner, and word had quickly spread among the ranks as to his presence. Soon enough, the crew was completely enamored with Gunner's stoic personality and they shared renditions of his "heroic" exploits—some of which were simply not true, but Gunner didn't once correct the sailors or tell the stories himself. I realized this was how outlaws such as him earned their monikers and became household names, so I let it all slide without comment. I worried at first that we'd hardly be docked in New York before coppers would be notified to come and arrest Gunner, since this crew appeared to be the respectable sort, but it turned out the men were far more thrilled to have something to boast to other airship crews about over drinks than they were about collecting a reward bounty.

One of the younger sailors—he couldn't have been a year or two beyond twenty, with blond hair that was nearly white from long hours on deck and working in the sun—had timidly shared a stick of Black Jack with Gunner, at the egging-on of his fellow crewmen, like it was some rite of passage. Later that first night, however, as I'd been stowing goggles, collar, and cuffs in my bag before turning in, there'd been a knock at the door. Gunner had opened it to reveal the same lad, his face a crimson mask of nervousness as he'd stuttered a request to speak in private. So Gunner had stepped into the passageway, and when he returned a minute later, his composed expression gave no hint as to their brief conversation.

"What did he want?" I'd finally asked.

Gunner had said, in his typical monotone as he unbuttoned

his waistcoat, "A tumble."

"A—wait, what?"

"Are you jealous?"

"It very much depends on what you said."

I'd been treated to that there-and-gone smile of Gunner's before he'd answered, "I told him I was attached." He crouched before me on the bottom bunk and had put his hands on my knees. "Does that make you feel gross?"

I shrugged a little before shaking my head.

"Then it makes you happy?"

"More than I can say," I'd whispered.

He kissed me, and said against my lips, "Me too."

It was nearly eleven o'clock that Monday night when our cargo airship docked at the piers along the southeastern edge of Manhattan. The original structure of Pier 17 still existed, but after the city remodeled the seaport for import and export via air instead of water back in '75, the pier was merely a boardwalk by which to reach the ramps and pneumatic lifts to the docked ships overhead, their steam engines chugging and creating a constant but not unpleasant drone. We thanked the captain for his goodwill, Gunner paid him of course, and we departed before the skeletal crew who worked throughout the night to accept international deliveries could notice that the captain had been hauling more than bolts of fabric.

I was always mindful of Cherry Street when I was down this way—the destitution and depravity that never failed to make my blood run cold in ways the rest of this wicked city could never scare me was just a few minutes east of Pier 17. I hastily led the way west along Water Street, which boasted the same fares as along the Bowery—spirits and sex—but due to the sheer number of airship crews who frequented these watering holes, the neighborhood was also home to river gangs who gave the Whyos a run for their money in terms of brutal viciousness. There was no easier target to rob, fuck, or kill than a lower-class transient man, whose captain wasn't in a position to delay flights and search for him among the dilapidated tenements—ergo, no charges were ever brought down upon these thieves and murderers. Their numbers and territory were small in comparison, but I didn't have to tell Gunner to unbutton his coat for easy access to the shoulder holster he preferred to wear in the city.

When we'd reached the El train's South Ferry station, we paid fare for the Sixth Avenue line, joined the few other passengers heading uptown at the late hour, and sat beside each other in a comfortable silence until Fourteenth Street, where the train picked up a belligerent drunk who zeroed in on a young, well-dressed woman traveling on her own. Gunner and I stood at the same time, and I walked across the car, held out my hand, and asked if she would care to sit at the other end. She offered a relieved smile and accepted, hardly out of her seat before the drunkard started in, slurring vile comments about her person that were so disgusting even sailors would have winced. Gunner promptly punched him in the face, dragged him to the car doors, and calmly held the scum upright by his jacket collar while his nose and mouth bled and he covered himself in snot as he cried. Once we reached Twenty-Third Street, the doors opened with a hiss of steam and Gunner threw the drunkard onto the platform. When the young lady departed a few stops later, Gunner tipped his hat and bid her a good night.

We remained on the Harlem-bound train, which transferred tracks and hopped onto the Ninth Avenue line, before stepping out of the car at the Seventy-Second Street platform. Gunner followed without question as I once again led the way down to street level and one block north to an apartment hotel towering between avenues. The Globe was impressive in both its sheer size and flamboyancy in design. It was the first of these bachelor accommodations to embrace the opulent, overblown, hyperaccentuated Beaux Arts aesthetic over the Renaissance Revival motif seen in my former home of The Buchanan. A combination of limestone and brick on its exterior emphasized the ornate, balustraded balconies and sloped, copper roofs, of which was the inspiration behind the structure's name.

A doorman met us at the gates of a small courtyard. "Good evening, sirs," he said.

"Good evening," I replied. "May I be permitted to call on Loren Moore? Is he home?"

"The Globe doesn't allow guests after ten, sir," the doorman answered.

"It's pertaining to federal business," I said next, unswayed by his dismissal. "If you could let him know Misters Ackerman and Gaylord are here, per his request."

Dropping "federal" as a means of making a point tended to work wonders on the honest sort, and luckily I'd pegged this doorman's reaction accordingly. He told us to wait a moment and disappeared into The Globe's bright and warmly lit lobby.

"Why Ackerman?" Gunner finally asked, a plume of cold air settling around him on the exhale, visible via the red and green lampposts along the sidewalk.

"It was the false name Barrie had provided for my airship ticket."

"I see."

"You don't like it?"

"I do not."

I laughed under my breath.

"How is it you knew Moore's home address?" Gunner asked next.

"Oh. I'd been renting a room for years, here and there, you know? As families moved and landlords changed. And I was preparing to find new accommodations once again, when Moore told me about these new apartment hotels being built throughout the city. I was rather dubious, because it sounded like the worst of two worlds: the publicness of a hotel and the overcrowding of a tenement. So he brought me uptown one day to show me The Globe," I concluded, motioning with one hand. "I found my way to The Buchanan about a month later."

The front doors opened and the doorman stepped outside, his footfalls echoing on the cold stone and crunchy snow of the courtyard.

Gunner said, "Moore was angling for you to rent here, my dear."

"He what?"

"Gentlemen," the doorman said as he opened the iron gate and gestured us into the courtyard. "Mr. Moore will see you. 7C—the lift is available at the end of the hall, to the left of the stairs."

I thanked him as we stepped toward the main entrance. Inside, the lobby was far grander than my own had been—marble and colored tile floors, gilded molding along the ceiling, and premiere-quality mosaics covering every inch of available wall space. The cogs and screws, gears and wheels all gleamed in the overhead steam-powered lighting, the parts moving in a perfect and silent synchronization so that as we crossed the long hall, it shifted with us. The brass and copper and silver and gold mechanics all together created the New York cityscape, with airships chasing the rise and fall of the sun and moon, and silhouettes of men and women ballroom dancing on the bank of the East River. We passed two doors, one marked Mailroom and the other Newsroom before reaching the lifting apparatus.

When we stepped inside, I pulled the gate shut and cranked the brass handle to level seven. As the lift rose, the passing floors quiet at the late hour, I murmured, "I'd have never been able to afford a place like this."

"Moore pulls in that State Director paycheck."

"You really think he wanted me to move here?"

Gunner glanced down, a careful sort of expression on his face. "He loved you then. He loves you now."

"I wish he didn't. No, I don't mean how that sounded. It's only—"

"I know what you meant," Gunner answered.

At the seventh floor, we exited the lift and walked to the corner apartment with a gold plate naming it 7C. I knocked quietly, and like he'd been waiting on the other side, the door opened suddenly and Moore—still larger than life and as handsome as ever, with his ash-brown-and-steel-gray hair and out-of-date but well-groomed beard—stood in the threshold. He wore a waistcoat and tie, but his sleeves had been rolled back, so the transducer connected to his PDD headset around his neck had been tucked into the front pocket instead of being hidden up the sleeve. He took the pipe from between his teeth and leaned forward to check the hallway at our backs. Moore took a step inside and motioned us to follow with a tilt of his head.

He shut and locked the door behind us before asking, "Did anyone see you?"

"Only the doorman," I said, removing my cap.

Moore nodded, but like he'd only half heard my response. He was staring at me so intently, I felt I was about to wilt like a summer flower who'd had too much sun and not enough rain. He reached forward and gave my shoulder a hard squeeze. The touch lingered until wisps of smoke rose from my jacket as our magics reacted to each other, and if it hadn't been for that limitation, undoubtably Moore would have pulled me into a back-breaking embrace.

"It's good to see you again, Hamilton."

"You too, sir."

Moore looked over my shoulder and said to Gunner, "And I suppose you're part of the package?"

"You had your chance, Director."

Moore's expression darkened, but when he looked at me again, his tone was gentler than I expected. "Hang up your coats and come sit." He stuck the bit of his pipe between his teeth and walked into the parlor just to the left off the foyer, a heady, cherry smoke trailing behind him.

Gunner silently took my carpet bag and set mine and his atop a marble counter before we both hung winter jackets and hats on the brass rack beside it. I glanced down the hall straight ahead—two closed doors on the left and one on the right. I suspected there was no kitchen, much like how The Buchanan had been designed, and that the top floor featured a restaurant for the tenants. The air in the parlor was warmed by the steam radiator along the far wall beside a large, eastern-facing window that still hadn't had its curtains drawn closed for the night, so colored lamps from the street below cast a sort of fantastical and kaleidoscopic glow about the room.

I took a seat on the settee, a pretty thing of vibrant yellow with a corresponding armchair, both of which matched the dark mahogany furniture and wall paneling. Gunner didn't join me. Instead, he went to the window and peered out into the city night. Moore stood opposite of me at a brass cart, his back turned. The clink of glass and slosh of liquid told me he was mixing drinks. His pipe rested in a glass tray atop the table beside me, the ember dying without Moore there to puff and tamp the tobacco.

The first thing Moore said was "We took Barrie into

custody this evening."

I let out a breath and nodded to myself. "Good."

"So far he's not talking, but a night behind bars is bound to soften him to the idea. You said nothing about showing up on my doorstep, Hamilton."

"I couldn't very well ask you in advance," I said.

"Because I would be aiding and abetting?"

"At the very least."

Moore glanced over his shoulder at me. "I'm already in plenty deep."

"Pardon?"

"I didn't want to say so over unsecured airwaves," he began, "but on February the eighteenth, I was ordered to dispatch agents to the city ports and apprehend Simon Fitzgerald, who the FBMS claimed had caused critical magic injury to both person and property while attending a routine health screening at Bellevue and was now on the run."

I shook my head in disgust and said, just shy of a whisper, "I was never at Bellevue."

"I know that now," he replied, returning to his drink-making. "I didn't then."

"Who'd the report come from?"

"That's the thing." A clink against glass as Moore stirred the contents. "D.C. council sent me the directive. It'd been the first time in over a month you'd been spoken of, but I knew something wasn't right. Because the council had also been the ones to tell me you'd quit and left the city—so why did they know about your routine health screening *in* the city?" Moore turned and walked across the room with a crystal tumbler. "Be it Fitzgerald or Hamilton, the man I knew would never hurt innocent people and would never willfully cause chaos or destruction. So I went out to Bellevue myself." He handed me the glass. "To confirm the situation. And you know what?

There was no damage, no injuries. No one knew anything about a Simon Fitzgerald." He pointed to the drink and said, "Old-fashioned. That's a cherry, by the way. Much better than an orange peel."

"Ah, thank you," I said hastily before continuing with the more important matter at hand. "But you mean to tell me the council has now falsified evidence against me and presented it to a State Director as gospel *more than once*?"

Gunner snorted from the window but didn't interject with his own comment.

Moore had resumed mixing two more drinks. The strong line of his shoulders dropped a little—deflated, even. "Yes." He carried a glass to Gunner, who accepted it without a word, and then Moore collected his own drink and took a long sip. "If it had been in regard to any other agent, I might not have realized. But a lie about *you*, Hamilton?"

"Lies are a pretty accurate assessment of my person," I said.

"A lie about your name is not the same as a lie about your character." Moore took another drink. "I didn't know what to do, other than if you were on the run, to let you get where you needed to be."

I raised my eyebrows. "Sir?"

He said again, in that professional but indifferent tone, "I was only able to spare three teams to conduct the search and apprehension of Simon Fitzgerald. One for the East River ports, one for the Hudson, and one for Grand Central. So far, they have been… unsuccessful."

"Agent Plunket," I whispered. "She knew to look the other way."

Moore smiled, stroked his beard, and said, "Let's just say that Plunket is still making amends and did me a favor."

"Sir, if the council learns about this—"

"They'll what?" Moore countered. "Take my badge too?"

"*Yes!*"

"I welcome them to try. I've given the Bureau seventeen years of my life because they promised protection, integrity, and opportunity for our community. And now I learn they want to ruin one of their best men because… what… they'd rather charge you with war crimes?"

Hot, sour bile rose up my throat, and I focused on the hardwood floor of the parlor, somewhere at the middle point of the room, but what I really saw was the blood-soaked battlefield. Smoke from cannon fire was so heavy, it made my eyes sting. I could smell the lingering stench of destruction—of ozone from too much magic, of gunpowder, of ruptured bowels, of charred flesh. I could hear a eulogy of rage whispering across Antietam: *Kill the monster, kill the monster, kill the monster, drop the curtain on his life.*

This horror was to forever be the soul of my plot.

I slammed the tumbler down on the table and clamped a hand over my mouth to keep from retching.

"Hamilton?"

But it was Gunner who reached me first, strong hands gripping my biceps as he drew me to my feet. He tilted my chin up, forcing me to meet his gaze, to acknowledge the naked honesty of his concern. "Gillian?"

I sucked in a deep breath through my nose and was briefly overwhelmed by the Sandringham perfume Gunner wore, the hint of black licorice on his breath, and the fine wool of his suit coat warming after being in the cold. I lowered my shaking hand and said, "I'm fine." I pulled free from Gunner's touch and looked at Moore. "May I use your water closet?"

"Second door on the left," he answered somberly.

My legs felt about as firm as custard as I left the parlor. I hurried down the hall to the door Moore had indicated, shut it behind me, and was promptly sick into the toilet. I was never prepared for how I would or wouldn't react to those war-torn recollections, but I was certain the more people who knew I had been born Simon Fitzgerald, the worse it got. Because even if my darling and my friend insisted it was not a burden I had to keep shouldering, even when they called me Gillian Hamilton, I couldn't help but remind myself that when they looked at me… they knew.

They knew I took all those lives.

A violence forced upon me, yes.

But I had still been the one who aimed and pulled the trigger.

And if the federal government had it their way, I would do it again.

I was sick a second time, the knots in my gut lessening some after that. I flushed, washed my mouth and face, and silently left the closet. I moved down the hall and neared the open doorway of the parlor before I picked up pieces of Gunner and Moore's low but fierce discussion.

"—Soldier's Heart—" That was Gunner.

"—didn't know," Moore retorted.

"—wanted since '62."

"Fitzgerald—casualty of war."

Gunner said something decidedly in the negative, and I moved to stand in the doorway as he asked Moore, "Do you think you and Inspector Byrnes are the only law enforcement with a rogues' gallery?"

"What does that mean?" I interrupted.

Both of them turned quickly, guiltily, in my direction.

"What does that mean?" I asked again, aiming the question at Gunner.

And for perhaps the first time since we'd met, he looked wholeheartedly uneasy. "My dear—"

I shook my head. "*Don't.*"

"This isn't the time or place."

"You just made it so."

Gunner didn't move, but all at once, there was a sensation of him having drawn himself up, much like the way he'd stared down Tinkerer's deadly devices in Shallow Grave and not blinked. And while Gunner almost always spoke in a monotone, I had learned how to recognize his very real emotions in between the words. But this time, those breaths were distant, empty. "It means, until a dead body is presented, the Pinkerton Detective Agency has considered Simon Fitzgerald an ongoing and active case since the Great Rebellion."

I felt as if I'd been submerged in an ice bath and someone was holding my head under. "And you know because…?"

"Because I was a Pinkerton," he concluded.

"*What?*" Moore interjected.

Gunner didn't break eye contact with me. "For eleven years. During the war, I worked with Allan Pinkerton as part of his Union Intelligence Service. When Simon Fitzgerald went missing after the Battle of Antietam, I was tasked with locating and returning him to the Union Army." Gunner took a step toward me, and his tone changed—something akin to an animal in distress. "I refused the assignment."

Moore said, boldly, defiantly, "You'd have us believe you worked as a Pinkerton for nearly a decade, and no one has questioned the probability of Detective Gunner and Gunner the Deadly being one and the same man?"

Gunner's gaze cut to his left, listening to Moore at his back, but he looked directly at me when he answered, "I worked under an assumed name as a detective."

"Hogwash," Moore spat.

But I shook my head, saying, "Gunner doesn't lie." To Gunner, I asked, point-blank, "When did you leave the agency?"

"'72."

"Why?"

Gunner narrowed his eyes. "Because who I was before did not allow for self-respect."

"That's not enough of an answer," I said.

"It's what I'm comfortable sharing." He held his hands out slightly, indicating our surroundings, while adding, "I gave you my word I'd explain, and I'd hoped that was enough for you. With Blackwell's, the FBMS, and let's not forget Barrie, *this* was an undue stress to our current situation that I wanted to avoid."

I ran a hand through my hair, swore under my breath, and strode toward the settee. I picked up my abandoned drink from the table, knocked it back in one long swallow, and put the glass aside. I pushed my suit coat back, set my hands on my hips, and walked to the window. I took Gunner's drink from the sill and sipped it as well, but more appreciatively. I watched the reflection of the room—Moore shaking his head as if disagreeing with some inward conversation, and Gunner approaching, footfalls silent.

"I know the exact moment," I said, turning partially to meet Gunner's gaze. "At Dead Man's Canyon. You had such an odd expression on your face. I knew you wanted to speak, but then you clammed up. I'm right, aren't I? That's when you knew who I was?"

Gunner nodded.

"Why didn't you just say so? We could have avoided… so much bullshit."

"Would we?" Gunner countered. "You introduced

yourself as Gillian Hamilton. You had reinvented yourself, as I had. That was good enough for me. But when I began to notice how certain circumstances afflicted you, I realized I was wrong in my prior assessment. It wasn't that you wished to merely reinvent yourself—you wanted to be someone else entirely."

"The things you said," I whispered against the rim of the glass.

"I wanted you to know love. I wanted you to know that I could be trusted." After a beat, Gunner added, "I admittedly got frustrated once or twice, when you were on the verge of divulging and then backed away."

I took a swallow of the bourbon. "You really refused the assignment?"

"McClennan wanted to court-martial me, but I was a civilian." Gunner gently took the tumbler from my hand and set it back on the sill. "I promise you, I've never been privy to any additional information about your life. I only knew, and still know, the basics. Simon Fitzgerald was a weapon of war and disappeared after Antietam. On paper, the government did consider Simon a casualty of the Great Rebellion, but they also employed the Pinkertons to find proof either way." Gunner touched my balled-up fist and then visibly relaxed as I wrapped my hand around his. "If you never want to speak another word of that life, I will respect your decision. But I want you to understand, when I was asked to apprehend Simon and was given the description of a ten-year-old boy…." Gunner's very-blue eyes caught the colorful lights from outside when he looked away, and I realized he was about to cry.

"What?" I pressed.

"Let's say that my difference of opinion with law enforcement began in September of 1862." Gunner cleared his throat and hastily wiped one eye. "I'm sorry for upsetting you, my dear."

I shook my head. "I wasn't—I was surprised, is all. *Really* surprised." I looked up at Gunner, and even though I felt exhausted, managed a smile. "You being a detective."

"Once upon a time."

"The unblinking eye. It explains a lot about you."

"Hamilton," Moore interrupted.

I looked across the room, but was not oblivious to the way Gunner drew his hand up my arm and held my elbow, a suggestion of both intimacy and territoriality. It was a blatant warning to Moore. "Sir?"

"Are you okay?"

I nodded. "Yes. I'm sorry. It's been a long few—" I almost said 'days,' before laughing and opting instead for "—decades."

Moore offered a sympathetic expression. "Do you have accommodations in place?"

"Oh. No, not yet. There's bound to be lodgings—"

"Stay here."

I blinked. "Pardon?"

"I have a spare bedroom," Moore answered.

I looked at Gunner, who said nothing. To Moore, I said, "I, uhm… that is…."

"These aren't transient affections, are they?" Moore asked. He didn't need to motion between us to make his point.

"No, sir."

"Stay here," Moore reiterated. "Barrie isn't going anywhere. Get some rest, and we can decide in the morning our next plan of action." His gaze shifted to meet Gunner's. "And since I can't shake the man of many faces…."

"It's just the one, Director," Gunner corrected, letting go

of my arm, pocketing his hands, and turning to face Moore head-on.

"Is that so?"

"I make no attempt to hide who I am."

"And so who might that be?"

"America's most-wanted outlaw, and Hamilton's darling—Gunner the Deadly."

XI

February 24, 1882

It was one o'clock in the morning when I said good night to Moore and shut the door to the bedroom he'd offered us. It was furnished with quality and care, but I couldn't imagine—given Moore's bachelorhood, tendencies, and lack of extended family—the room had ever seen any use. I turned, leaned back against the door, and watched Gunner remove his suit coat. If how I felt was any indication of his own state, he was more than ready to get a few hours' rest.

"You antagonize him," I stated.

"Moore?" Gunner asked. He removed his pocket watch from his waistcoat, checked the time, then carefully laid it out on the bureau. "I respect his heartbreak—he respects my affections toward you. Anything more is because he makes it so easy."

I smiled to myself.

"What?"

I glanced up to see Gunner staring intently. "It's nothing." I pushed off the door and approached. "If I asked what name you worked under as a Pinkerton, would you tell me?"

"There are matters in my own past, Gillian, that I don't necessarily want to dredge up. But of course I'll tell you." Gunner waited, cocking his head. "Are you asking?"

"No. I suppose not." Feeling both bold and in love—a recipe for disaster, if there ever was one—I put my hands on Gunner's hips, drew him close, then fiddled with the buttons keeping his braces in place. "I think I'm addicted to you, is all. I have to remind myself that if you don't push me, I can't push you."

Gunner leaned down to kiss my mouth. "I might be addicted as well. And I very much enjoy the taste of bourbon on your lips."

"I've grown a fondness for the taste of Black Jack on yours."

Gunner turned me around and tugged the suit coat from my shoulders. "Come to bed," he said, his voice its usual huskiness and not a suggestion of something more lying in wait.

I was halfway out of the coat when the magic atmosphere prickled, tightened, and felt as if it were digging under my flesh. "Stop, stop," I said to Gunner, who immediately paused in trying to undress me. I hunched over, gripped my left hand hard, and dug my thumb into the palm to try to alleviate the pain.

Gunner stepped in front of me.

I shifted perception and watched the currents of raw magic the apartment was full of. Heavy sparkling bands of energy were drawn through the wall and in the direction of Moore's bedroom, but the rest lingered here—so much of it attracted to me that my vision was nearly washed out by the powerful glow. I reached my left hand out, fingers rigid and locked in unnatural positions as the disturbance raked painfully along my damaged nerves, and let the magic coil around me. I forced my hand closed into an awkward fist, and my consciousness followed the energy like a gunshot—cutting through Central Park, shooting downtown, and exploding at random intervals along the Bowery like unattended firecrackers. A painful shiver went down my spine and gooseflesh made the hair on my arms rise as the metaphorical smoke dissipated from the discharges, leaving behind pulsing tears in the atmosphere.

I hadn't noticed Gunner exit the bedroom, but the next thing I knew, Moore was standing before me, mouth moving in words I couldn't hear. I blinked, and my perception snapped back to the mundane. I noted that Moore was partially undressed for the night, and that if there was a *type* I gravitated toward, it was apparently men with chest hair. I quickly looked at his face and asked, "Sorry?"

Moore raised both eyebrows in apparent befuddlement. "What's wrong?" His tone suggested he'd already asked this question at least once.

I looked over his shoulder to see Gunner in the doorway, then down at my hand. I gave it a cautious flex, but the nerves still hurt like a son of a bitch. "It's Barrie."

"He's locked up at the field office."

I shook my head. "No."

Moore turned and left the room, and seconds later, his booming voice was speaking into his PDD.

Gunner resumed his position in front of me, took my hand, and began to gently knead the palm. "It's the quintessence?"

"Yes. Every time it's used, the magic atmosphere convulses. Like… I don't know how to explain it… a festering sore that's broken open."

"Lovely," Gunner said dryly.

"Before I had a name for it or understood how the quintessence was being used, I thought this sensation was due to only the artificial spells fused into the ammunition being shipped into the city," I explained. "But now I'm beginning to understand it's more the quintessence that's damaging, rather than the illegal fire or lightning spells. When Barrie injected you with that morphine… same sensation as now. But it's like, until the quintessence is activated, it's almost undetectable."

"Almost?" Gunner echoed.

"Hm-hm. Quintessence has this… weighted effect."

"It forces a reaction."

"Right, but I also mean literally. If the tangible item that's been infused with quintessence sits in one place too long, it leaves a signature. Just like when Fishback was murdered—the spell terminated at the office, but originated in the facility that later exploded on Hester Street."

Gunner narrowed his eyes.

"It'd been stored there for at least a few weeks," I explained. "So when the ammunition had been taken from storage and brought uptown, it left a—"

"Breadcrumb trail," Gunner concluded, letting go of my hand.

I murmured a quick thank-you before saying, "Yes. Exactly."

"So is there a trail to follow now?"

"Not really. Other than something's happened along the Bowery. The spell is too fresh to trace any kind of starting point." I looked around Gunner's shoulder as Moore returned to the doorway, pulling the headset around his neck. "Well?"

"Barrie's still behind bars. There's been no less than two agents on guard duty all evening."

I shook my head again, more fervently this time. "No. It's him. Something's very wrong."

Moore admired automobiles as much as I actively loathed them. He was the proud owner of a behemoth of a machine, all black with a blood-red interior and open-hood design meant to show off the polished brass and chrome steam mechanics of the engine and radiator. The rakish angle of the roof, like the brim of a bowler pulled low, combined with the long front body, gave the auto a decidedly devious aura, like its owner was most certainly up to no good. Despite my disinterest in riding in automobiles, I had to admit, given the current circumstances, the ability to facilitate expedience was much appreciated. Moore took advantage of the near-empty streets and sped downtown along Ninth Avenue, all while more savage tears in the atmosphere along the Bowery kept exploding at random.

"It's still happening?" Moore asked.

I glanced sideways from where I sat in the passenger seat.

"You keep flexing your hands."

I realized I had balled my hands into fists and consciously relaxed, smoothing out the wrinkles in my trousers. "It is, yes."

"You can really sense it all? Illegal magic? Artificial? Even the raw current?"

I declined disclosing that I not only felt the raw magic, I could see it if I so wished, I could identify the signature of other casters, and I could pick out every single magic user in a crowd without fail. "Yes," I said again. I looked at Moore as he made a sharp turn east on Twenty-Third. "Can you not sense the resistance when casting?"

Moore took one hand from the wheel and briefly stroked his beard. "I've noticed a time or two over the past month that I've needed more energy than normal to cast certain spells. I thought it was the typical reasons: overworked, overtired… too much drinking."

"It's the reactivation," I explained. "Once the quintessence is cast into a tangible item, such as, for example, fire ammunition, it lies dormant until put into play. It's the reactivation process—magic being utilized by someone without magic abilities—that causes the spell to pull energy from the atmosphere."

"Bypassing the required step of a caster replacing the raw magic with their own lifeforce," Moore said, picking up my train of thought. "And it's killing the atmosphere, isn't it?"

My silence was answer enough.

Moore came up on the looming structure of the field office at the corner of Fifth Avenue, its outline a chaotic mixture of greens and reds and purples from the steam-powered lampposts. He drove past the front entrance, turned down Broadway, and parked the auto within walking distance. The three of us exited the relative warmth of the interior and got that initial shock of cold winter air in our lungs before silently walking back uptown. We kept as far right as possible, so as to remain outside the pools of light dotting the sidewalk. Moore's steps along the frozen bluestone were heavy—he put his full weight on the heels of his shoes—mine lighter, and Gunner's nothing but a whisper against the smooth surface as he brought up the rear. We passed the office of Dr. Lillingston, which was dark and shuttered for the night. When she'd opened her practice years ago, she'd smartly chosen real estate within a stone's throw of special agents working active, and often dangerous, cases on the city streets, making her the field office's on-call physician. The decision had first simply been due to convenience. Now it was because of her top-notch capabilities and trustworthiness.

When we'd returned to Twenty-Third Street, Gunner asked, "Fourth floor jail cell, is it?" His mouth twitched in his usual ghost of a smile before he addressed the look on Moore's face. "You're very predictable, Director."

"Wait, where are you—?" I began as Gunner turned to walk farther east instead of toward the side entrance of the field office.

"I'll find my own way up," he said over his shoulder.

"Come on, Hamilton," Moore grunted. He led the way across the cobblestone street and down the dark and narrow, dead-end passage illuminated by a sole security lamp overhead. He stopped, collected his ring of skeleton keys, and looked at me. "I'll see that the agents on guard are dismissed. Give it a sixty count so you don't pass them in the stairwell."

"It's too risky," I replied.

"I don't know how else you expect to get upstairs, unless you intend to scale the building like our second-story criminal is likely doing this very second," he said.

"That's not my style. I don't have to lie about my skill level anymore, right?"

Moore raised a quizzical eyebrow, but he agreed.

"Then please be sure to open the window when you get upstairs." I snapped both hands and used the motion to point my palms toward the ground, conjuring a heavy gust of wind in the process. I was lifted off my feet by the spiral of air and rode it upward, passing the overhead fire escape before effortlessly weaving in between illuminated windows so as not to be noticed by agents working late-night hours. I reached the ledge of the fourth story well before Moore had made his way through the intricate twists and turns of the field office. I landed softly on the brick-and-metal outcropping, then terminated the wind spell with a casual wave of my hand. I'd hardly reached the other side of the ledge where the line of windows were—my arms out to balance myself like a tightrope walker—when I heard the crunch of old snow and a solid *thud* at my back. I startled and turned as Gunner raised himself from a crouched position on the roof several feet over my head and just to the right.

He jumped down onto the ledge beside me, tilted the brim of his bowler back, and said, "Fancy meeting you here."

"Did you *jump* from the neighboring building?" I asked.

"The alley was a strategically poor choice, if the intention of the FBMS was to maintain defense and impenetrability." Gunner then added, "Anything is possible with a running start."

"I'll remember that," I answered before crouching beside the third window. The two windows behind me, unreachable as the ledge terminated in that direction, were the half bullpen where I'd had it out with Henry Bligh on New Year's Eve, in the wake of Fishback's murder.

God, that felt like a lifetime ago.

The windowpane was drawn suddenly, Moore glanced out, then motioned us inside with the flick of his wrist. I climbed through first and Gunner quickly followed. Despite having more height to maneuver through the window than myself, Gunner managed to be far more graceful about it, which really solidified how routine such behavior was in his everyday life.

We followed Moore to the last of the three cells along the left wall, and when I saw the man sitting on the bunk in the cramped space, I blurted, "Who's this?"

"Eugene Barrie," Moore said in not quite a questioning tone.

"No, it's not," Gunner answered.

The stranger was middle-aged, tall and thin like a stork, with blond hair, round spectacles, and a suit that was decent enough, but those familiar with the latest in men's fashion would know it was half a decade out of style. Most importantly, however— "He's not even a magic user," I stated, looking up at Moore.

"What're you talking about?"

"This man," I said, emphasizing by jabbing my finger in the stranger's direction, all the while not looking away from Moore, "is not a caster."

"I am so!" the stranger barked suddenly.

"You are not," I retorted. "My prick has more magic in it than you do."

"*Well…,*" Gunner murmured with a thoughtful nod before the comment trailed off and he left it open to considerable interpretation.

Moore shot Gunner a vicious glare before saying, "He had a ticket in the name of Dr. Eugene Barrie. Airship crew identified him. He identified *himself* to my agents."

"As if any first-class man aboard Bartholomew Industries would be caught dead wearing a mismatched frock in 1882," I muttered, turning toward the cell and wrapping one hand around an iron bar as I leaned in. "How much were you paid to pretend to be this man—Dr. Barrie?"

The stranger crossed his arms defiantly, but visibly jumped when thunder cracked outside, sending a shiver through the entire building. Lightning jumped from my hand and spread across the cell, snapping and crackling against the iron. He swallowed audibly before stuttering, "I-I am D-Dr. Barrie." He shrieked and threw himself to the floor as I unleashed the lightning spell and it exploded against the wall, leaving varying degrees of blackened plaster behind that looked vaguely like an archery target. "Okay, okay!" he screamed from where he was curled into a ball. "I crossed paths with a man on the promenade deck early this morning—I was just stretching my legs, is all—he stopped me and said he'd pay me a hundred dollars if I'd switch tickets with him for the rest of the flight and go along with how folks addressed me." He tentatively raised his head and peeked from between his fingers like a child. "I'd get another hundred once we landed in New York, and if I was arrested, not to worry because he worked with, I don't know, you all, I guess, and he was playing a hell of a prank on everyone."

"He said he worked with us?" I repeated.

The stranger nodded vigorously. "Said to sit here, and in the morning, I'd be released and given the second hundred. Look, I didn't think… I mean… he was so sincere. Do you know what airship travel is like in first-class? I ate wild pheasant and olives before we landed! And I really need the money. It isn't illegal to switch tickets if the guy *wants* to sit in the overcrowded second-class cabin, eating cold sandwiches for lunch."

"Describe the man," I demanded.

"Auburn hair, a bit long. Freckles. He had a really soft voice."

"That's him," Gunner confirmed, more for Moore's benefit than my own.

"What's your name?" I asked next.

"Bert Parker."

"Occupation?"

"I'm an… out-of-work grocer."

"This is ridiculous," I said, turning my back on Parker so as to address both Moore and Gunner. "How could Barrie have possibly gotten tipped off midflight?"

"Perhaps he didn't," Moore said. "He might simply have more thought toward self-preservation than we originally surmised."

"Eugene Barrie is not a man who hides," Gunner said thoughtfully.

"That's true," I said next. "Gunner said that during the war, men opted to die rather than be brought to Barrie's field tent. He earned the nickname Sawbones twenty years ago, and yet he continues to blatantly practice medicine out in the open. He doesn't seem to care. And as far as travel is concerned—his first-class flights and a room at the Fifth Avenue were both in his legal name."

Moore frowned and stroked his beard. "Where'd he get that sort of money?"

I glanced at Gunner and said, "St. Margaret was a church-run hospital. Certainly they weren't paying for much beyond his boarding and meals. And the lecture tour was a lie, so it's not as if visiting hospitals were seeing to his expenses either."

"Tick Tock might have paid quite handsomely for his mechanical men, shortly before his demise," Gunner suggested. "Barrie could be living off those funds."

"True," I admitted. "But he spends as if he were an Astor and the well won't eventually run dry." I turned to Parker. "Were you told *who* was to release you from jail tomorrow?"

Parker's expression scrunched up as he tried to place the only hours-old detail. "Ah… I was told it'd be a gent everyone called Boss."

"Boss? As in, Boss Tweed? I hate to be the bearer of bad news, Mr. Parker, but Tweed has been dead since '78. He won't be helping you anytime soon."

"I wasn't told nothing about no Tweed, fella," Parker retorted. "*Boss*. That was it. No other name."

When I turned away from Parker a second time, I caught a look of uncertainty on Gunner's face. Subtle, of course, but it was there in the crow's feet around his blue eyes and the slight vertical crease between his dark brows. "Something wrong?" I asked him.

Gunner quickly met my gaze, hesitated for a fraction of a second, then said, "Trying to place the moniker."

I opened my mouth with the intention of asking Gunner if that was all, because he looked… troubled, but Moore interrupted.

"I suppose this Boss fellow could have arranged communication with the airship if they had noticed my agents at the Depot earlier today. Which means Barrie could have slipped out with the second-class passengers," Moore concluded.

"Why would the airship crew misidentify him?" Gunner asked.

"If Barrie arranged for meals to be delivered to his sleeper, the crew might never have had a chance to see him until Mr. Parker here went to the dining cabin himself," I answered thoughtfully.

Moore said, "Barrie's had close to a ten-hour head start. He could be anywhere in the city."

I shook my head and looked up, saying, "No, I find that doubtful. Sir, I think you should put in some calls. Bartholomew Industries, for one—see if you can obtain a transcript of any communications that ship received, originating from within Manhattan. We might be able to pinpoint who Barrie is clearly working with, if not for. I'd also check with some of the luxury hotels—see if he's checked in under his own name again." I considered my last thought for a moment, then added, "Please also send an inquiry to Blackwell's." I moved around Moore and took a step toward the window at the end of the hall.

"Hamilton, wait a moment. Blackwell's?"

I turned. "I think there is a distinct probability that whatever scheme Barrie is part of, he needs additional casters." I put a hand to my chest and added, "Unfortunately for him, I escaped, and now he's having to adjust course."

"Where will you go?"

"I'd like to examine whatever is currently happening on the Bowery."

"You're no longer a special agent," Moore said.

I studied him curiously.

"What I mean is, I can't order you to investigate."

I let out a slow breath before answering, "No, you can't order me—this is true. And I wish I had an inkling as to what I'm going to do with my life, being outside of the Bureau now." I took a step toward Moore. "For me, our relationship hasn't changed. You're still my closest friend and superior— I'll do whatever, whether you order me or not."

"That's very sweet," Parker spoke suddenly.

"Shut the fuck up," I snapped.

"Hey—seeing how I'm not actually this caster fella," Parker continued. "How's about letting me go?"

Moore ignored Parker's request and gave me a confirming nod. "The Bowery, then. I'll loan you a PDD. I'll start sending out telegrams too, and Mr. Parker and I will be here in the morning to greet this Boss gentleman in person."

XII

February 24, 1882

The middle of the night was when the Bowery was the loudest and deadliest. Most of the singing, dancing, and boxing that entertained customers of all different tendencies was winding down in favor of pounding back drinks at the bar or finding someone to heat a bed—or at the very least, a dark corner—for a short time. Music from competing halls drifted into the street as clients in various degrees of inebriation stumbled from the front doors in pairs or groups. Some were friendly drunks, laughing and talking merrily as they tried to find their way home. Others were the angry sort, picking fights with one another or complete strangers, their shouts and swears rivaling the fiddles and bodhráns.

But the vast majority of people lurking the street at this hour were gangsters, mainly Whyos smoking fat cigars and polishing their steam-powered brass fighting gloves. They prowled the neighborhood—some like Big Red Kate, a woman who wore her red-tinted goggles day and night, a bright rouge on her cheeks that matched the color of her hair, and carried an Excalibur, a pistol that shot superheated steam bullets that left behind her signature big red blister—

clearly hunting for a rival gang who might have accidently staggered into their territory and so needed taking out. The less respectable Whyos—thugs, really, who paid no mind to leader Danny Driscoll—were looking for nothing more than some excitement and chaos, and it didn't matter who they had to fight, fuck, or kill to scratch that itch.

Gunner and I had taken the Third Avenue El to Canal Street and were walking uptown along the Bowery in search of evidence of quintessence, when another flare struck the atmosphere. This one was so close and so powerful, it made my teeth ache, like I'd bitten down on a sheet of tin. I grabbed Gunner's coat sleeve as I came to an abrupt stop, adjusted my vision to take in the tumultuous fray of raw magic, and reached to grasp the closest tendrils. The magic sparkled brightly and then shot around the corner on Hester Street.

"Hamilton?"

"This way," I said, breaking into a run.

Gunner's long legs allowed him to keep easy pace as I bolted toward the end of the block, dipping in and out of light from streetlamps and dodging drunkards unable to walk a straight line. I turned left, pushed off the wall of a club when my shoes skidded along the frozen cobblestones, and kept running toward the intersection of Hester and Elizabeth Street. A dark form was hunched on the ground, hardly more than a murky outline, as the city spent less on lighting side streets in this neighborhood than they did the main thoroughfares. My pounding feet startled the individual, because they stood abruptly, and I realized there was another form on the ground, motionless.

"Federal Bur—*damn it*—stop right there!" I shouted before hurling a ball of lightning. But the little criminal ducked, dodged, and scampered out of sight. I blew past the prone body, continuing until I was halfway toward Mott Street, when Gunner called my name. I lingered a moment, checked the doorway of a tenement, an alley on the northside of the street, and behind a few monstrous piles of rubbish, but whoever the culprit had been, they'd successfully eluded me. I returned to Gunner at a jog. He was crouched beside the body and hoisting them onto their side. "They're still alive?" I asked.

Gunner didn't have a chance to respond before the poor bastard began profusely convulsing and retching. Something dark and wet pooled around the man's backside, and then the overpowering stench of loose bowels permeated the air. Gunner and I both took immediate steps backward in opposite directions, and we looked toward each other with a sort of helplessness until the man suddenly stopped seizing and went still. Gunner retrieved his bandana from a pocket, tied it around his face, and cautiously approached.

I opened my mouth to speak, but the stink of blood and stool and vomit had me gagging. I doubled-over, hands on my knees, and spat a few times to get the taste out of my mouth. "Christ Almighty."

"I think he was poisoned."

"With *what*?"

"Arsenic. A lot of arsenic."

I glanced over my shoulder, watching Gunner pat the body down. "Any money or valuables on his person?"

Gunner looked up, a question in his expression. "No."

I straightened and motioned in the direction the culprit had escaped. "Victim of a knockout gang." I paused, considered that statement, and furrowed my brow as I murmured, mostly to myself, "No, that can't be right."

"Knockout gang," Gunner repeated.

I glanced at him and hastily pointed to the body. "Rich sorts like him come downtown to slum, and one of these little street rats slips a poison into his drink. Once the victim's unconscious, they rob him. What isn't cash, they fence nearby."

Gunner was squatted on his haunches. "Was it a knockout gang or not?"

"I—well—it looks like it."

"Except if unconsciousness is the end goal, arsenic is a curious choice," Gunner answered. "It doesn't typically sedate a victim."

"No. Certainly not as fast-acting as morphine or chloral either," I added. "Which are the poisons of choice around here."

"Someone wanted him dead," Gunner concluded.

I hesitantly crouched beside the body, holding a hand against my mouth and nose because of the smell. "I'm certain this is where the quintessence spell was cast." Reluctantly, I wrapped my hand around the dead man's wrist. I expected to pick up the wriggling sensation of the quintessence— could practically feel that oily leech squashed between my fingers again—and the spell's slow dissipation after the death of the individual it was cast upon. Instead, I felt something entirely different. Quintessence, yes, but very much alive and writhing just under the surface, with the sensation of aether mingling—*interwoven*—into it.

Aether was the strongest magic to exist, a literal manifestation of all the raw elemental currents consolidated into one. Despite its ability to annihilate, intentions and skill level of the caster taken into account, aether was light and life. So to feel such a whole and pure magic butchered and defiled by something illegal and… *hollow*—it was sickening.

None of this made any sense. Arsenic had been what killed this man. The infused quintessence enforced an immediate death by weighting the overdose symptoms, but the aether spell was distinctly cast with healing intentions—with another layer of quintessence cast to essentially sandwich the aether in place. And to what end? To… reinforce life? The man was deader than Julius Caesar. Aether couldn't bring the dead back to life, because no caster could withstand the amount of power required.

Without warning, the soiled body gave a sudden lurch and bolted upright into a sitting position. The man's head jerked to the right, tilted at an unnatural angle so as to look at me. His eyes were very dead. And yet, he reached with his left hand and clamped it over mine, which had been holding his wrist, the still-warm skin flaring with a renewed burst of quintessence and aether. I screamed and yanked my hand free from his hold, fell onto my backside, and crabbed backward until I'd put enough distance between us that I could stumble to my feet.

"What in God's name?" I shouted.

Gunner jumped to his feet, unholstered his Waterbury, and cocked the pistol. He tugged his bandana down around his neck as he raised the weapon and pointed it at the dead man, who was staggering to his own feet. "What do I do?" he asked, his voice far calmer than my own.

"Shoot him!"

The dead man turned to face Gunner, and so Gunner shot. Three aether bullets tore through the man and blew his head apart. It was a perfect hit.

Perfect, except that the dead man was still standing.

"Hamilton?" Gunner asked, a touch warier now.

The man took a few ungainly steps forward, like he was simply a falling-down-drunkard and not a recently deceased individual, covered in their own blood and shit, with his head blown clean off. He reached an arm in Gunner's direction, to which Gunner answered with another shot, this one hitting the undead man square in the chest. He reeled back a step or two, but remained on his feet.

"I'm wasting good ammo and running out of ideas," Gunner called.

"I don't—" I was about to say, *I don't know*, but a moment of crystalline clarity hit me so suddenly, so intensely, it was like being pelted in the side of the head with a stone that had a sharp edge. I touched my temple, half expecting my fingers to come away bloody. "Barrie's been experimenting with medicinal aether, but it's never been legalized due to the uncertainty of how magic might interact with medications, or concern that the spell was performed by an unskilled caster and will hurt patients more than heal them."

"The point, Hamilton?" Gunner asked before he shot the dead man in the knee, which only hindered him enough that he was now dragging his right leg while continuing to move after Gunner.

"Quintessence has been the missing ingredient! Put it in elemental bullets, in the armor of mechanical men, or in poisons and medicines—it's a binding ingredient that keeps the spell from falling apart while being used by a noncaster."

"What does this have to do with our friend here?" Gunner asked as he holstered the Waterbury.

"Barrie's attempting what's always been deemed impossible—bringing the dead *back to life*." I raised both hands and fire erupted from my palms. "Move away!" I ordered.

Gunner ran to the south side of the street, giving the dead man a wide berth, before coming parallel with me and running for where I stood. As the undead turned around to follow Gunner's movement, I unleashed an explosive fireball, completely engulfing him and lighting up Hester Street several blocks in either direction. The stink of burning hair and flesh was dreadful and the black smoke stung my eyes, but despite this torture, the dead man didn't utter a scream, a cry, a single word. He just kept dragging his ruined body toward us.

I swore and made a cutting motion with one hand, which dissipated the spell at once. With how the two magics were interconnected inside this atrocity, it was a perfect cycle of the aether keeping the quintessence from having dissolved after death, and the quintessence fueling the aether at a consistent rate, more than any caster could ever perform on their own without overtaxing, even killing themselves. And it was this bypassing of the caster entirely that made resurrection possible.

This was Barrie's plan. And he needed a caster of my skill level to provide the aether so the stress didn't fall upon him when he was already charged with casting quintessence. Eugene Barrie had succeeded in surpassing the villainy of Mary Shelley's Victor Frankenstein, because at least his Creature could think, rationalize, respond—all indicative of a soul being present, however violent or terrifying or ghastly it might have been.

But this undead man?

This *monster* Barrie fashioned?

There was no soul present.

Just a husk.

The memory of pulling the quintessence spell out of Gunner—the living, writhing thing inside that'd nearly caused a fatal overdose in my darling—gave me an idea. If I removed the spell from this undead, the aether would lose its potency and he'd cease moving, surely. And because he was already quite dead and I didn't much care about salvaging his body, I opted for a less labor-intensive spell than what I'd performed on Gunner. I conjured a wind spell and hoisted the burned, blackened man up into the air before slamming him down on the cobblestone road. I cast gravity over the prone body, his bones snapping and the stones chipping and cracking as the weight bore down. A crater formed underneath him before the charred flesh began to slip and *squelch* free. That's when I could see the quintessence being pushed up and out of the hole in the dead man's chest, courtesy of the shot from Gunner's Waterbury. Like an oily finger reaching toward the sky, a spell the size of an eel made itself known, and the sheer volume of pressure being asserted on the body caused the quintessence to pop free.

I lowered my hands, turned to Gunner at my side as he immediately drew out his Waterbury again, and said, "If you will."

Gunner shot the flopping, wriggling mass, and the quintessence exploded in a spray of slimy refuse all over the cobblestone road, what was left of the dead body, across the front of a shuttered storefront, and even on the toe of my shoe. He holstered the pistol in a quick, fluid motion, then looked down at me.

"Well," I stated into the passing silence. "That was new and wonderfully horrifying."

XIII

February 25, 1882

"You're joking," Moore said, his voice a touch tinny in the PDD headset I wore. "Tell me you're joking."

"I've never had much of a sense of humor, sir."

It was morning on the Lower East Side—one of those bright blue sky, sun-shining sort of days that was also ridiculously cold. But despite the brutal bite in the air, the weather didn't keep the daily grind from happening. As the clubs, bars, and dance halls closed after a long night, the shops serving these poor neighborhoods opened for business. The pushcarts came out, stray dogs barked, and gangs of homeless children roamed in search of a breakfast they could pilfer. I stood in the doorway of a theater—its overhead marquee advertising evening shows of "the drollest and lewdest material to ever be performed on stage!"—where I could have a private conversation with Moore and also observe Gunner speaking to an older couple with a pushcart of knishes.

A small gaggle of children had been drawn to Gunner, each taking turns pointing to the grip of his holstered pistol and shrieking and jumping in delight. One girl made a motion like she wanted a cigarette, to which Gunner shook his head, and a cocky boy managed to get a hand into Gunner's coat pocket, but when Gunner met his look, the boy stumbled backward several steps and sheepishly rubbed his hands together. It was so easy to see myself in those babes, to imagine what it must be like to marvel at a character like Gunner in their neighborhood. A larger-than-life man of few words, who was mysterious and powerful and all grown up. That last one was the real reason for the awe in their eyes. Because when you lived in this shithole, when your shoes were several sizes too small, when you had to eat from the trash… no one made the empty promise to wretched children that they'd one day grow up.

"But resurrection? Aether *can't* raise the dead," Moore replied, beyond belief as I reported last night's incident.

"I think the correct statement is, no *caster* is capable of utilizing aether long enough in which to allow it to raise the dead," I replied. "You and I both know that setting broken bones with aether is nearly impossible. It just takes too much out of the caster. Barrie's found a workaround to what is arguably most requested of the magic community. 'Bring my dead father, mother, brother, sister, uncle's cousin twice removed, back to life.'"

Gunner paid the pushcart couple, accepted a handful of knishes, then handed two of the baked goods over to the gang of children. He waited to make sure broken pieces were evenly distributed among all of the hungry mouths, then crossed the busy street and returned to me. I couldn't help but imagine, for just a passing moment, how different my life might have been if a man like Gunner had shown me kindness as a boy. But then again, hadn't he? Because he'd refused a direct order to apprehend a war criminal when he'd learned I was only ten years old. He'd given me my first chance of growing up.

I turned to face Gunner and discreetly set my free hand on his hip before pressing my palm against his lower belly, where waistcoat and trousers met. Gunner winked and tugged the brim of my cap down playfully. I accepted one of the two knishes, the dough and mashed potato filling still warm, and tuned back in to what Moore was saying.

"—is that right?"

"Sorry?"

"You said this victim wasn't quite alive, though," Moore repeated.

"By that, I mean to imply there was no soul inside the man. He was walking, acting like he wanted to fight Gunner, but he never spoke. His body was wrecked, and yet it didn't seem to cause any pain. So he didn't appear... *alive*, if you understand."

"Like he was merely reanimated?"

"Yes, I suppose so," I concluded before taking a bite of the knish.

Moore swore under his breath. "First the mechanical men and now reanimated corpses. This Dr. Barrie is performing act after act against God like he's planning for an exhibit of new technologies at the World's Fair."

I swallowed my bite and asked, "Can I safely assume that while I was... away... word spread about our dearly departed Henry Bligh?"

"News from Bottle Alley is that Driscoll has sworn war against any gangster, associate, sneak thief, or Tammany Hall politician who opts to utilize a mechanical man, or who finances the man responsible for their production—which we now know to be Barrie," Moore replied. "I'd go so far as to claim the Whyos are downright afraid, and that makes them doubly dangerous."

"So really, with the attention Driscoll brought to the

New Year's fiasco, anyone with a connection to the criminal underground, as well as considerable funds, could have made contact and hired Barrie after Bligh's untimely demise. And this… bringing back the dead… this is far more sick than the brutal amputations of his early days, or building mechanical abominations for a power-hungry, spoiled brat. I suspect Barrie couldn't care less who hired him and what their own end goal is. He wants to play with blood and guts and maintain this new, expensive lifestyle he's gotten a taste of."

Gunner nodded absently in agreement as he ate his breakfast and listened to the one-sided conversation.

"It's a compelling argument," Moore murmured. "By the way, a few hotels have gotten back to me—nothing under Eugene Barrie. I'm still waiting to hear from Bartholomew and Black—"

"Sir," I interrupted. "What are the chances that Barrie's contact—*employer*—could be someone on the FBMS council?"

Silence crackled over the line.

Gunner brushed the pad of his thumb along my jaw.

"Sir?"

"I'm here."

"Barrie claimed the resident physician of Blackwell's wished to show me off, but…." My voice unexpectantly caught in my throat as I recalled those dark, dark days. "But I think Barrie asked for me specifically. I think he was told Simon Fitzgerald was on the island. And if he needs a caster capable of holding their own when casting aether…."

"The council lied to me. The council put you on Blackwell's," Moore finished.

"Yes," I whispered.

He expelled a long breath, and it distorted over the line. "Gillian, if this is true—"

"I don't have hard evidence."

"But if it is," he insisted. "This is beyond you, beyond me. It goes to the very top. It shakes the very foundation of everything we've vowed to uphold." Something slammed in the background of the call, and I could imagine a door swinging wildly as much as I could Moore putting his fist through a wall. "The fact that I can't immediately refute your suggestion...."

"Let us both keep an open mind and work toward verifiable facts," I suggested. "Tell me about this Boss fellow. Has he made an appearance yet?"

Begrudgingly, Moore muttered, "Not yet. If it happens, I'll be certain to ping you. What about you? What's your next step?"

I glanced at Gunner as I said, "All those isolated activations of quintessence—we picked up gossip that there were at least half a dozen hits by knockout gangsters last night, but only the one we came across ended in death and reanimation. I believe Barrie's experimenting with different volumes of magic to see how much it takes to bring the dead back to life."

"And he sold magic-laced poison on the Bowery?"

"Sold? Hell. He probably gave it away, just to ensure it got onto the street and he could observe the results. We're going to visit a nearby fence and see if we can locate the thief who robbed our victim. They might be able to tell us where they met Barrie."

Thoughtfully, Moore asked, "Which fence?"

"Old Mother Marm."

"Hamilton, she won't talk to you. She knows you've been a special agent for a decade. She'll give you the same spiel she gives every other honest copper: I have never knowingly bought stolen goods. I have never stolen anything in my life.

I have—"

I laughed quietly. "It won't be me talking to Ma," I assured Moore. "It'll be Gunner."

Kleindeutschland, or Dutchtown, as I had known it growing up as an Irish outsider, was east of the Bowery and the original settlement of German immigrants in the city. The neighborhood was settled along Avenue B, a major artery for business, and so boasted a plethora of artisans not found in such quantities in other wards of Manhattan: steam technicians, tobacconists, bakers, brewers, even the cog and gear artisans responsible for the living murals inside apartment hotels—they were skills and trades many brought with them overseas. In contrast, my father had been an illiterate laborer who worked the El train track construction for a few cents a day, when he wasn't out cold from too much raw whiskey the night before. My mother could at least read somewhat, enough for her own needs anyway, but she'd always tell me: *World ain't gonna pay you to read, Simon.*

Practical skills or not, the Germans were still outsiders like everyone else living this far south, and among the storefronts, social clubs, and beer gardens were blocks and blocks of cramped and overcrowded tenements, packed to the brim with families getting by but never enough to pull themselves to the next rung of the social ladder like those who'd managed to move uptown. All except for one woman—Fredericka Mandelbaum—known on the street as Old Mother Marm or Ma. Every burglar, panel man, pickpocket, and thief was a regular at her dry-goods shop on the corner of Rivington and Clinton Streets, and every special agent and copper alike knew it. But because Ma never actually did any of the stealing herself, our hands had always been tied by the law. We couldn't arrest her without proof, and considering she dealt in anything from mundane bolts of silk, pinched timepieces and jewelry, to the highly illegal aether ammunition, brass fighting gloves, and one highly inventive steam-powered lockpick kit meant for bank safes, you'd think the odds of her being caught red-handed would be in our favor.

And yet, here she was, half a decade after her husband's passing, making more money with each passing day, having high society ladies over to her home for tea, even hosting extravagant meals with guests she knew worked in politics and law enforcement. Mother Marm was fearless, self-assured, and didn't much like me.

The overhead bell rang as Gunner and I entered the shop. I shut the door behind us, flicked the lock, and turned the sign hanging on the glass front from Open to Closed.

There was a gruff clearing of the throat to my back, and I turned around to see a short, heavyset, dark-eyed woman with a thick neck and naturally rosy cheeks. She stood behind the counter, directing that piercing gaze right through me. "Hamilton," Marm said, her German accent understated but still detectable.

"Good morning, Mother."

Marm narrowed her eyes. "I heard around the Bend that you left the FBMS."

"Did you?"

"No one's seen you."

"I'm right here, aren't I?"

Her expression was still tight as Marm flicked her gaze to Gunner, to me, then back to Gunner. The heavy lines in her face softened and then a smile threatened to crack the tough façade. "Detective," she said sardonically.

Wait—what? I looked up as Gunner tilted the brim of his bowler to Marm in acknowledgment. "I thought... hang on.…"

Marm made another gruff sound that this time could have been a laugh. "But it hasn't been 'Detective' for a long time, has it? What're they calling you these days… Gunner the Deadly?"

"It's a pleasure to see you again, Marm," Gunner replied.

I grabbed Gunner's arm and whispered loudly, "You've known her since you were a Pinkerton?"

"Until the New Year, I hadn't been to an East Coast city since '75," Gunner reminded me. "When else would I have met her?"

I shrugged awkwardly. "I don't… I mean, I thought you knew her via criminal word-of-mouth?"

Gunner's lips twitched in amusement.

"*Criminal*," Marm repeated with disgust.

"Yes, Mother," I said, turning my attention back to her. "When you break the law, you're known as a criminal."

"I'm just a widow selling ready-made handkerchiefs and remnants, Hamilton."

Gunner said to that, "I was sorry to hear of Wolfe's passing, Marm."

She nodded in acceptance of Gunner's condolences, but said, "I was relieved to hear you'd left the Agency. I was sick of having you come around here, trying to arrest me."

"That's part of the game, Marm."

I was still trying to digest the fact that Gunner had once been actively working in the city as a Pinkerton, had in fact tried to arrest Marm on more than one occasion, and while I had already been employed by the FBMS too. How close had we come to crossing paths on these very streets? Would we have stopped? Or merely looked at each other, recognized those tendencies that Gunner referred to as *survival instincts*, and kept walking? Would we have ever worked together as fellow law enforcement agents? Would we have still found our way into a courtship? I supposed it really didn't matter, but I had a certain weakness for imagining how different—*better*—my past could have been, if only I'd known to take a left instead of a right at certain intersections.

Marm had let out a vicious snort of a laugh and was asking Gunner as I returned to the conversation, "—part of the game as well?" She waved a meaty finger between us.

"We have an arrangement," Gunner replied. "The law stays out of my affairs, I stay out of their pocket, and we can deliver on some mutual objectives."

"It's more than business, Gunner the Deadly," Marm chastised quietly. She was giving him a significant look. "A mother knows."

Gunner didn't remark on the suggestion, and I sort of came to realize he was doing so for my sake. Because I was the one still struggling to accept who I was and where I fit into the world. He knew I was trying, and Gunner was content with that, but I remembered the way he had smiled the night I'd kissed him at the FBMS field office. He'd stopped caring about secrecy once we'd become involved—didn't care if the whole world knew where his heart lay—and my God, did I want that same freedom.

That same courage.

That same happiness.

Of course, there was a danger in the world knowing of our love, of this neither of us would deny. But the world had already been so dangerous and so cruel to me at every opportunity thus far. It wouldn't stop of its own accord. I had to *commit* to breaking that cycle and to standing up for myself.

No more feeble attempts when only the situation was

most conducive.

No more inspiring self-talks I couldn't commit to outside of my own mind.

No more allowing others to abuse my magic or my tendencies because that was the status quo.

No more.

I slid my hands into my trouser pockets in an attempt to give off an air of bravado I didn't entirely feel, cleared my throat, and said matter-of-factly, "It is more than business, yes."

Marm's black eyes were on me again. "You turned in your badge for an outlaw?"

I swallowed audibly, could feel my face burning, but only said, "It's a bit more complicated than that."

"I always thought you were a touch like those boys on the Bowery, Hamilton," Marm answered. Then, to my utter surprise, she cracked another rough smile. "But I never thought you were so romantic."

I let out a quiet breath and could feel my insides shaking with the release.

With the suddenness of a steam lamp blinking to life, my truth had earned a respect from Marm that I'd never seen her dole out to anyone, let alone a once-special agent. "Let's speak in the back," she said before going through a dimly lit doorway.

Gunner touched my shoulder before I could take a step forward. "Are you okay?"

I was smiling before I could catch myself, and said with relief, "Yes." To his uncertainty, I added, "Finding which shade of gray suits me best, is all."

Gunner's expression softened.

"Let's not keep Ma waiting."

I walked across the protesting floorboards, around the counter, and down a tight passage that opened onto a massive storage room. Every square inch of shelf space was crammed with basic, cheap, and forgettable wares Marm stocked the front of the store with so as to keep up appearances of being a respectable business, but behind and in between was the good stuff, the stolen stuff, the illegal stuff. There were men's wallets and coin purses, baskets of loose jewelry—everything from plain gold and silver bands to stylish, some bordering on garish, brooches, necklaces, and earrings of precious gemstones—high-quality muffs, candelabras, snuff boxes, porcelain this and that, to an entire goddamn wall of weaponry hidden behind bolts of silk.

"Christ Almighty," I muttered.

"Impressive," Gunner countered.

Marm moved around another strategically placed counter, reached her short, chubby arms overhead, and finagled free a mean-looking silver machine that was Gatling gun in setup and overinflated rifle in size. She said to Gunner, "I hear you favor that little Waterbury, but if you're looking for an upgrade...." Marm trailed off as she pulled the trigger. The cylinders began to slowly revolve, picked up speed, steam screamed from the backend, and fire shot out of the barrels. "Pull the trigger twice," she shouted over the noise, "and it releases a fireball! No magic—only steam and phosphorus." Marm took her finger from the trigger and the barrels slowed and the fire ceased. "Well?"

Gunner nodded his head in my direction, saying, "I rely on him for such necessities, Marm."

Marm glanced at me.

I raised one hand and fire erupted from my palm.

She harrumphed, grunted, and returned the weapon to its shelf. "Then what're you looking for, Gunner the Deadly? They say you've no interest in riches."

"Information."

"Information isn't free," she warned.

Gunner reached inside his inner suit coat pocket and removed a coin purse. He took out several double eagles, set them in a careful stack on the countertop, then stated, "Knockout gangs."

"I don't supply poisons," Marm said firmly.

Gunner had the tip of his index finger on the coins. "No. But they come here with their loot."

Marm looked contemplative, shot me one last look like she was priming herself to share secrets before the eyes and ears of the law—which was how she and most others of the criminal class would always view me, badge or not—and then she gave a curt nod.

Gunner picked up the first coin and slid it over. "Have any shown up with last night's spoils?"

"Three."

Gunner slid another coin toward Marm. "Any belongings from a man?"

"Two."

Another coin. "Either of those two thieves magic-users?"

"One."

Gunner pushed the last coin over while looking at me.

I understood his process of elimination and shook my head, because no, the thief from last night had no magic in their bones—they'd merely utilized poison infused with it.

Gunner said to Marm, "We need to speak with the nonuser. Where can they be found?"

Marm looked at the pile of coins now on her side of the counter, then gave Gunner a pointed look. "I work in round numbers, Gunner the Deadly."

Rolling my eyes, I reached into my own pocket and

found the coins Moore had thrust into my hand alongside the borrowed PDD—with the added caution that it was unsafe to wander the city without means. I joined Gunner's side and set the heavy gold coin down with a satisfying *thump*. The inclusion of my own money in this barter… it was difficult to explain, but criminals like Marm had a code of conduct, just as Gunner had, and underlings often followed lead. Because of my show of goodwill, proof that I'd abide by her rules and respect her business, Marm would, in return, certainly tell any copper who might happen by looking for a man whose description was startlingly similar to my own that she'd seen no one of such account. Because without knowing why I was no longer with the FBMS, she would realize in an instant that a uniformed beat cop inquiring after me was suspicious. And Gunner? Forget it. Gunner the *Who*?

Marm accepted the fifth coin, slid them into her palm, and said, "Shy Phoebe. She lives over in Gotham Court."

I felt my heart skip a beat. A few beats, actually. "Gotham Court?" I repeated.

Marm nodded curtly.

"No."

"*No*?" she drawled.

"We're not going to Gotham Court. Where does Shy Phoebe ply her trade?"

"The Sausage and Clam," Marm answered. "On Mulberry."

A sudden and sharp, ear-piercing scream echoed from the street, interrupting our conversation. I didn't think as I instinctively ran out of the back room, down the hall, through the empty storefront, and tore out the door. The intersection was congested with morning traffic and pedestrians, but the ambiance of this usually low-key chaos was heightened by a miasma of terror. People were looking toward and rushing away from the north end of Clinton Street, so I shoved my way through the crowds and parting pushcarts, reached the cobblestone street, and realized what was putting the fear of God into the neighborhood.

Three undead men stood several yards away, one still dressed for an evening out, the other two in their nightshirts. All three were stained with their own vomit and blood—signs of a delayed but equally as painful an overdose as the gentleman from last night. The proof that Barrie was testing different potencies of magic in order to find that perfect combination of quintessence and aether could be seen in the way these undead held themselves.

One in a nightshirt had that same distant, empty expression as the undead man from last night. His stance was loose-limbed, shoulders awkwardly slumped to one side, and jaw slack. The other was a bit more… I don't know how to say it, other than *cognizant*? Not quite alert, but his gaze stared through me rather than somewhere over my shoulder, and his steps were quicker, sturdier. The man in the suit, however… if it wasn't for the bodily refuse his clothes were stained with and the fact that he hadn't spoken a word, I might have considered him to be as living and breathing as myself.

"Hamilton." Gunner's back pressed against mine. He cocked the Waterbury, and the aether ammunition activated. "Two more to the south."

"Suffice it to say we found the rest of last night's poisoning victims."

"I think it's more accurate to say, they found *us*."

I made a sound of annoyance in the back of my throat, raised one hand overhead, called down a massive bolt of lightning from the clear and bright sky, and when the undead lunged forward, I released the spell in one direction and Gunner fired his pistol in the other. There were more panicked screams from the crowd, warnings to cross themselves in the presence of magic, because biases were still alive and well in communities of limited education, but mostly the street was filled with the *crack* of electricity and the *bang*s of gunfire.

The lightning dropped my three undead to the ground, sparks dancing between limbs and bouncing along the ground as the bodies convulsed with shocks. I yanked my goggles on before casting aether, pulling the blinding-white light between my hands until it resembled the arc of a rainbow, and then I twisted my arms and released the spell. It spun forward like a blade, slicing two of the undead in half as they struggled to regain their footing. The body parts flopped to the ground, still trying to drag themselves toward me as the quintessence magic slopped out from their innards and made a mad squirming dash in my direction, almost like it was attracted to my presence… my magic.

"If you'll be so kind," I called to Gunner over my shoulder, "as to switch places with me?"

We were like a ballet, Gunner and I, so in tune with each other that our movements became one. It must have come off to spectators as carefully rehearsed and choreographed. I cast aether again as I took a step back, pivoted on my heel, and spun to release the spell on the two undead Gunner had been shooting at. In that same fluid motion, Gunner whirled around, aimed, and fired twice at the scurrying quintessence magic I'd released. Sounds that I can only describe as the burst of grease confirmed Gunner had hit his mark both times.

When the next two bodies collapsed to the ground in several more revolting pieces, quintessence crawling free like a parasite in search of a new host, Gunner took his cue by sound alone and spun again to shoot the magic. That's when I realized the mistake of taking my eyes off the man still dressed for a night on the town. I turned to find him directly in front of me, staring, blinking, dried vomit crusting the corners of his mouth.

"*Fiiitz—geraaald,*" he groaned.

I didn't know the man, was certain he hadn't known me when he'd been… well, *alive.* But the amount of quintessence and aether in his system was drastically different from the others, and I was nearly convinced that upon this monstrous reanimation he'd been forced to endure, a portion of his soul had been recalled in the process. The fact that Barrie's latest abomination somehow recognized me, either by face or by magic, was no longer of any surprise.

And while speaking seemed to still be a struggle, movement wasn't. He grabbed for me, got a fistful of the collar of my jacket, and yanked so hard that it threw me off balance and I tripped and spun without form or grace. He began walking away, dragging me with him, like I was very much wanted alive and unharmed. I tried to slip free from the sleeves, but he had a grip of my shirt collar too, making an easy escape more problematic.

"Gunner!"

But Gunner didn't need prompting. He was racing toward me with a policeman's nightstick in one hand. He swung down hard on the undead's arm, breaking the bone with an audible *crack.* The undead stopped, turned, and with physical strength that surpassed that of any living man, kicked Gunner in the gut, sending him flying. Gunner crashed hard onto his backside, but still drew his Waterbury, aimed, and blew the man's head off.

I will admit, the fact that this headless corpse was still walking, still dragging me along behind him, alarmed me considerably. I craned my neck to look back at the ragged bone and flesh and what remained of a lower jaw and saw the tip of a wriggling black eel poking out from the meat. I raised one hand, focused a very small and dense gravity spell directly above the undead while attempting to keep myself out of the magic's range, and drew in raw energy from the atmosphere.

Under the intense pressure, the undead's shoulders drooped and his knees buckled. He was still walking—trying to, anyway—as the gravity spell began to flay the open wound of his neck in two, forcing the massive quintessence spell up and out of the body.

It dropped to the cobblestone road and the man immediately crumpled into a dead heap. I yanked myself free, got to my knees, and scrambled to my feet as the quintessence, longer and bigger around than my arm, perspiring some sort of syrupy, viscous fluid, seemed to be looking me up and down with an eyeless, bulbus shape I took to be its face. Then it flip-flopped like a fish out of water, hurling itself toward me like it was desperate for a new host before it withered and died. But a final round of aether bullets blew the oily creature apart, and then it was just me, Gunner, and a street full of dismembered corpses.

A shiver strong enough to chatter my teeth worked its way up my spine as the quintessence spells dissipated and the atmosphere pulsated in pain. And as the adrenaline waned, my limbs a touch weak and shaky in its aftermath, I took in the grotesquery around me: the severed torsos and deluge of guts that'd been my doing, my brutality, my butchery—

Gunner stood in front of me, his hands on my shoulders. "Look at me," he ordered, his voice a careful balance of concern and demand. "Don't—no, only at me."

He knew. He knew immediately that while my mind saw the undead bodies who'd attacked us on Clinton Street, my heart saw piles of severed limbs in a hospital tent, a ravaged battlefield, my bloody hands, every ghost I was haunted by.

"Are you here with me?" Gunner asked.

I drew in a breath like I'd been hit in the solar plexus by a pair of fighting gloves, and said, while staring at his face, "I-I dream about how blue your eyes are."

"I dream about all of you," Gunner replied, profoundness

in his blunt simplicity.

His response was humbling, overwhelming, and I had to close my eyes a moment and recollect. "Where did you find a nightstick?"

Gunner removed his hands from my shoulders. "I relieved a copper of his responsibilities."

When I looked up, I followed the quick dart of his eyes toward a man in a blue uniform, sheepishly watching from among the frightened crowd.

"He called me Fitzgerald," I said after a moment, pointing in the direction of the massacre without looking. "The—the one who—" I figured Gunner understood when he nodded curtly, and so I declined to finish the thought aloud.

"They attacked me," Gunner replied. "But not you. Barrie needs you safe and sound if you're to be of use."

"I'd sooner find the courage to kill myself than be used again."

"Neither of those will happen, my dear." Gunner caught sight of something over my shoulder and walked toward what was left of the mob that hadn't run.

I turned to watch him accept a wrapped parcel from Marm—aether bullets were my first guess—tuck it into his coat pocket, and then Gunner inclined his head for me to follow him out of *Kleindeutschland.*

XIV

February 25, 1882

We reached the Sausage & Clam at noon.

"Why do I have to be the lure?" I asked Gunner.

He leaned casually against a lamppost, several feet from the bar, and popped a stick of Black Jack in his mouth as he considered me. "Because you haven't yet realized the suggestion behind the name."

I furrowed my brow, glanced at the sign above the front door, and then it hit me. I felt a rush of blood go straight to my face. "*Oh*. That's extremely lewd." I looked toward Gunner again, and from the glint in his eyes, I knew I was being laughed at. "But I—flirting with women is not—you're much better at talking with them than I am."

"That's exactly why I won't be targeted. Shy Phoebe is going to be looking for, as her name implies, a shy man. And you have a sort of helpless yet endearing charm about you, as far as when the opposite gender is involved."

"I'm not sure I appreciate that description," I muttered.

"I'll follow in a few minutes," Gunner promised.

I huffed and stamped a bit of dirty snow from the toes of

my shoes before squaring my shoulders and starting for the door.

"And Hamilton?"

I turned.

"Don't drink the beer."

I snorted. "No kidding." I grabbed the handle and stepped inside.

The Sausage & Clam was dimly lit and the steam lighting flickered now and then, suggesting they were illegally syphoning power from the city's grid. The floor was covered in sawdust, and the tables and bar had a decidedly greasy film to them that was visible when the yellow glow caught the wood just right. The establishment smelled like how most of these Lower East Side businesses did: of sweat, raw whiskey and hops, and a hint of copper I could practically taste— recent blood. The clientele was still light, given the time of day, but there were a few older and ragged men scattered among the tables, two women sitting at the far end of the bar, and one man tending.

I removed my cap and cautiously approached the bar. I didn't even need to act the part of timid, because that's exactly how I felt when I caught the interested stares of the two women. It's not that I was uncomfortable around women, but that I'd always struggled with how to interact with them. I supposed that innate understanding of how to speak and flirt and conduct myself was the equivalent of Gunner's survival instincts when it came to picking out the man in the crowd who'd be willing to entertain your interests. But because I was hardly experienced or shrewd even when it came to men, there was a sort of... loss in translation when I attempted to apply that same interaction to the opposite gender. All I could think about whenever I dealt with a woman was: What can I say that won't make her uncomfortable or suggest I was... one of *those* men? And that's why, for years, I'd bought and read editions of *The Delineator*—a woman's magazine—simply as a way of grounding myself in subjects that were of interest to them, so that if they spoke about it, I could react accordingly.

One of the women was already on her feet and rounding the bar. She was my height, the same brown hair, sans my gray, with big brown eyes like a doe. She smiled coyly at me and asked, "Thomas?"

"Pardon?"

"Oh. Sorry, sir. I thought you might've been the gentleman I've been waiting on." She had a rough, lower-class inflection to her words that she was trying to hide. "I suppose I've been stood up."

"You were meeting a man for a date… *here*?"

She looked chagrined. "Men have no class or character these days."

"I suppose not."

She blushed prettily and put a hand to her mouth as she laughed. "My goodness! Present company excluded, of course."

"That's nice of you to say." She was lingering, and it took another half a second for me to realize that this was Phoebe, she was probably used to already being offered a free drink at this point in the conversation, and I was missing all the expected cues. "Ah, would you—?" I was still standing, but pointed to the stool beside me.

"That's mighty kind of you." She tugged up her skirts and climbed into the seat. "My name's Phoebe."

"Malcom," I answered, taking the next stool. "Would you allow me to buy you a drink?"

"Certainly."

I made a gesture to the bartender, and Phoebe gasped. I looked at her. "Is something the matter?"

She quickly reached for my hand and clasped it in both of hers, and I completely froze at the touch. "What on Earth happened?" Phoebe asked, stroking my scarred palm. "You *poor dear*!"

I tried to tug my hand free without coming across like a panicked animal, but the stammer in my voice did not go unnoticed. "I-I—it's nothing. An old accident."

Phoebe made a sympathetic sound as she pursed her lips.

The bartender set a large brown bottle and two relatively clean glasses in front of us before leaving Phoebe to her task of drugging and robbing me. I picked up the bottle and poured us each a drink. When a hand slid between my legs, I startled so violently that I spilled what was left from the bottle across the bar top.

Phoebe giggled and whispered, "Aren't you delightful, Malcom."

My face felt as if it were about to spontaneously combust. I tugged her hand free, but not before she managed to get a decent fondle. "M-Miss Phoebe—"

"Do you think I'm pretty?" she asked, leaning too close.

"I—yes, but—" *Where the hell are you, Gunner?*

"But what?" Phoebe purred.

"But I'm not interested in *that*," I blurted before I could stop myself.

Phoebe narrowed her eyes, studied me a moment, then said, "You're one of those fairies, ain't you?" I bristled, but didn't have the chance to reply before she smiled, leaned in again, and whispered in my ear, "You'll forget the taste of cock when I'm done with you."

The door opened at my back and Phoebe's attention shifted minutely to the new customer. I glanced in the opposite direction in time to catch Phoebe pouring granular contents into my beer from a glass vial she'd likely kept tucked up one sleeve. I grabbed her wrist and said, "Tell me who—"

Phoebe reactively seized the empty beer bottle from the counter with her free hand and whacked me upside the head.

"Jesus fuck!" I let go of her in reflex and fell off the stool. I crashed to the floor as Phoebe's feet hit the sawdust and she turned to run for what I assumed was a back exit. I raised a hand, cast a wind spell, and knocked her sideways into one of the tables. Her skirts flipped up like a cheap cancan performance, and Phoebe went head over heels across the nearest tabletop. I heard the bartender cock a rifle; then aether ammunition activated at my back in response.

"Drop it," the bartender ordered.

"Try me," Gunner replied calmly.

I scrambled to my feet to see both men holding each other at gunpoint. I rolled my eyes and snapped my fingers, setting the sawdust under the bartender's feet on fire. He was yelping and swearing up a storm as I maneuvered around a few tables and approached Phoebe, still sprawled on the floor. I crouched beside her, patted the sleeves of her dress, and pulled free a second poison vial. "Who'd you purchase this from?"

She groaned.

I tugged her into a sitting position, gripped the back of her neck, and put the vial in front of her face. "Who. Is this. From?" I reiterated.

"I don't like the way you're touchin' me," she spat, no longer trying to mask that coarse and brutal inflection I, too, had grown up with in Gotham Court.

"Miss Phoebe, you grabbed my prick, then hit me over the head with a bottle. You're quite lucky I'm a gentleman about the whole matter." I glanced over my shoulder. Whisps of smoke curled around where the bartender stood. He had both hands raised. Gunner kept his Waterbury aimed in one hand, the other holding the confiscated rifle. I noted that the second woman who'd been sitting with Phoebe upon my entering was gone, but the haggard older men were still nursing beers and watching us like we were some much-needed entertainment in their lives.

"You got thirty seconds before Mary comes back through that door with a score of Whyos," the bartender told Gunner. "I'll be cleaning your blood off my floor for a week."

I could only imagine the wicked, dangerous smile Gunner gave him—like, finally, there was some real fun to be had—because I heard the man choke and swallow from where I stood.

"Hear that?" Phoebe said, glaring sideways at me. "Them Whyos are—"

"I certainly hope they try," I replied. "Because I've had a hell of a week, and I wouldn't mind taking some frustration out on a handful of two-bit, Five Points thieves. This is your last chance to tell me who sold you this poison." I gripped her neck hard enough for her to wince and hiss.

"It were free! I didn't pay a damn penny."

"And what sort of enterprising man gave you his wares for free?"

She cocked her head just enough to eye me through a bit of hair that'd fallen free from its do. Phoebe's stare was dubious as she said, "You ain't slummin'. I can tell—you too comfortable in these parts. I bet you're a canary bird. How much can I make by turnin' you in to the pigs? A century? Maybe more?"

A spark of fury lit my belly afire, and I leaned close, hissing through clenched teeth in a dialect and accent I had worked so hard to hide my entire adult life, "You nothin' but a diver mab with Venus's curse. Tell me now, and I won't string you upside down to a fuckin' lamppost where the whole Bend gets a sight of your crotchless drawers."

Phoebe's eyes glinted with unbridled rage and her face flushed at the insult, but she snapped out, "I ain't *got* a name."

"What's he look like?" I asked, giving her a shake.

"Hamilton?" Gunner called.

"A moment," I replied, losing the street-rat cadence for those two words.

Phoebe sniggered. "Aye, that's what I thought."

"I'm done bein' gentlemanly." I stood and hoisted Phoebe up with me. I began dragging her toward the door.

"Wait, wait!" She flailed wildly. "Fairley! Said his name was Fairley Holloway."

"Fairley?" I repeated, trying the name out, but it felt foreign to my tongue. I glanced toward Gunner, and sure enough, he'd heard the exclamation. To Phoebe, I kicked the Gotham Court accent a second time and asked, "Auburn hair? Soft-spoken?"

She twisted unsuccessfully in my hold and, chest heaving, said, "No. He were tall—rich and proper-looking. Gray hair and a busted eye."

I felt the aether in the Waterbury ammunition diminish, and when I looked to Gunner again, he'd lowered his pistol and was staring at Phoebe.

"Busted eye, like, how?" he asked.

Phoebe glanced in Gunner's direction. "It were milky." She tapped under her own left eye in emphasis.

Gunner met my gaze, holstered his Waterbury, and said, "Let her go." He made quick work of disassembling the bartender's rifle, tossed one piece at the man, the other in the opposite direction, and headed out the front door.

I gave Phoebe a shove, and she fell into the seat of the nearest chair. I had reached the door by the time she called after me, "Come back home sometime, ya coward!"

I ignored her and slipped outside. Gunner was already half a block uptown on Mulberry and I had to run to catch up. When I reached his side, he immediately took me by the sleeve of my coat and hustled me down an alley packed with broken, warped, and rotten wooden crates and barrels. Patches of frozen dirty snow pockmarked the cobblestones, and overhead, two old women called to each other from the respective windows of their listing tenement homes. Gunner backed me into the outer wall of the closest building, a few feet from the rickety wooden steps leading to a back door.

"You recognized that name, didn't you?" I asked, pushing back the brim of my cap. "Who's—"

"Listen to me for a moment," Gunner interrupted, quiet but resolute.

I hesitated, nodded, and waited, but Gunner remained silent. *Picking his words*, I thought.

"*Why-o!*" came a sharp cry from somewhere on the block. The pseudobird call was the warning of nearby Whyo gangsters—no doubt those answering Miss Mary's call for necessary backup at the Sausage & Clam.

Gunner *tsk*ed under his breath. He shifted his stance so that he towered over me, one arm resting on the wall, his back to Mulberry Street. He removed his bowler, leaned down, and kissed me as a second, piercing *Why-o* cry echoed from somewhere around the Bend.

Distantly, I acknowledged the rising voices drawing close—young men whooping and hollering and cussing—the cracking of thin ice along bluestone sidewalks and slipping of worn soles across cobblestone, and the definite sound of bullets being chambered. But more immediate than my sense of sound was that of touch, of smell, of *taste*. A single kiss from Gunner was an all-consuming experience: my hands on his slender hips, drawing his warm body closer, the woodsy, neroli scent of Sandringham mingling with fresh sweat and wool, and the bitter, herbal aftertaste of Black Jack on his tongue as it slipped into my mouth.

The clamoring gangsters seemed to have passed the alley without a second look at the two faceless people ignoring the rules of kissing etiquette while in public. After all, it wasn't exactly the neighborhood that such standards were upheld or consequences were delivered for breaking them. That's why men and women of our tendencies made their home along the nearby Bowery.

"That's certainly one way to hide in plain sight," I whispered as Gunner let up.

The tip of Gunner's tongue poked out as he licked his lower lip. "Fairley Holloway was my assumed name while working as a Pinkerton. And the man who supplied last night's poisons—who has a milky eye—his name is Magnus Prince. He was older. We used to call him Boss."

"Who's *we*?" I asked.

Gunner shifted, putting his bowler on.

"*Constantine.*" But the PDD around my neck began to ping and I swore. "Magnus gave your old name to the knockout gangs because… it was a message?"

"Obviously."

The PDD continued giving off a set of high and low tones, indicating Moore was on the other end of the call.

"Obvious how?" I countered.

Gunner turned sideways, studying the mouth of the alley. "Barrie recognized me the night aboard the airship. This is a warning for me to back off."

"And Barrie is working with this—*Christ*—Magnus, and told him you were… hang on." I yanked the headset over my ears, flicked my wrist to reveal the transducer kept up my sleeve, and answered, "Sir, I'll have to—"

"We've got a goddamn situation here, Hamilton," Moore shouted. There was commotion of some sort that distorted over the line, and then he said, "Bert Parker was just escorted out of the office, and now we've got three agents acting exactly like those undead you described!"

My heart plummeted to my stomach like I'd jumped off a ledge. "Who escorted Mr. Parker?" I asked over the noise.

"*Sonofabitch*!" Moore shouted. "Plunket, barricade the door."

"*Sir*," I tried again.

"I could really use your trick for stopping these horrors," Moore answered curtly.

"Gravity."

"*Gravity*," he echoed sardonically. "That's an illegal spell I don't have the skillset to cast."

"I'm on my way," I answered.

"Hamilton," Moore bit out, which was preceded by the sound of something exploding. "It was that new councilman the FBMS hired last year."

"I'm not familiar with all the councilmen," I admitted, grabbing Gunner's arm with my free hand while running out of the alley.

"His name's Magnus Prince," Moore answered.

XV

February 25, 1882

Black smoke carried with it the scent of burning infrastructure and roasting flesh.

Gunner slammed down on the brakes of the automobile he'd appropriated from some poor bastard who'd not thought to lock its doors. Traffic on Twenty-Third Street had come to a standstill. Just ahead loomed the FBMS field office, where the smoke billowed from a fourth-floor window. A sizeable crowd of pedestrians had gathered along the perimeter in the way which any disaster draws spectators, and water tankers on the scene were currently deploying leather hoses.

I shoved open the passenger door, climbed out, and ran through the disarray of haphazardly parked automobiles and motorwagons without waiting for Gunner. I barked orders for civilians to move from my path and outright shoved them aside when I was ignored. Glass shattered from overhead as I reached a clearing that'd been provided to the fire department, and I'd hardly time to look up and stumble backward several steps as a body engulfed in flames was flung from the fourth floor and slammed down into the road.

A visceral panic nearly undid me then and there when

I immediately picked up Moore's magic signature from the broken body before me. But one deep breath, then another, and I was in touch with all my faculties again. The fire was magic. The magic was Moore's. He was still alive. Which meant this once-fellow special agent before me had, *somehow*, become a victim of the poison and reanimation and now required… permanent elimination.

Gunner entered the enclosed space next, briefly touching my shoulder as a means of identifying himself, and then I heard him draw the Waterbury and demand the firefighters to back up because he knew what was going to happen with this human burning before us.

Whispers and speculation charged the air like a sudden and incoming thunderstorm.

"Who's that?"

"What a handsome rogue."

"A new gangster?"

"That's Gunner the Deadly!"

Over the excitable voices, crackling fire, and overwhelming chaos, I heard my name—distant and carried on the wind. I raised my head and pinpointed Moore leaning out the broken window, waving his hand for my attention. He pointed, shouted a second time, but this time said, "*Watson.*"

Onlookers gasped and cried out, and I spun toward the body in time to see Special Agent Watson, Plunket's new caster partner, pick himself up from the ground. He was still on fire as he faced me, staring through one good eye.

"*Oh God,*" I whispered.

Watson raised both hands and held them forward, conjured a wind spell, and shot it toward me and Gunner and the firemen at my back. It carried the flames of Moore's magic right at us, and among the shouts to ready hoses—which would do little against magic fire—and the panicked cries of the crowd realizing the situation had escalated into one of life or death, I held my hands out, palms forward, and cast a wall of shimmering, crystal blue water. The wind and fire crashed into my magic, and while Watson wouldn't have held a candle to me in a regular fight, he was fueled by endless aether that kept him from overexertion, and Moore's high, level-four energy had been mingled into his own spell. I remained standing, although the blast forced me back nearly a foot, my shoes skidding along the slick road.

I checked over my shoulder and saw Gunner and firemen alike had braced for the attack, arms raised and heads turned away. Luckily, my magic had shielded them all. I turned back to Watson, brought my hands together, and the water mimicked my motion by forming a tunnel.

Despite the flames, I saw Watson grin. He reached a hand toward me and called, "*Fitzgerald*!" It was clear that Barrie had perfected his poison and magic ratio, the end result being this undead creature that seemed to be controlled from afar, felt no pain, could only be stopped by the removal of quintessence from the system, and possessed enough intelligence to move and speak almost as if they weren't actually *dead*.

Watson cast another wind spell.

I released the volley of water.

The magics hit in an explosion of brilliant white and blue light. Wind bent the bare skeleton limbs of trees along the street and knocked civilians off their feet, but the water spell barreled directly into Watson, dousing the flames and throwing him far enough that he slammed into the front doors of the field office. Despite his smashed body, Watson climbed back to his feet. He looked at me, at Gunner, as the latter moved to stand beside me, then raised his hand overhead. The wind began to spin viciously around Watson as he pulled the freezing February day around him like a blanket, which mixed with moisture in the air. He was promptly surrounded by dozens of jagged, deadly, and nearly translucent ice spikes. Watson flashed that malicious grin again, one he had never worn while alive, and released the spell directly at Gunner.

Gunner shot a triple round directly into Watson's chest, but the magic kept its target.

I threw an arm in front of Gunner, fire flowing from my shoulder to fingertips, eviscerating Watson's magic. I looked at Gunner in time to see he hadn't flinched as a shard of ice with a point, molded by the cold and wind, dangerous enough to plow right through a human body, had been melted just inches from his face.

Gunner caught my gaze and nodded once. *I'm okay and thank you* was what it conveyed.

Watson's behavior was like the other undeads: remove Gunner from the equation at all costs, while I remained unharmed. And if there was one fear more intense, more feral, than that of being abused for my magic again, it was someone coming for Gunner's life.

I yanked my goggles on and ran toward Watson. I cast aether, drew the magic out in a long arc between my hands, then leaped into the air. I rode a current of wind up before crashing down on Watson, driving the aether through the hole in his chest and out his back. I didn't have the heart to use gravity on this man I'd once known, didn't want to see his body ruined any more than it already was. This option was harder on me physically, but kinder to my soul. And I needed that.

"I'm sorry, Watson," I said, staring into his dead eyes as we both crashed to the ground.

He was still trying to grab at me, so I jerked the aether hard, digging it into the front steps and pinning him like a bug on a slide in someone's curiosity cabinet. I cast more aether on myself, reverse engineering the spell until I could pump him so full of magic that the quintessence began to ooze out from around the spike of aether stuck in his chest. I didn't let up until the gelatinous black magic, spilling out like blood, coalesced into another big, fat, eel-sized creature. I released the aether, stood, and staggered back as the quintessence lunged after me.

And then it exploded as a round of aether ammunition hit it.

Gunner holstered his Waterbury and raced to join me. He grabbed my biceps before my knees gave out. "Whoa, hang on. I've got you." He eased into a crouch to help me sit on the top step beside Watson's body. Gunner wiped my face with his hands and rubbed the black, oily residue on his trouser leg.

I put my head between my knees and closed my eyes as my equilibrium went off-kilter and the city felt like it was riding the waves of a storm at sea. I fought the unconsciousness that was slinking ever-closer, because we weren't done here. There was no time for a long recovery period. Moore was still inside. He said there'd been *three* afflicted agents. I had to save him, tell him about Magnus Prince—that he possessed the power and authority to have imprisoned me on Blackwell's, that he'd have had access to our reports on Henry Bligh and could have made contact with Barrie with relative ease, that Barrie was in cahoots with a top official of a federal agency and now no one in our community was safe.

Gunner's arms came around me, but I weakly shoved him off. "I'm going to pick you up," he said calmly.

"No." I shook my head, but the motion made me dry heave a few times.

I turned my hand palm up and focused on the magic plane. I felt the raw current encircle my wrist, twine around my fingers, soothe the constant ache in my palms. I gently closed my hand around the tendrils and opened myself to absorbing the energy without giving the stream anything of my own in return—a grave skill to have, one I hadn't used since the Great Rebellion. It didn't leave a wound in the atmosphere, but instead reduced the amount of magic available to everyone else. I had promised myself to never use it again because it set an unbelievably perilous precedent, but seeing as I was literally on a mission to save magic as we knew it....

The effect was immediate, like being blinded by headlights of an oncoming automobile before the chrome grille barreled into your body. I was thrown onto my back, my eyes shot open, and I gasped for air. I raised a shaky hand and yanked the goggles down, losing the purple-tinted world in favor of crisp, winter sunshine.

"Gillian?" Gunner had one knee on the step as he leaned over me. "What's happened? Are you okay?"

"I'm okay," I agreed in between gasps for air.

Gunner glanced over his shoulder at the onlooking crowd, at the firefighters blasting the upper windows with water, and then he took my hands and helped me to my feet. "Not that I'm unhappy to see your beautiful green eyes, my dear, but why aren't you unconscious?"

"Let's circle back on that later." I turned, threw the front doors open with a gust of wind, and ran inside with Gunner at my back.

In the event that an FBMS field office's defenses were breached, protocol was that scholar agents secured all confidential documents, studies, and records, while architect agents acted as their defense. Meanwhile, casters went on the offense, while their bruiser counterparts fortified all ingresses and egresses so the criminal stood no chance of making a successful escape. The fact that I expected to blow the front doors open and climb over a barricade but did not was concerning. No doubt the fact that agents had been assaulted by their own had confused protocol. After all, our manuals never did include a chapter on how to handle undead special agents striking from within.

I raced up the main set of stairs, giving each landing only the most cursory of once-overs. Furniture was overturned, sheafs of paper marbled the hallways, and here and there a body lay unmoving. I kept going until I neared the fourth floor. I could make out the scholar bullpen on my right as I slowed on the steps. The door was shuttered and a small army of architects and a smattering of casters were guarding the agents and sensitive data on the other side of the door. Ahead was the open doorway to the half-bullpen and jail cell that Bert Parker had spent the night in. In the threshold was a body hacked to pieces with what had likely been an axe. Blood and innards painted the walls and floor, and another one of those quintessence eels—withered and quickly dissipating without its host—flopped weakly in the pooled vile. Gunner, still a step behind me, shifted to his left, aimed, and shot it to smithereens.

One of the nearby casters reacted to the gunfire, and a bolt of lightning hit the balusters and handrail right beside me. Wood splintered, fractured, and exploded as we both dropped to the steps and out of sight.

"Hold your fire!" I exclaimed before cautiously rising. I shook my head and wiped my shoulders of debris while reaching the landing.

"Agent, er—I mean—Hamilton?" the woman caster, Special Agent Cooke, cautiously called. "What're you…?" I suspected that Cooke had been one of the agents Moore had trusted to oversee the piers and look the other way if I was spotted trying to leave the city. I based this fact on nothing more than she appeared to struggle with what to say—not only to me, but in the presence of agents who hadn't heard the council's absurd story about my supposed havoc wreaked upon Bellevue.

"Where's Director Moore?"

She pointed at the hall to my back. "He—he drew Agent Watson away from the scholars. He was going toward the private offices."

I motioned Gunner to move ahead of me, so that if some knucklehead thought to open fire on America's Most Wanted Outlaw, they'd first have to come to terms with shooting me in the back. We hurried down the hall, its walls and ceiling blackened from charring, and the deeper we went into the building, the more steam-powered lamps were broken or flickering at random. At Moore's office, I glanced inside, but it was empty. I instructed Gunner to take a right onto a corridor of private offices, which included the one I used to call my own at the end, beside the busted window. Water rained down from the ceiling in the aftermath of the fire department's dousing, and steam mingled with the remnants of black smoke.

Moore stumbled out of one of the offices suddenly, coughing lightly. His usually so carefully set hair was in disarray, and his rolled-back sleeves and waistcoat were wet and plastered to his body, but otherwise he didn't seem worse for wear. He turned and reached into the room to help Rachel Plunket climb over what was probably an overturned desk.

"Sir," I called, quickly approaching the two. I grabbed Moore's arm instinctively, then jerked back when he hissed in pain and an electrical arc snapped between us. "I'm sorry."

"It's fine," he said. "I'm just easily conductive at the moment."

An embarrassed laugh died in my throat, and I clasped my hands together. My emotional reaction to Moore being alive and well had been so extreme that I'd nearly drawn him into an unwarranted embrace, in front of Plunket, no less. Belatedly, I took in her appearance, and seeing her absolutely *drenched* in blood about caused my death by apoplexy then and there.

"Plunket," I cried.

She held up her hands, which were nearly black, there was so much blood. "It's not mine," she said in such a calm and rational voice that I suspected she was in shock. "I had to do it," Plunket continued, nodding to herself. "Agent Phillips. He killed Agent Evans and then started after Director Moore when—when Watson was already trying to—to kill—" Tears spilled down her usually rouged cheeks, instead now spattered with Phillips's blood.

My heart crumpled in on itself as I watched her break into pieces. Was this helplessness I felt akin to what Gunner suffered when my Soldier's Heart reared its ugly head? Knowing that a decent person survived something so brutal and ghastly, something that no human should ever endure, and now that moment was left on repeat over and over and over, like a broken steam pneumatic, forever trying to propel forward and never able to break from its locked cycle.

"Come with me," I said, ushering her forward. To Gunner, I said, "Give us a moment?"

He understood. But of course he did. What *didn't* Gunner see? His eyes softened and he grabbed my hand, gave it a quick squeeze, then let go.

Plunket was giving me an odd, sideways stare as I escorted her to the nearest water closet. I motioned for her to sit on the toilet lid, then fetched one of the hand towels from the cabinet beside the sink and soaked it thoroughly. I crouched in front of her in the cramped quarters and hastily wiped blood from Plunket's hands in the way no one had ever done for me.

"I recognize him," she said, still sounding detached.

"Do you?"

"He was here in January. Gunner the Deadly."

I made a noncommittal noise under my breath as I rolled her sleeves back to make certain her wrists were clean too.

"He's in love with you."

I glanced up.

"I wish I could say someone has looked at me the way he just did you."

I said nothing of that and returned to the sink to hold the towel under the cold tap until the water ran clean. I murmured an apology before touching Plunket's chin in what was a fairly intimate gesture, then began to gently scrub her face.

"I'm so sorry, Hamilton," she whispered.

I briefly met her dark eyes, and they were filled with more unshed tears. "For what?"

She swallowed hard; it looked like it'd hurt. "I could have been anything to you, and I chose bully." Plunket took a strangled breath and the tears fell, streaking through the blood I was washing away. "Because all you can think, in moments like that, is *thank God it's not me they're laughing at*. And you'll do anything to keep them from finding out."

"Finding… *oh*." I lowered the hand towel and studied her ruddy face. "Really?"

Her chin quivered and she nodded once.

I rinsed the towel again as I mulled over my words. I'd denied my tendencies for thirty years. I'd chosen a life of celibacy and solitude, and it'd nearly killed me. But then again, what had been the alternative? Those like us would be lucky to only lose their jobs, their homes. So many were jailed, beaten, even killed. It's why we haunted the city's most dangerous neighborhood, because society and coppers alike tended to avoid the area like it was home to the latest epidemic. It's why men had developed the skill to gauge the interests of others with a mere once-over and women moved to the middle of goddamn nowhere to simply lay their heads down on the same pillow at night.

I turned around and finally said, as I scrubbed Plunket's neck, "It's hypocritical of me to say this, because I'm afraid every single day, but you must be courageous."

"You're a caster too," she murmured.

A wry smile crossed my face. "Yes, I know a thing or two about oppression. But so do you. So do a lot of people. And the only way to change society is… to not allow it to bully you anymore."

"Does he know?" Plunket asked.

Practice what you preach.

"Yes."

Plunket drew her gaze back to mine. Her chin quivered again, but there was a hint of a smile somewhere in there.

"He's… well… he's my darling."

A sudden ghost of a laugh escaped Plunket.

"It wasn't intended to be humorous," I answered, briskly finishing with the last spots of blood I could find on her face. I tossed the sodden towel into the sink.

"No, no. It's only…." That whisper-laugh again. "You were always such a stickler for code and law and regulation, and yet, your darling is *Gunner the Deadly*."

"He's not as bad as the papers would have you believe." I took Plunket's hand before I could overanalyze and second-guess myself. I recalled the sensation of wasting away, when denied human touch, only too well, and unsurprisingly, she startled, but gripped my hand almost painfully. "Don't give up. And when you find the one who makes you feel safe, you fight to keep her."

"Okay," Plunket whispered.

"I'm sorry about Watson."

She nodded, and the tears were back. "Is he… you didn't have to…."

"No. It was quick." I pulled her to stand. "You're a good agent, Plunket."

Plunket studied me, studied our joined hands—perhaps with that same curiosity I often had regarding the other gender—studied how strange her thin, delicate fingers looked against my rough, battered ones. Then she met my eyes a final time, said, "You were better," and stepped out of the water closet.

I followed, watched her pick her way down the dark and ruined hallway, then returned to Moore and Gunner.

"Is she all right?" Moore asked as he mopped wet hair from his eyes.

"Probably not," I answered truthfully. "Where's the third undead?"

Moore's expression was appalled at the description, but he said, "Dispatched on the second floor."

"Did you take out the quintessence?" Gunner asked.

"If you're referring to the bloated worm that crawled out, then yes. I set it on fire and it exploded."

"How did this happen?" I cut in.

Moore settled his hands on his hips. "I put two teams on Parker and stepped out to make a few calls from my office. Plunket and Watson were one of those teams. When Councilman Prince arrived, Plunket slipped out to fetch me— said someone from D.C. was releasing the prisoner without any intention of speaking to me first, not that I'd have had power to stop him. But when we reached the room, the jail was empty and the three agents were dead." Moore shook his head like he was mentally rewriting his narrative. "Well, they weren't dead for long, anyway. I found a puncture mark on Watson's neck, but didn't have time to inspect the other two. I assume I'd have found the same." Moore said to me, "I don't understand. Is Barrie trying to raise the dead, soul and all, or is he trying to control the dead?"

"Perhaps both," I suggested. "Given the circumstances."

"You didn't speak with or see Prince yourself," Gunner said to Moore.

Moore shook his head.

"Then how do you know it was him?"

"Plunket recognized him. She had a hearing before the council in January regarding Bligh's actions and subsequent demise. I met him then too, for that matter. He, ah, stands out in a crowd."

Gunner considered this for a moment, removed his bowler, then said, "The foundation of your Bureau is being tested, Director. Your decision right now will decide if the rotten apple spoils his companions."

Moore's stare was steely.

"I've let my own matters with Prince rest for the better part of a decade," Gunner continued, "but unfortunately for us both, he's now involved Hamilton."

"What business could you *possibly* have with an FBMS councilman?" Moore countered.

"We've all lived lives," Gunner answered. "Prince wasn't always a councilman."

"He used to be a Pinkerton too," I clarified quietly.

"Prince believes me a murderer," Gunner said, and a hush fell over us, so intense that the dripping water sounded like a storm in the absence of conversation. Mildly, Gunner added, "For the wrong reasons. And I was even determined to look the other way after Prince sent Milo Ferguson to belittle my reputation and kill me. I've already lost one love in my life. I'll be damned if I allow it to happen again, and at the hands of someone like Magnus Prince."

Moore studied Gunner, stroked his beard thoughtfully, then said to me, "As State Director, I have the authority to temporarily deputize regulated casters, if the FBMS faces an imminent threat to its structure, agents, or its capacity to fulfill its duty in the supervision of magic and steam in the state of New York."

I shook my head and opened my mouth to protest.

Moore spoke over me. "Gillian Hamilton, I temporarily authorize you to work on behalf of the FBMS, to assume all the responsibilities of an active special agent, and to accept orders from a superior—who, in this case, happens to be Director Loren Moore."

"You can't do this, sir."

"I just did."

"But I'm not—"

"*Simon Fitzgerald* isn't in the regulation records," Moore stated. "Gillian Hamilton is. I've seen the documentation myself. And this way, your actions won't be viewed as vigilantism."

"Sir—"

"Let me deal with the consequences, Hamilton," Moore said softly, and he smiled with the courage and bravery of a captain who kept his hand on the wheel, even as his ship was going down in flames. "Dr. Eugene Barrie is an immediate and dangerous threat to not only the health and stability of the magic community, but he has demonstrated a cruel indifference toward the lives of innocent civilians as well. He's to be handled in whatever manner proves successful."

"Yes, sir."

"And there is considerable evidence that can be used to build a case against Councilman Prince for his involvement in Barrie's undertaking. This is a direct violation of our ethics and abuse of the power he commands as head of the FBMS.

He's to be detained at any cost."

"Yes, sir."

"Then shall we pay Barrie a visit?" Gunner asked, settling his hat back on his head at that rakish angle he preferred. He looked down at me. "Blackwell's?"

"An entire asylum of casters at his disposal to abuse for their aether skills, and at the behest and protection of the FBMS? Yes, I do believe that's where Barrie, and possibly Prince, are currently holed up." I began to lead the way down the disaster of a hallway.

"Gunner," Moore called. We both turned, and he said, before tossing Gunner a ring of skeleton keys, "Take my automobile."

Gunner snatched the ring out of the air one-handed.

"But I expect you to return it. In person."

"I've not been shot yet, Director."

"For Hamilton's sake, you'd best keep it that way," Moore warned.

XVI

February 25, 1882

"The steam shuttle won't make its evening commute to pick up staff from the island until…." I paused, leaned over to tug Gunner's pocket watch from his waistcoat, and concluded, "…seven o'clock. That's not for another five hours." I tucked the timepiece back and settled into my seat.

"I prefer to abide by my own timetables," Gunner replied. He made a smooth turn uptown on First Avenue, shifting gears and feeding the engine steam power as easily as when he'd directed that black Morgan stallion in Arizona. Gunner was always so utterly composed, calm, in control of every situation. From gunfights to automobile chases to jumping off the railing of a moving airship. He never hesitated, never showed doubt, and somehow, as if to add insult to injury for the rest of us, maintained devilishly handsome good looks while doing so.

"Are you ever afraid?" I asked.

Gunner briefly took his eyes from the road. "Of course."

"Really?"

"You don't think so?"

"You don't show it," I answered.

"I've been afraid," he confirmed.

"When?"

"When I was scouring the country for your whereabouts. For over a month, there wasn't a single scrap of evidence you were even alive." Gunner looked at me again. "I was afraid then."

"I wanted so badly to give up," I admitted.

"I'm glad you didn't."

I briefly squeezed Gunner's thigh before a curious thought surfaced. "How *did* you board the Ora Continental?"

"I've made a career out of robbing airships, my dear."

"Uh-huh."

"A gentleman never tells."

I rolled my eyes but had to look out the passenger window to hide the smile on my face.

Gunner parked the auto on the side of the road at Thirty-Fifth Street and First Avenue. He climbed out and made a point of locking the door before tying his black bandana around his face. He crossed the front of the auto as I got out, said quite simply, "Stay here," and then marched onto the squat boardwalk that overlooked the East River.

I slipped my hands into my trouser pockets, leaned against the auto, and watched with a shake of my head as Gunner jumped off the boardwalk, caught ahold of the steel anchor chain belonging to the docked and hovering shuttle, and showed off some impressive upper-body strength as he climbed up and snuck onto the deck. Nothing happened after that. Traffic ebbed and flowed at my back. The shuttle's steam engine chugged along in the cold air. I noted that the blimp's canvas was patched here and there, and the aft propellor looked dented. I thought idly, if this was the best shuttle the city could afford for tending to the doctors, nurses, and guards who worked on Blackwell's, it spoke a great volume as to how much money was reserved for the actual patients. A few cents per head, I guessed. And that was being generous.

A sudden yelp startled me out of that cynical spiral, and I looked toward the railing around the deck in time to see someone flail, fall overboard, and hit the icy waters like a cannonball. Two men immediately slid down the anchor chain, charged full speed along the boardwalk, and skidded right past me while shouting:

"Holy Mary, Mother of God, that was Gunner the Deadly!"

"I don't get paid enough for this!"

They vanished into the afternoon sun just as the engine of the shuttle roared to life. The anchor was weighed, the dinky ship took flight, and it was maneuvered over the tops of several trees before descending into the middle of First Avenue. I put my goggles on, held tight to my cap, and approached the shuttle as the propeller kicked up snow and debris from the road. Automobiles and motorwagons came to a screeching halt, horns blaring and steam screaming from their exhaust pipes.

Gunner jumped down from the bridge, wearing his own goggles, and settled his arms on the deck's railing. He tugged the bandana down and asked, "Would you like a ride, Special Agent Hamilton?"

"First, that title is only temporary."

"We'll see."

"Second, you threw a man into the East River."

"He wasn't nearly as smart as his companions." Gunner reached a hand out.

"Third, you're showing off." But I said this while taking his hand and allowing Gunner to hoist me aboard.

"I wouldn't do it if you didn't enjoy it." Gunner removed

his bowler long enough to lean down and brush his lips against my own, and then he was returning to the bridge. He stood at the wheel, jostling a brass lever until it seemed to unstick itself, and the shuttle once again rose into the sky. He shifted gears on another mechanism, and the engine sounded as if it cranked into overdrive. Within a minute, we were soaring over the choppy river toward Blackwell's.

"Clever trick," I called over the wind. "Is there anything you can't pilot or drive?"

Gunner held the massive brass wheel with one hand as he considered the question. "I've yet to have an opportunity to conduct an El train."

"Lord save us from that day," I muttered.

"Gillian."

"Hmm?" I looked up.

"What will be the best method for entering the asylum?"

"Well… our only options are the front doors or basement. I'm not familiar with the layout of the rotunda, though."

"What do you mean?"

I shrugged a little and clarified, "Patients are brought in through the basement."

"How are patients housed on the upper levels?" Gunner asked.

"They're separated according to the elemental default for the caster. For example, I had initially been placed on the second floor, because it's reinforced with bronze, which is the least conductive metal."

Gunner shifted various levers again. "Even though you can cast every spell across the board?"

"What can I say—Dr. Ashland should have heeded the warnings he'd been given about me."

"Where would they place casters who use aether?"

"Aether isn't an inherent skill. It's a spell usually obtainable by level threes and higher. It takes a great deal of patience and practice to master. In the occurrence such a caster must be interned, platinum is the metal of choice. But the asylum is only three floors—the third is reinforced with iron. And practical experience has taught me that the asylum simply confines problematic higher-levels to the cells in the basement. They employ platinum restraint gloves, but there are other… less humane options available." I hastened to add, "All that being said, I don't believe Barrie will be in the basement. There's simply not enough space for him to work. And given his recent palate cleanse, I doubt he's willing to work in conditions similar to what we found at Higgins's warehouse on Bayard and Mulberry."

"Then what are you suggesting?"

"Well… the rotunda is the asylum's pièce de résistance. It's meant to charm the social reformers who come to inspect the property. It's quite large, I hear, and very opulent. 'Even our undesirables are treated like royalty!' You understand?"

"I do," Gunner said gravely. "The front doors, then."

We wasted no time with subterfuge, landing the shuttle on the dead and frozen front lawn of the asylum. Gunner swung down from the railing and hit the ground with a quiet *thump* before he offered his hand as I followed suit.

I said to him very matter-of-factly, "This is where Barrie wants me."

"I'll have your back."

"I know." I took Gunner's arm as he began to move. "Tell me something."

"What's that?"

"I don't know. I don't care. Anything. Just in case."

"This isn't where our story ends, my dear." Gunner drew close and cupped my face in one hand. "It's only now begun."

I nodded but couldn't speak around the unexpected knot in my throat.

Gunner leaned down, whispered against my ear, "I love you," and kissed my cheek.

I supposed there wasn't anything else worth him saying.

"I love you too."

Gunner flashed that wicked, charming smile he so often hid and unholstered his Waterbury, and we walked to the front doors of the Asylum for the Magically Insane. We climbed the grand staircase that flanked either side of the rotunda entrance, each grabbed one of the brass handles, and shoved the heavy double doors open.

The rotunda was five stories, built in an octagonal shape of the same stone that dominated the island. A grand spiral staircase wound all the way to the top, with each floor looking down at the ones below it. Stained glass windows all along the roof's perimeter let in colorful sunshine that created fantastical mosaics across the floors and walls. On the ground floor, two corridors, one to the left and the other on the right, no doubt led to the wings of the asylum proper. The welcome desk was unmanned—the rotunda so quiet that the blood in my ears was louder—and the squirming and festering sensation of quintessence was so overwhelming that it nearly bowled me over.

"Something's not right," Gunner whispered. "Where are the patients?"

I pointed in either direction at the halls. "Beyond multiple access points so their screams don't echo where polite society may hear."

"Okay, but what about the staff?"

I shook my head, and taking a few steps across the lobby,

said, "Good question." Upon reaching the middle of the room, I raised my head back and studied the floors overhead. I could make out the tops of doorframes at this angle. Most appeared to be open, but there was definitely a closed room on the third floor. I heard the quiet scratch of rustling paper and glanced over my shoulder to see Gunner picking up a loose sheet from the floor that I must have stepped right over. He studied it a moment, then calmly folded it a few times. "What's that?" I asked him.

He shook his head while tucking it into his coat. "This is a trap."

"No doubt."

Gunner joined me. "What do you want to do?"

I pointed. "Third floor. The atmosphere here is pulsating." I started cautiously up the beautifully curved decorative staircase.

At the second floor, we paused long enough to check a few of the rooms. They varied from exam rooms to treatment rooms to some sort of recreational area. All of them looked brand-new, never having once been used since the asylum opened a decade before I was even born. It was confirmation for me that they were for show, to placate the worries of the occasional upper-class woman who'd recently joined a committee or three, as well as nosy journalists. The reality was the actual hospital wings were crowded with double the patients the building was meant to hold, and they had no choice but to live here. They were prisoners—not only mentally, but physically.

We returned to the stairs and cautiously rose to the third floor. Each step felt like I was walking through deeper and deeper water, the current working against me, but with the added sensation of hundreds—*thousands*—of fat, bloated, disgusting worms crawling all over me. There was so much recently activated quintessence in the rotunda that there was a permanent tear directly over the island. The atmosphere was bleeding out, and there was no way heavy-hitting casters like Moore or even Barrie couldn't sense this.

"You're white as a ghost," Gunner murmured as we reached the landing.

There were fewer rooms here, but all were open and empty except one. Quintessence seeped out from under the crack of the door.

"Magic," I answered. "We're about to find out what Barrie's been hacking and sawing." I stared at the doorknob as I considered whether I was about to vomit, but there was no turning away from this. Barrie wasn't only a criminal—he was the true monster, the true butcher. He delighted in this brutality and torture and needed to be stopped.

At whatever the cost.

I grabbed the knob and threw the door open onto an operating theater. Elevated seating had been built into the rounded shape of the building along three-fourths of the room, and the half a dozen steep, wooden rows overlooked the center stage with its menacing table. What was perhaps more mentally and emotionally crippling for me was that there were *spectators* in the rafters and a… sort of body on the table. Beside the haphazard mess of laid-out flesh and bone, stood Barrie, his arms bloody up to his elbows.

Behind him, lined up along the wall of the auditorium seating, were several men and women, dressed as patients, securely fastened to their chairs. Attached to each of the patient's hands were box-like brass and silver structures around their palms, a hose protruding from the middle, and a series of ticking mechanisms that looked almost as if it was tightening, twisting, *wringing* the magic from their hands. A bright white light—aether—was steadily pumping through the tubing, all of which was attached to the mass of body parts on the table. Tentacles of quintessence twisted and squirmed inside the rib cage, and as the aether spread throughout the skeletal structure, I realized I was literally watching organs, muscle, and flesh form right before my eyes.

Eugene Barrie was not only bringing the dead back to life—he was working with the bones of the deceased, not a still-fresh body—and the intensive process appeared to be sucking all of the magic out of the caster patients. Barrie was going to murder half a dozen helpless undesirables for the sake of a science experiment that allowed him to play God.

"Simon Fitzgerald" called a voice to my left, and a man who I could only presume to be Magnus Prince was taking steps down from the amphitheater seating at a leisurely pace. His tone was cool, clinical, even. He was as Shy Phoebe described: tall, at least Gunner's height, with conservatively cut and styled gray hair. He was handsomely dressed in a charcoal suit with a waistcoat of cobalt blue that heightened his air of riches and authority. Prince's left eye did indeed have a milky sheen, and the skin underneath was puckered, like a wound from a long-ago fight. Stopping on the second to last step, he smiled and said, "You've been awfully disobedient."

"I'm not mad," I said sternly. "There's no reason to speak to me as if I were a child."

Prince's eyebrow rose in what was clearly delight. His gaze shifted from me to Gunner and he said, "Fairley. You didn't heed my warnings, I see. I wish I could say it was a pleasure."

Gunner lifted the Waterbury and cocked the pistol. "Hamilton's here to arrest you, Mag. I'm here to kill you. Take your pick."

Prince chuckled lightly and set his hand on the railing. "Arrest me. Under what authority, Mr. Fitzgerald?"

I squared my shoulders and said, "My name is Gillian Hamilton, and under the deputized authority provided me by State Director Loren Moore, I'm arresting you on behalf of the Federal Bureau of Magic and Steam."

Prince's smile grew into something frightening. "*Moore* authorized my arrest? How interesting. And what exactly do you and him hope to present to the council that *I* sit on?"

"False imprisonment, for one," I answered.

"No. The council agreed you were a danger to both yourself and the general population."

"You lied!" I shouted suddenly. "You lied about my faculties—to the council, to the staff on Blackwell's, to my director! You turned me into a criminal overnight."

"You did that all on your own, Fitzgerald—"

"Stop calling me that!"

"—on September 17, 1862."

"That wasn't my fault," I protested, breathing heavily.

"And then you fled," Prince continued. "And the shine of rising star, Fairley Holloway, dimmed when he refused a direct order to retrieve a war criminal."

"I don't hunt children," Gunner replied, still holding his pistol trained on Prince.

"No. You and your warped sense of ethics and ideals," Prince countered. "So warped, in fact, that you're now on the complete opposite side of the law. Gunner the Deadly, isn't it? *Charming.*"

"You've been harboring Dr. Eugene Barrie, also known as Sawbones, who's been a wanted criminal since the New Year," I said, trying to regain both control and composure. "You used FBMS documentation to find the doctor, and instead of overseeing his arrest and imprisonment for involvement in the usage of highly illegal and dangerous magic, never mind the multitude of deaths he's contributed to, you've chosen instead to hire and protect him while he continues to abuse the magic community."

"What do I care about the magic community?" Prince retorted, and that terrifying smile was back.

I was momentarily nonplussed by the comment. Yes, it was quite obvious he cared little of me, but the community as a whole? "It's your *job* to care."

"It's my job to maintain law and order among the magically inclined," Prince corrected. "In the year I've sat on the council, do you know what I've learned? The whole lot of you are dangerous and defective human beings. If we cannot rid this country of you entirely, then I aim for complete control. And I'll start by removing casters from positions of power they've abused. Like Loren Moore."

"Moore is the most honest—"

"And what would you know about honesty, you monstrous little fairy?"

"What the hell is wrong with you?" Gunner snapped. "Do you even hear yourself?"

Prince studied Gunner, seeming to outright ignore the weapon still trained on him. "I hear myself quite clearly, Fairley. I hear myself wishing to protect our modern society from the hazards and depravity that magic wreaks upon the innocent. Discipline and control. That's what this city—what all American cities—need."

"Magic wasn't responsible for his curiosity toward men," Gunner said in an abrupt subject change that lost me, as I was quite certain he wasn't referring to me.

"You *tormented* him!" Prince roared unexpectedly. Promptly, he collected himself, cleared his throat, and said, in that once again aloof voice, "Dr. Barrie?"

The man in question momentarily overlooked, I turned to the surgical table to see that what was once old bone and haphazard piles of flesh was now, quite nearly, a completed man. I also saw that two of the strapped-down patients were, without question, dead. Meanwhile, Barrie had both hands on the table as he leaned over the body, watching with a sickening fascination as patches of skin fused together and hair sprouted from pores.

"He's nearly there," Barrie responded excitedly.

"What're you doing, Mag?" Gunner asked with a discernable amount of wariness.

"Finally making use of this godforsaken community," Prince answered. "What was it Milo used to say? Anything is possible with 'silver and steam and a little magic in between.'"

The body on the table let out an abrupt gasp and sat up in a sickening rush. The tubes pumping aether into his body were still attached—now embedded in the muscle—but otherwise the man before us looked... *alive*. And by that, I mean, there was life in his brown eyes. He wasn't the metals and mechanics of Barrie's earlier work, nor was he merely flesh and blood and bone behaving like a puppet on strings. He had a soul.

He was a striking to look at too. Tall and lean, perhaps a few years my junior, with hair that was either a natural ash brown in coloring or had subtle hints of premature gray.

The nude man before us tilted his head and said on an exhale, "*Fairley?*"

I shot Gunner a glance. His complexion had gone milk-white, like he was about to be sick. He looked... utterly *horrified*. "Oh my God...."

But then Barrie raised a bloody hand in the air, and the seated audience all rose like musicians at the command of a conductor. They were the staff of the asylum, from the matronly nurse, Miss Louise, to the brutal and unforgiving Dr. Ashland. And as all of them growled in unison, "*Fiiitzgeraaald,*" I realized that they had been on the wrong end of arsenic or morphine and existed in this now-familiar, undead limbo.

"And so begins the discipline and control." Prince ordered, "Annihilate Fairley Holloway."

"It's Gunner, you sack of shit."

Prince cast a final grin in our direction and said, ignoring Gunner's retort, "I want it to be absolutely *agonizing* for him. But spare Fitzgerald. You'll need him." To Barrie, he concluded, with an idle wave of his hand in the direction of the tethered patients, "Considering how quickly all of these gave out."

Barrie pointed a bloody hand in our direction, and the undead staff leapt from the rafters.

A nurse cast a fire spell, and the ball of flames hit me square in the chest as I shoved Gunner to the left of the doorway. I flew in the opposite direction, was knocked off my feet, and was so busy coughing and patting out the flames on my clothes that I barely caught Prince's movements from the corner of my eye. He ran down onto the surgical stage and tore the tubing from the man's body. Blood spurted from the open wounds, and the man cried out in pain—so he was nothing like these undead who felt nothing. Prince was quick but noticeably gentle as he aided the man to his feet and shuttled him toward the exit.

"Mag!" Gunner shouted from across the room. He was crouched, Waterbury raised.

Prince moved so that he was shielded by the nude man. "You wouldn't dare pull that trigger," he called.

The fire nurse grabbed me by the front of my suit and hoisted me to my feet in a display of strength an otherwise-diminutive woman shouldn't have possessed. She got an arm around my neck, slid behind me, and started dragging me toward Barrie. I grabbed her forearm, tucked my chin, then drilled my elbow into her ribs over and over until her footing faltered and I was able to tear free. I spun around, raised her into the air on a current of wind with one hand, fed fire into the whirlwind with the other, then slammed her body down in the upper seating so hard that she broke right through the floor and was stuck within the structure of the amphitheater layout.

I turned in time to see Prince dart out the door, using the nude stranger as a human shield. As the door slammed shut, Gunner jumped to his feet and ran to throw it open, but it didn't budge. Gunner threw his shoulder against the door, backed up, shot the lock plate, then banged on the door furiously when the aether bullets made no difference.

"Magnus! Don't do this," he screamed. "Open the door!" I rushed toward Gunner, and at my approach, he said, "The door locks are reinforced with silver."

"Move out of the way," I ordered, casting fire a second time. My hands glowed red, orange, yellow—

The floor shaking under our feet was my only warning of approach from behind, and then Barrie had my shoulder in his grip, and our magics drew swords against each other. He spun me around as my lightning lashed out, but by the way my teeth were chattering, like there was an earthquake inside me, I knew his elemental default was earth, and I was more prone than he was when we touched. The wooden floorboards underfoot pitched and moaned and cracked. Gunner was flung against the door when Barrie cast wind on me and threw me into the rafters.

"I have to admit," Barrie called from below, still in that soft and unassuming voice. "Pretending to go along with you to California was, if nothing else, amusing."

I grunted and rolled onto my back under a broken bench as an undead doctor leaned down to grab me. I yelped, kicked him in the chest, then cast gravity. I scrambled back, one hand extended to maintain the spell. The doctor's legs *pop*ped, *snap*ped, he folded in on himself like a stick of Gunner's Black Jack, and the quintessence eel spurted out his back. It flopped angrily against the floor.

"Losing you to the likes of a vigilante was less amusing," Barrie continued.

Why the hell isn't Gunner blowing this sonofabitch's head off? I rolled onto my knees, rose, and saw exactly why. Gunner must have dropped the Waterbury when Barrie attacked, because now the mad doctor was holding the pistol, checking the cylindered rounds, and Gunner was surrounded by three undead. He held a long piece of metal in one hand to defend himself—a thin, sharp knife meant for amputations. Just seeing the blade made me dry heave.

Barrie saw my reaction, glanced curiously over his shoulder, then looked back to me as he said, "They say you murdered a thousand men in Antietam. And yet, *that* makes you squeamish?"

"Unlike you, I didn't enjoy it," I spat.

Barrie smiled coolly. The Waterbury was covered in the blood that coated his hands. "Once I'd informed Mr. Prince that Gunner the Deadly was involved, he all but promised me of your return. Why do you think that is?"

Gunner stabbed the blade through Dr. Ashland, slicing him open from chest to belly. He turned and smashed his elbow into the face of another undead before kicking him in the chest.

"My guess?" Barrie continued. "*Secrets.* You have secrets too, don't you, Fitzgerald? I, on the other hand, do not. I'm an open book. A medical man who honed his skills at the worst possible moment in our nation's history and discovered a few dark desires within myself along the way." Barrie spun, raised the Waterbury, and shot at Gunner.

I screamed something inarticulate as a gravity spell tore

from my hands. The magic grabbed everything in the room short of Gunner and one undead, and hurled them into the wall below the first row of seats, the midair triple aether round included. In fact, the bullet's change in trajectory blew the head off a nurse and her blood spurted everywhere. I hoisted myself over the amphitheater railing and jumped down to the stage. I grabbed the Waterbury from Barrie, who lay against the wall, momentarily stunned, and threw it to Gunner. I cast a second gravity spell and dropped Dr. Ashland like a ton of bricks had crushed him, while Gunner caught the pistol and promptly dispatched the quintessence spell. That bastard deserved far worse, in my opinion, but beggars can't be choosers.

Gunner lowered the Waterbury, grabbed my arm, and drew me into a quick, hard kiss. "You're incredible."

Smoke was beginning to fill the operating theater at that point, and I nearly asked where the origin was so as to put it out, considering we were still locked inside, but then that undead nurse I'd set on fire broke through the wall she'd been trapped in. Her body was charred black—nothing left of hair or clothes, and she smelled awful—and yet she still moaned something horrible, likely meant to be "Fitzgerald," and came stumbling toward us. I raised one hand and made a striking motion, gravity following the movement and crushing her body into the floor. A blackened and burned eel wiggled free from the husk of what was once human, and Gunner shot it too.

I cast a water spell next, moving my hands far apart and growing a large, glistening, and gently churning sphere of water, before directing it into the wall, where it made quick work of dousing the flames.

"There's still smoke," Gunner warned, and he pointed to the front door, where thick gray plumes coiled underneath the door and into the theater. "*Mag.* He's destroying evidence.

Witnesses."

"But he needs Barrie," I protested.

Gunner shook his head. "No. He knows about Weaver. He's a councilman. He has access to all of the FBMS reports. He doesn't need Barrie for quintessence. He can go directly to the source. Losing you will be tough, but if it means getting rid of me in the same breath—he'd do it. And then there's no one to report him."

A noise interrupted Gunner—protesting hinges and a heavy *thud* and *bang* against stone. We both looked toward the steps in the amphitheater seating in time to see Barrie at the top of the risers, scrambling out an access hatch and onto the lower roof. In his wake, the remaining undead had recovered from their body slam into the wall and were racing across the theater toward us.

"Stop Barrie," Gunner ordered.

"*What*? I'm not leaving you here!"

"How much longer can the magic atmosphere withstand the assault of quintessence?" Gunner countered.

I hesitated.

"I'll be right behind you. I promise." He immediately shot a huge, lumbering man, who was likely another criminal on loan from the penitentiary, in the head and then drove the amputation knife into his gut, spilling out the oily sack of mucus and magic the old-fashioned way.

With the momentary opening Gunner had supplied me, I ran up the steps and climbed out the open hatch. Immediately, I sucked in a lungful of air that stank of incoming East River low tide and Blackwell's Island sickly malaise, but at least it wasn't more of the blood and soot from below. I turned in search of Barrie—the madman was wielding a hefty tree limb that must have fallen from the bare trees surrounding the front entrance. He smashed it into my side, knocking the air from my chest, and I dropped to one knee. Tossing the limb aside, Barrie approached, grabbed a fistful of hair, and yanked my head back. My teeth were chattering from the rumble of the earth, and lightning bit at Barrie's hand, but it was almost like he didn't *mind* the pain.

"I can practically *smell* the aether in your veins," Barrie said, dragging his other hand down the side of my exposed neck, digging his nails in hard enough to leave a welt. "I knew. In Tucson. You were someone special." He pulled my head up closer as he added, "But who'd have ever imagined I opted to save *the* Simon Fitzgerald. The most powerful caster alive." Barrie glanced down at my clenched fists. "There's still pain. I can tell. You shake your hands after casting." Barrie whispered in my ear, "I suppose I just can't help myself sometimes."

"You—*ah!*—you did that to me on purpose?" I studied his passive face and asked, "W-why're you helping Prince? He doesn't care about you. He's using you."

With a terrifying sense of welcomed fatalism, Barrie replied, "We all die someday."

He grabbed my wrist, wincing as sparks sizzled and shot between us, but he didn't let go. He forced my hand palm up and put enough pressure on the sensitive tendons of my wrist that I was forced to release the fist. He made a kind of pleasured sound in the back of his throat as he studied the latticework of scars. "We could have achieved wonderful feats together. Sawbones and the Butcher."

"My *name* is Gillian Hamilton," I gritted out.

"That's not what anyone will remember."

I'd stood on a stoop in the rain, clutching immigration documents that were truly my last hope. The door had opened, and a woman warily looked me up and down as I said, "Good evening, ma'am. I'm here about the room for rent. I'm Gillian Hamilton."

Loren Moore was massive, even seated behind his desk. He'd studied me intently from where I stood in the doorway of his office, puffing away on his pipe. Eventually, he removed the bit from his mouth, closed a folder he'd been poring over, and leaned back. "You must be my new level-five caster."

"Yes, sir. Gillian Hamilton."

Gunner the Deadly had kicked up a spray of orange dirt as he slid behind the wagon, while the Ten-Barrel Self-Propulsion Arachnids busily turned Shallow Grave into swiss cheese. He'd rolled out of the scatter of bullets and pointed his Waterbury in my face the same instant I'd revealed my pinned badge and said, "You're under arrest."

"Who are you?"

"Special Agent Gillian Hamilton."

The sky blackened overhead, the wind picked up, and thunder boomed as I said darkly, "From this moment on, I promise you, *no one* will forget the name Gillian Hamilton."

And lightning exploded from my entire body.

It hurled Barrie up against the looming dome structure that housed the final two stories of the rotunda. His back snapped loudly against stone and tile, but he caught himself on a window ledge before falling back to the roof. I stood as Barrie—bloody, burned, and smoking—climbed the ornate architecture around the window. Something fell in his haste, and I briefly studied the three fingers that had fallen from his hand and landed at my feet like a sacrificial offering.

Rain began to fall—heavy, ice-cold sheets that all but blotted out the world surrounding Blackwell's. Thunder and lightning crashed overhead. Barrie was hoisting himself onto the window ledge of the fifth story, scaling the roof to reach the very top. I let the wind lift me off my feet and shot up to the widow's walk ahead of him. I stood in the gale, wind whipping and tearing at my coat, cap long since lost, and watched Barrie struggle to haul himself up without the use of all his fingers. He was gasping for breath as he finally got his legs working underneath him and shakily rose. Whatever color was left in his face drained away when he met my gaze.

Barrie raised his bloody stump of a hand, palm toward me, and cast quintessence. The atmosphere churned in on itself, a silent scream of pain and protest as magic that was as black as the clouds that I'd manifested above began to pour from his hand.

I lunged, grabbed Barrie's wrist, despite the ricocheting pain of our magics, and yanked him close. "One thousand and one murders," I said. "And yours is the only one that'll bring me pleasure." I thrust his hand against the asylum's lightning rod and let go as a crack sounded overhead, the world turned white, and millions of volts tore Eugene Barrie apart.

"*Gillian!*"

I looked away from what remained of Sawbones, leaned over the edge, and could just make out Gunner on the fourth-story roof. I jumped from the widow's walk and landed safely at his side.

"Barrie?" he asked over the raging storm.

"Dead" was all I said.

"We have to get out of here," Gunner said next. "The fire—"

"What about all the patients?"

"I don't know how we'd reach them."

I shook my head, ignored Gunner's protests, and closed my eyes. I held my hands palm down at my sides, concentrated on the frozen dirt, the blue-gray stone deeper in the earth, the very foundation of this pit of despair and tragedy, and then I jerked my hands upward. I felt the windows burst, doorframes warp, and hinges and bolts scatter. Mortar cracked, support beams listed, and walls crumbled. The fire within the building was most definitely out of control, and I couldn't be certain if anyone in the wings was even alive, considering smoke inhalation alone could have gotten to them before the flames, but this way, they at least had the option to escape.

The building shook ominously underfoot, and the storm overhead was still raging. I pulled Gunner against me and said, "Don't let go."

"I won't."

The wind lifted us both, and we shot across the sky and open water.

XVII

February 28, 1882

I had stressed upon Moore how vital it was that he not remain in the city. That Magnus Prince had escaped Blackwell's and washed his hands of all witnesses, save for us. And who even *were* we? A vigilante, a caster thought more dangerous than God's wrath, and a director who'd tried to have an FBMS councilman arrested. But without evidence of Prince's doings—receipts, a money trail, the frightening devices Barrie had built to suck the magic from unwilling casters, *hell*, even the bodies of those patients he'd murdered for the aether—how on Earth was Moore to stand before the rest of the D.C. councilmen and convince them that one of their own was crooked and unhinged? That Prince was drunk on power and spiteful toward an entire group of humans simply trying to exist? And what had become of the resurrected man Prince had fled with? Was that stranger in peril now as well?

"I will not leave this office," Moore had replied, as stubborn as he was tall.

"Sir—"

"No. We are the only witnesses who can attest to what's

unfolding. We can't run away." Moore smoothed his beard with one hand in a self-soothing gesture.

"They're going to remove you as State Director," I protested. "Prince will see to that. He's going to use these events against us—against casters. It's his argument for cracking down on the community. If Prince can get his hands on quintessence magic again, use it to weaponize more undead, he means to use them as a form of policing! Can you imagine that?"

Moore had smiled a bit twistedly and said with a note of finality, "Then you'd best find this mysterious architect before he does, Hamilton."

That was how, three days later, I'd found myself once again outside of my home and comfort zone, and in Dodge City, Kansas.

More specifically, I was in the second-story flat that Gunner rented—or might have actually owned outright, he was never particularly forthcoming with that sort of information—of an otherwise completely unassuming boarding house owned and operated by an elderly couple who'd introduced themselves as Ma and Pa Gordon. After the two days of air travel aboard a clunky steamer hauling European furniture and linens to the well-to-do families out on the West Coast, Gunner had requested this moment of reprieve and had, uncharacteristically, been asleep for the better part of a day.

Based on Gunner's reaction to learning of Prince's involvement with the FBMS, as well as having been part of their inauspicious reunion on Blackwell's, it took very little imagination on my part to conclude that his past wasn't dead and buried where Prince was concerned, and it was deeply upsetting Gunner. Naturally, I wished to understand the situation so that I could perhaps ease some of his hurts. Because while a broken heart might have been my daily existence, seeing those same emotions play out in the blue of Gunner's eyes was like a sucker punch when I was already down. But I couldn't demand of him what he didn't wish to share....

I removed the stove lid and muttered under my breath, "Steam-powered range, my backside." The water reservoir in the cast-iron stove was still ice-cold, even though I'd checked the drafts and dampers twice. "*This* is why I dislike kitchens," I told the stove, under the impression I was alone and safe to speak to household appliances and not be mocked for it. I snapped my fingers and the water instantly came to a boil. "Ha. There we go." I set the siphon pot on the burner and glanced toward the bedroom door, only to find it open with Gunner standing in the threshold. "Oh! Good morning."

Gunner was doing up his black shirt, although he left the top open enough that I could glimpse his chest hair. His braces were buttoned to his trousers, but they hung loosely at his sides. Seeing him standing there, silent, in his stocking feet... there was something deeply human, almost fragile, about it. Gunner quietly stepped into the room, bent to kiss my cheek, then sat at the table without a word.

"Coffee will be ready soon," I said with a lightheartedness I'm sure he saw right through. "There's nothing in your pantry, but I can go downstairs and see about buying some eggs and meat off Mrs. Gordon... although I'm not so certain you want me in charge of actually cooking—"

"Gillian."

I turned.

Gunner was holding a folded square of paper in one hand, and I recognized it as what he'd collected from the floor of the rotunda on Blackwell's. "I need to speak with you."

I slowly moved to the table, much like a floating, disembodied spirit, and sat in the chair across from Gunner. My heart was hammering in my throat, and I prayed he didn't notice the erratic pulse point just above my collar.

But Gunner wasn't even looking at me, instead he was still staring at the paper he gripped in one hand. "The three of us were Pinkertons together. Me, Mag, and his younger brother." Gunner unfolded the paper once. "I was madly in love with him." He unfolded it again. "And when I'd finally gathered the courage to tell him, he swallowed an entire bottle of strychnine in response."

Gunner glanced up. He slid the paper across the tabletop.

I didn't want to read it. I wanted nothing to do with it. But I was compelled, *possessed*, and took the sheet into both hands. It read: *Fairley Holloway fucked and murdered my brother.*

I looked at Gunner.

"The man who Barrie resurrected?" he asked with a small nod of confirmation.

No.

"That's him."

Please, God, don't do this to me.

"Danny Prince."

Gillian Hamilton and Gunner the Deadly return in:

The Councilman
(Magic & Steam: Book Four)

C.S. Poe is a Lambda Literary and two-time EPIC award finalist, and a FAPA award-winning author of gay mystery, romance, and speculative fiction.

She resides in New York City, but has also called Key West and Ibaraki, Japan, home. She loves Romanticism artwork, Gilded Age New York, the films of Buster Keaton, coffee in the morning and whiskey in the evening, true crime, and cats. She's rescued two cats—Milo and Kasper do their best to distract her from work on a daily basis.

C.S. is an alumna of the School of Visual Arts.

Her debut novel, *The Mystery of Nevermore*, was published 2016.

cspoe.com

ALSO BY C.S. POE

SERIES:
Snow & Winter
The Mystery of Nevermore
The Mystery of the Curiosities
The Mystery of the Moving Image
The Mystery of the Bones
The Mystery of the Spirits

Snow & Winter Collection
Interlude

Magic & Steam
The Engineer
The Gangster
The Doctor

A Lancaster Story
Kneading You
Joy
Color of You

The Silver Screen
Lights. Camera. Murder.

Memento Mori
Madison Square Murders

An Auden & O'Callaghan Mystery
(co-written with Gregory Ashe)
A Friend in the Dark
A Friend in the Fire

NOVELS:
Southernmost Murder

NOVELLAS:
11:59

SHORT STORIES:
Love in 24 Frames
That Turtle Story
New Game, Start
Love Has No Expiration

Visit cspoe.com for free slice-of-life codas, titles in audio, and available foreign translations.

Join C.S. Poe's mailing list to stay updated on upcoming releases, sales, conventions, and more!
bit.ly/CSPoeNewsletter